THE HYPNOTIST

His name is Darmanian.

He is master of Woodlands, a Victorian estate and healing clinic in upstate New York. Through Woodlands' ornate iron gate pass some of the world's most beautiful and powerful people—churchmen, senators, athletes, models, actresses—all seeking miraculous cures induced under hypnotic trance.

Eric Storm has come at Darmanian's personal request—to write the famed hypnotist's life story.

The night of Eric's arrival is filled with dark omens. First there are strange hypnotic regressions into the past, and bizarre sexual rites . . .

And then Eric learns that Darmanian believes he has lived before . . . as the most ruthless Satanist of seventeenth-century France.

Is it mere delusion? Or has Darmanian's coven already reassembled in rural New York?

One chilling fact is certain: Darmanian is prepared for yet another incarnation—this time as the most feared presence the world has ever known.

THE
HYPNOTIST

Brad Steiger

A Dell/Quicksilver Book

Published by
Dell Publishing Co., Inc./Quicksilver Books, Inc.
1 Dag Hammarskjold Plaza
New York, New York 10017

Copyright © 1979 by Brad Steiger

All rights reserved. No part of this book may be reproduced or transmitted in any form or by any means, electronic or mechanical, including photocopying, recording or by any information storage and retrieval system, without the written permission of the Publisher, except where permitted by law.

Dell ® TM 681510, Dell Publishing Co., Inc.

ISBN: 0-440-13771-3

Printed in the United States of America

First printing—September 1979

For Francie,
my Star Maiden,
who expanded both my awareness
and my universe.

Chapter One

Under the best of circumstances reality can only be dealt with in measured dosages. That is why man must sleep and, more importantly, dream.

But there exist monstrous forces that can upset this delicate and vital balance. One's reality can be transformed into a waking nightmare, and his dreams can become feverish encounters with hideous shadow creatures.

The time has come when I must face the truth of what occurred and tell my story, fantastic and frightening as it may seem, so that others may gain the knowledge of a terrible alternate reality that pulsates at the edge of our mundane world. I am not ashamed to admit that I was terrified on several occasions during my virtual imprisonment at Woodlands, and, for a time, I was fearful that I might be going mad. Believe me, I have seen the dark side of the soul, and I have returned with a frenzied vision of depravity and unmitigated evil.

It all began on March 24, 1978, when I received a letter from a man whom many believe to be one of the greatest minds of our time. Although most would recognize the name of Darmanian as an innovative hypnotherapist, I knew that he was also an accomplished pianist, composer, and inventor. I was flattered that he should write to me and ask me to be the author of his biography. His letter was brief and direct:

My dear Eric Storm:

I hope it will please you to learn that I have been following your career as a biographer with great interest. Your earlier historical portraits of such men as Emerson and Napoleon III bore evidence of meticulous scholarship. Your most recent work has demonstrated your ability to ferret out the facts as doggedly as a persistent detective and to argue your case as effectively as the most convincing trial lawyer. I greatly require an author of your skills to present my work fairly before the public. Just as your re-creations of the lives of the Swedish mystic Swedenborg and the faith healer Quimby made them sympathetic and believable figures, so must your biographical talents translate my unconventional life into acceptable standards.

I, too, am something of an unorthodox healer; and many of my critics decry my use of the "black magic spell of hypnosis." And my empathy for my patients has, of necessity, made me something of a mystic. It is time that I have my own Boswell to record my accomplishments for posterity.

As you are certain to know, I have utilized a

practical hypnotic therapy for several years. Let me entice you further by informing you that I stand now on the very precipice of a quantum leap forward in exploring the innermost reaches of the human mind.

I am summoning you, Eric, to witness the development of a breakthrough technique in raising human consciousness. Your recent books have shown me that you have begun to explore a new reality, but you have yet to cross over to higher levels of awareness. Come join me in a great adventure.

If you decide boldly and answer my challenge, please be advised that you must arrive at my clinic in Saratoga Springs prepared for work no later than April 18th. Time is of the essence.

Yours faithfully,
Darmanian

There are times in one's life when it seems certain that destiny or an all-pervasive intelligence must be directing the more intricate movements of the cosmic clockwork. Darmanian's invitation to assume the mantle of his biographer came on the very eve of the deadline that I had set for a final decision on my next writing project.

Although I was familiar in a general sense with the hypnotist's work, a couple of telephone calls to psychotherapist friends and a trip to the New York Public Library provided me with a small dossier of impressive data.

"Are you familiar with the work of a hypnotherapist named Darmanian?" I asked my agent, Naomi Birnbaum, when I called her just a few minutes past three.

"Certainly, darling," she said. "He's that rather eccentric hypnotist who has a clinic up in the wilds of Albany or Buffalo or somewhere up there."

I could visualize Naomi, her large green eyes crinkling at their edges, a determined forefinger sliding her overlarge glasses higher on her nose. She was a buxom, silver-haired lady just touching sixty, but she maintained the pace of a career girl in her twenties.

"His clinic is called Woodlands, and it is in Saratoga Springs," I said.

"Some people say he's a genius," Naomi commented. "Others say he's a madman. I've learned some pretty wild stories about some of the therapies he employs up in those woods."

"Could we sell a book about him?" I asked her. "He's written to me and asked me to be his biographer."

Naomi made tiny clucking noises as her mental computer took a few seconds to assess the market possibilities. "It would be controversial," she decided. There was the off-key music of her bracelets clinking together as she lighted a cigarette and puffed noisily into the receiver. "He's a doctor, too, isn't he? Books about unorthodox therapists are so much easier to sell if the people are real doctors."

"Darmanian never completed his doctorate," I replied. "Nor did he pursue his medical studies."

Naomi sighed her disappointment. "Too bad. It would be easier to get you a really good advance if he were a doctor."

"My friend, Dr. Ralph Miller, told me an anecdote about Darmanian in that regard," I said. "A couple of years ago there was a big conference on hypnosis and medicine in Las Vegas. Although it is supposed to be very difficult to lure Darmanian away from his clinic, he had consented to give one of the main addresses. While he was there, a bunch of his detractors jumped him about the lack of a 'doctor' in front of his name. Darmanian looked the spokesman for the group full in the eye and replied: 'But who would sit on my examination board? Who would presume to test me when I am in the process of rewriting the textbooks on what is possible in hypnotherapy?"

"Well," Naomi suggested, unimpressed by Darmanian's arrogant squelching of his colleague, "maybe we can get a doctor to write a foreword."

"I'm quite certain that we can," I agreed. "According to Ralph, Darmanian seems to be quite judicious about working closely with medical doctors and psychiatrists in his more difficult cases."

I leaned back in my desk chair, glanced out at the meager portion of New York skyline alloted to me by my apartment window at 709 Central Park West. Dark clouds were gathering for a March rain. I would have to remember to pick up my coat at the cleaners.

"Darmanian often makes the news with his dramatic cures," Naomi considered, "so we shouldn't have too much trouble getting you a good advance. Let me check out the idea with a couple of publishers. Fix yourself a cup of coffee or something, and I'll call you right back."

I cradled the receiver, decided to take my agent's advice. It was a bit chilly in my apartment. Hot coffee would taste good. I pushed away from my desk, took my clipboard with me to the kitchenette.

While the water was heating on the small gas stove, I found the sheet of paper on which I had typed a list of the references that I had gathered that morning at the library.

In July of 1973 Darmanian had been interviewed in *Psychology Today*. Later that same year both *Time* and *Newsweek* ran brief articles on the rehabilitative work that the hypnotist had accomplished with Vietnam veterans who had been hooked on drugs while in service. A *New York Times* magazine piece had carried a long appraisal of his innovative drug-weaning hypnotherapy. Early in 1975 *Human Behavior* carried a cover article on Darmanian, praising his work with insomniacs and alcoholics.

Interestingly, Darmanian had published very little material himself. There were a few obligatory articles in professional journals that dealt with the value of hypnosis in difficult psychotherapies, but it appeared that the hypnotist had established his reputation at an early age with two controversial monographs. In 1957, when he was still in his twenties, he published a paper based on his work with brainwashed and combat-damaged Korean War veterans, "Rebuilding the War-Shocked Personality Through Hypnosis." Darmanian acquired his master's degree in psychology in 1959, then in 1967 he published his other important monograph, "The Care and Keeping of Flower Children." This paper dealt with the role of hypnotherapy in reclaiming young people from the abuses of unrestrained drug experimentation.

I was still on my first cup of coffee when Naomi called back.

"Talk about synchronicity!" She was laughing. "Would you believe that my very first call got us an offer of a contract?"

I tried to keep my voice professional and level, but I found it difficult to contain my own enthusiasm.

"As soon as I mentioned Darmanian to Larry Ashcroft, he literally cheered back at me," Naomi went on. "It seems that he has spent several weekends at Darmanian's clinic and is a wildly enthusiastic supporter of the man. He has suggested several biographers to the hypnotist, but Darmanian has declined to work with any of them. Larry considers it a real feather in your cap that Darmanian sought you out."

"Well, I am flattered," I conceded.

A tone of caution entered Naomi's voice. "Don't you think you should run up to Saratoga Springs and see exactly what Darmanian has in mind before we sign the final contract? You two could have a personality clash or something."

"Darmanian has already invited me. He wants me up there sometime before April eighteenth," I said.

"Then by all means, accept his invitation. You've got a lot to gain. What have you got to lose?"

"Nothing that I can foresee," I replied.

"Don't forget to make copies of any articles you have on Darmanian so I can attach them to the presentation," she reminded me. "And remember to file your income tax before you leave!"

"Anything else, Mom?" I teased her.

"Yes," she said. "Find out if he can help my insomnia."

If I had had the gift of clairvoyance, I would have realized that I was the sheep answering the wolf's summons to his lair. Naomi's sporadic bouts of insomnia were nothing compared with the terror-filled nights of sleeplessness I would soon have to endure.

Chapter Two

April in Paris or New York might inspire romantic ballads and lovers' escapades, but April in Albany is cloaked by a heavy, gray rain cloud that clings stubbornly to the Mohawk Valley and seldom raises its hem to permit sunlight to stream through to hopeful May flowers or the pale survivors of ferocious upstate winters.

"My God!" complained a man in the seat behind me as the wheels of our Allegheny commuter jet touched down on the Albany Airport runway. "It's always raining here. Every damn time I fly up to Albany, I have to get off in the rain."

The jetliner stopped approximately fifty yards from the terminal, and two attendants, hats crunched low over their ears, wheeled portable stairs against the forward door of the aircraft. Addressing myself to any responsible deities who might be listening, I uttered silent thanks for inspiring me to wear a hat.

The wind seemed unnaturally chilly as I took my

turn negotiating the slippery metal steps. My smile was a grim tight line that was but a reflex responding to the stewardess's wish that I have a good day. The rain pelted my cheeks and hands with what felt like an icy cutting edge on each drop. Since I had just descended to earth, I knew that somewhere above that angry, thick, gray blanket there existed the kingdom of the sun. But from my new vantage point beneath the belly of the jet, heaven was but a dark and hostile mass of spitting clouds.

In our exchange of letters Darmanian had told me that there would be a limousine waiting for me outside the baggage claim area. Woodlands Clinic was about a forty-minute drive from the airport, the hypnotist had said, and a gentleman named Worthington would be my chauffeur. Following Darmanian's instructions, I had packed clothing for at least a week's stay.

My baggage claim tickets entitled me to regain my three suitcases and portable typewriter. I had kept my tape recorder with me on the plane. The year before, a flight to Chicago had completely totaled a very expensive Sony recorder, and I had had no desire to replicate the experience by surrendering the tape equipment to Allegheny's baggage handlers.

A large man with a gapped-tooth smile approached me. His raincoat was badly soiled, and his white shirt and necktie were stained by coffee, but his black-billed cap and dark suit proclaimed to all his occupation: He was a chauffeur.

"I'm Worthington," he said grinning as if he were delivering the punchline of a joke. "If you're Mr. Storm, I'll help you carry those bags, and I'll drive you to Woodlands."

"You're on, my friend," I replied, handing him two of the suitcases. "How did you know me? I wasn't wearing a white carnation or carrying a poster."

Worthington emitted a peculiar wheezing laugh that sounded very much like someone coaxing a stubborn lawnmower into starting. "Mr. Darmanian gave me a picture of you," he explained, thrusting forth a blowup that had been made from one of my books' dust jackets. "Would you like to keep it?" he asked as he bent to pick up the two pieces of luggage.

"I have others," I told him. "How long has this miserable rain been coming down?"

He jerked his head across his left shoulder and cast a baleful eye upward. "It's the monsoon season, sir," he sighed. "It rains most of April. But then it also rains most of May, June, July, and August. It generally clears off for two weeks in September and part of October. But then the snow starts."

I paused a moment to turn up my collar against the weather, then matched Worthington's brisk pace to the black limousine parked outside the terminal.

After we had placed my luggage in the trunk and I was comfortably seated, Worthington slid behind the wheel. Within a matter of moments, he had negotiated the heavy five-o'clock airport traffic and had us on the correct highway headed north to Saratoga Springs and the Woodlands Clinic.

In spite of the rain and the woefully diminished late afternoon light, I was very much impressed with the fresh spring beauty of the area. There was something about the green, budding forests and the river valleys that reminded me of the Minnesota in which I had grown up as a kid.

Although I had been mainly occupied with my

mental survey of the rain-drenched countryside, from time to time I glanced at my driver and noticed that he was apparently studying me in the rearview mirror. I could not imagine what there might be about me that he should find so compelling.

"Is there something wrong, Worthington?" I asked after his examination of me had gone on for several minutes.

"Beg pardon, sir?" he asked, his eyes meeting mine in the rearview mirror.

"You keep glancing at me in the mirror as if you might want to ask me something," I said, hoping to prompt an explanation from him.

"Oh, it's nothing, sir," he said with a shrug, displaying again that broad gap-toothed grin. "It's just a little hobby of mine. I try hard to guess why my passengers are coming to see Darmanian."

His eyes pleaded with mine not to take offense. "It's strictly for my own amusement," he protested. He wore battered Ben Franklin glasses with a piece of transparent tape holding one of the lenses together.

"I drive for Mr. Darmanian quite a bit, you see," Worthington went on. "And I just make it a game to guess if the person is coming for smoking, weight, nerves—something like that."

"Actually I'm not coming to see Darmanian for therapy," I said. "I'm writing a book about him."

"No kiddin'!" Worthington said laughing. "I've heard a lot of folks say that they'd like to write a book about Darmanian! And you're actually going to do it."

"Who"—I wanted to know— "have you heard talking about a book about Darmanian?"

"Oh." He smiled boyishly and winked at me in the

mirror. "I just meant folks around Saratoga Springs. Not any real writers."

I couldn't resist asking Worthington the next question: "And just what do the good townsfolk of Saratoga Springs say about Darmanian? This isn't gossip now, Worthington. This is research for my book."

The driver suddenly became very serious. "You won't quote me, will you? I mean, you won't use my name in your book. All right?"

"I shall protect your anonymity," I reassured him.

"Oh, I don't care about that so much," he said. "I just don't want you to use my name."

I held up three fingers in the Boy Scout pledge. "I promise I will not use your name. Now tell me what people say about Darmanian, perhaps the greatest hypnotherapist of this century—or any other for that matter."

Worthington grimaced, as if deep thought and acute pain were synonymous in his lexicon of emotions. "Well, some folks say that Darmanian does some pretty weird things behind those high stone walls."

"From the viewpoint of the man in the street," I suggested, "Darmanian may well seem to do some 'pretty weird things.'"

"Naw," Worthington said with a scowl, adjusting the windshield wipers to a faster sweeping action. "They know about the hypnosis. They're talking about other things."

"Such as?" I persisted.

"Well, I've heard a lot of people say that Darmanian hypnotizes some of his pretty women clients into having sex with him," Worthington said, accidentally pressing the horn on the wheel, as if the statement needed a trumpet blast to herald its significance. "Some have claimed to have heard singing coming from the grounds and said that they saw Darmanian and some of his clients dancing nude and having a sex orgy."

I burst out laughing at the townspeople's stereotype of the lecherous hypnotist, jagged lightning bolts coming out his eyes.

"I didn't say I believed those stories," Worthington protested loudly over the sound of my laughter. "I even want my wife to go see Darmanian. I want him to help her lose weight. It'll soon be summer, and she likes me to take her and the kids swimming at Lake George. She's even heavier now than she was after last winter. She'll look like Moby Dick, the great white whale, when she comes out in her swimming suit."

I shook my head and scowled in mock disapproval. "What else do they say about Darmanian, besides his sexual control over his female clients?"

Worthington accelerated to pass a slow-moving Chevrolet station wagon. "Well, so much of the talk is because a lot of folks just didn't like Darmanian barging into the community and kind of, you know, taking over. I mean, he's real snooty. Talks fancy. And he looks so, you know, foreign. And then there was what he did to Esther Woods."

"Did he dance nude with her in the forest?" I asked jokingly.

Worthington didn't find the comment amusing. "Esther Woods was highly respected in this town, Mr. Storm. Her family owned Woodlands for generations. Then Darmanian moved to town, set up his clinic right in downtown Saratoga Springs. It wasn't long until Esther was coming to see him. I mean, everyone knew that she was always imagining herself to be sick. Right?"

I reminded Worthington that it was his story.

"Well," he continued, "Esther was soon bragging all over town about how wonderful Darmanian was. Pretty soon we started seeing the two of them going to concerts, plays, movies. Most folks figured Darmanian to be using Esther. I mean, hell, she was probably fifteen years older than he was. Not that that's a crime, but she was homely as a mud fence, so don't tell me it was love."

Worthington kept the limousine cruising at a steady sixty miles per hour and went on.

"Some folks claim they actually got married, but I don't think that's true. What is true is that it wasn't long before Darmanian had moved his clinic to Woodlands and taken over the entire estate. A lot of people figure that he hypnotized her and really put the whammy on old Esther."

"And what did Esther say about all these accusations?" I asked him.

"She didn't live much longer to say much at all," Worthington said, his voice suddenly soft, hoarse. "She died shortly after Darmanian moved into Woodlands. It was in her will that the entire estate should go to him. And there weren't but a couple of distant cousins to protest the will. That was about ten years ago. Folks still miss Esther and talk about what happened. People really liked the old girl."

"Are you suggesting that Darmanian might have placed some hypnotic suggestion on Esther Woods and bent her to his will?" I asked him.

The driver shrugged, but his eyes caught mine in the rearview mirror and held them fast. "If Darmanian can make folks lose weight and give up smoking," he argued, "why couldn't he have hypnotized Esther Woods into giving him Woodlands."

It was my turn to shrug. "I don't know if it is possible to make someone do something against his or her will when they are hypnotized. When men and women give up smoking, for instance, they are responding to the hypnotist's suggestion to do something they really want to do. That's not the same as giving up a family estate."

"I think it is possible to make people do things against their will when they are under a hypnotist's spell," Worthington said, his jaw working hard against a stick of gum he had just placed in his mouth.

"It's a trance state, a sleep, an alterated state of consciousness," I corrected him. "It's not a spell."

"When Darmanian hypnotizes anyone," Worthington said firmly, "it has to be classified as a spell, mister. Call it the evil eye, call it the whammy. Darmanian has it!"

"Worthington," I scolded him, "next you'll tell me that Darmanian's whammy was so strong that it killed Esther Woods."

"There are those who say that is the way it happened," he shot back at me without hesitation. "She was found peacefully lying in her bed, but I've got it on good authority that the coroner said that it was as if her heart had just suddenly burst. The attack was that severe. The coroner told my friend that it was like she had either been scared to death or like her whole adrenal system had got stuck on working overtime."

"And Darmanian was the cause. Is that what you're saying?" I asked my driver. "Heart attacks by hypnosis?"

"I'm not swearing things happened this way," Worthington said softly. "I'm only telling you that Darmanian will never win a popularity contest in Saratoga Springs. Sure, the cops like him well enough, because he helps them with police work once in a while. And the big shots like him because of the publicity his clinic brings to the town. But the rest of the townspeople cross to the other side of the street when they see him coming. Of course, that ain't often, 'cause he hardly ever leaves Woodlands."

Suddenly Worthington hit the brakes. Up ahead the red light atop a highway patrol car was flashing danger and emergency. A Buick sedan had skidded off the wet pavement and rolled down a muddy embankment. An ambulance had pulled over on the shoulder and two paramedics were bent over a blanketed man on a stretcher. A solemn-faced patrolman was waving traffic by.

"In the midst of life, we are in death," the driver said solemnly. "You never know when the grim reaper is gonna knock your feet out from under you."

We sat for several moments in silence, the only sounds the *swip-swip* of the windshield wipers and Worthington, who was making peculiar sucking noises with pursed lips.

As we moved slowly past the accident, I wanted to shift our thoughts away from the highway reminder of our mortality and return them to our discussion of Darmanian.

"If Darmanian is such a monster," I asked, "why do you work for him?"

"Listen, Mr. Storm," Worthington said, suddenly nervous, glancing quickly from side to side as he turned the limousine down an arterial road off the main highway. "I was only telling you the gossip. Right? Darmanian has always been good to me. Gives me business. Tips good. Please don't tell him that I said anything about how people in Saratoga Springs talk about him."

"You were only helping me with my research," I said, smiling. "There's no need to apologize for what you told me. Darmanian is a very controversial man on a national—probably international—scale. He has many detractors who have said very negative things about his techniques and his methods. I'm here to see and to learn for myself."

Worthington fumbled with an unpleasantly soiled handkerchief, wadded it in a loose ball, and wiped his forehead and cheeks. I had not noticed how profusely the man was sweating on such a chilly April afternoon.

"Darmanian seems to have ways of knowing things," he said. "You'll soon see for yourself. Woodlands is right up ahead."

Chapter Three

I had not noticed until we rounded a bend in the road how we had steadily been working our way upward on the blacktop. Now, sprawling before us as if it were some magnificent King of the Mountain was the estate. Perhaps it was its great size that made Woodlands threatening rather than inviting. I felt suddenly in awe of the great mansion that towered above us on the road ahead.

The splendid house had been built in the Victorian tradition, probably in the late 1890s. There were towers and turrets and buttresses of wooden lace literally thrusting themselves forward and upward to demand equal attention from each stranger or visitor who happened upon the grand edifice. Whether responding to prevalent style or to the indulgence of personal taste, the architect had left nothing undecorated. Gothic spires seemed to scratch the overcast sky, and gargoyles nested in every corner and leaned out from every ledge. The malevolent leers and snarls of the wooden demons only added to the atmosphere of foreboding that seemed to grow heavier as we drew nearer the massive iron gate.

"My God, Worthington," I managed to say at last. "I thought you said Esther Woods was a gentle and much beloved member of your community. This house looks like the home of someone possessed."

Worthington treated me to another broad grin. "It is kinda weird looking, isn't it? Well, there are a lot of these old houses in Saratoga Springs. Oh, not this big, of course. The Woods family had a lot of money. Esther lived here because it was her family home. If you think the place is spooky looking, believe me, it suits Mr. Darmanian."

Worthington stopped the limousine in front of the gate. The metalwork was tall, ominous, and very heavy. The gate had been thickly set solidly into a stone wall. A large padlock hung from the links of a thick chain that twisted around and through the bars.

"Why is it locked?" I said frowning. "Darmanian is expecting me. He said that I was to come straight to Woodlands for dinner."

Worthington opened his door, then turned to fix me with a harsh stare as if I was an impatient child. "He's expecting you, sir. The gate is locked at Woodlands promptly at five fifteen each day. After that time, no one goes in, and no one goes out."

I glanced at the forbidding gate and smiled wanly. "Then am I to scale the bars, or are you going to shoot the lock off?"

Worthington considered smiling, but it was obvious that he had finished with pleasantries. He seemed nervous, irritable. "Neither, sir," he said humorlessly, producing a large key. "Darmanian gave me the key before I left, and I'm supposed to return it to him when I drop you at his front door."

Worthington made for the gate as if he were running a gauntlet. He jiggled the key in the lock unsuccessfully. He glanced back toward me, as if embarrassed to be standing there in the spotlight of the headlamps and to fail at opening the padlock. The rain seemed to have grown heavier, and Worthington manfully set to his task with renewed vigor.

"Got the damn thing," I heard him say, then he turned to look full into the headlights with a smile of accomplishment. He ran back through the pouring rain to the limousine and slid quickly behind the wheel.

The driveway to the main house was lined with shrubbery that had been meticulously trimmed and cared for. Worthington turned to speak to me once more as he braked in front of the large front door: "You will tell Mr. Darmanian that I did a good job of driving you, won't you, sir?"

"Of course," I assured him, but my attention was on the intimidating architecture of turrets, towers, and perching gargoyles. As Worthington held open my door and I was leaving the limousine, I noticed that the large brass knocker on the mansion's front entrance was nestled in the chubby arms of a winged cupid.

"Ah," I said, smiling at the plump, beatific features of Love's errand boy, "I hope there are more of your number around to offset all those menacing gargoyles."

I was about to reach for the knocker and announce our arrival when the front door opened. I am certain that my mouth must have gaped at the woman's astonishing beauty. She was tall, clothed in a flowing dress of some gauzy, white material. Her long, brown hair framed exquisite facial features which were dominated by two of the largest brown eyes that I had ever seen. She appeared almost as if she were some doe-eyed forest creature that had been magically transformed into humanhood for the sole purpose of elevating the lives of whomever she touched.

And the touch of her proffered hand was softly electric. "I'm Delores Touraine, Darmanian's assistant. Please come in, Mr. Storm."

"Please," my bedazzled brain managed to say. "Call me Eric."

"Eric," she said, smiling warmly. "Won't you please come in?"

Worthington edged by me, set my luggage just inside the door, and handed Delores the key to the padlock. "I'll be sure to lock the gate on the way out, ma'am," he said. Then, without another word, he turned quickly, shut the door behind him, and was gone.

I shook my head in puzzlement and smiled at the tall, slender Delores. Her white hostess gown was trimmed with embroidered rosebuds, and the full-sleeved sheer material made her appear to be a one-woman protest against the dreary April weather. The very aura of the lady declared spring within her heart. Delores Touraine appeared to be a delightful mixture of innocence and sensuality.

"I do hope your trip was pleasant," she remarked. "We have certainly been looking forward to your visit."

As if anticipating my unspoken query, Delores told me: "Darmanian is in meditation. Permit me to take your lighter bag, and, if you can manage the others, I'll show you to your room so that you might freshen up before dinner."

I draped the strap of my tape recorder over a shoulder, bent to pick up my heavier suitcase. I permitted Delores to take my portable typewriter and a small bag that was filled with light articles, such as underwear and stockings. I indicated that she should lead the way and we set out across the entryway to the staircase.

From what I could see of the downstairs, Woodlands was overfull of dark wood and heavy antique furniture. The staircase was set against the same dark wood to shoulder height, then a blue figured wallpaper stretched to the ceiling. The banister and posts were engraved with leaves, grains, and an assortment of woodland creatures. The hallway that lay beyond the top of the stairs seemed dark and poorly lighted.

There were several doors on the second floor, and their decorative woodwork appeared to be alternately carved with cupids and with gargoyles. "I see you have rooms for both saints and sinners," I said to Delores.

She turned to look at me over a shoulder, understood my comment when I gestured toward a scowling gargoyle with a nod of my head. "If you will count the doors," she told me, "you will find more gargoyles. In fact, the third floor is mostly gargoyles."

I saw two large double doors at the end of the hallway which obviously led to yet another floor of rooms. The place was truly enormous. I was thankful when Delores stopped at a door that was second from the end.

"How nice for you," she said with a smile, glancing upward. "There's a cupid over your door."

"Thank God," I said. "I always feel more comfortable on the side of the angels."

Delores paused to turn her large brown eyes directly on mine. "Really?" she questioned. "There's no devil in you at all?"

"Never on Sundays," I replied. "Sometimes on Saturday nights, though."

She stood for a moment in silence, then she smiled as though she had a private joke. "Tonight is only Monday," she said. "You have five nights to go."

Delores stepped into my bedroom, switched on the light. She set my suitcase and typewriter just inside the door. "I'll let you freshen up now. Each bedroom has its own bathroom facilities. I'll see you in the library as soon as you're ready. It's the room at the foot of the staircase and directly to the left."

I thanked Delores for her kindness in helping me to my room, then I entered with my suitcases. Pale yellow curtains draped two windows, which looked out over the roof of the veranda onto the lawn. I walked to the windows to see what I could of the view in the gathering darkness of the rainy April evening. I could not see much more than the humped back and pointed ears of a crouching gargoyle leaning over the edge of the roof directly in front of my room.

The room was predominantly yellow. A yellow figured rug matched a yellow spread on the double bed. There was a yellow quilt folded neatly on a wooden chest at the foot of the bed. The walls were of the same dark woodwork to shoulder height, and yellow wallpaper with a design of tiny flowers or grain shocks (I couldn't determine which) extended above their horizon. A marble-topped dresser with elegantly carved legs stood against one wall. A full-length mirror served me on the opposite wall.

The adjoining bathroom was dominated by a magnificent, old-fashioned tub supported by four three-toed, clawed feet grasping large ceramic balls. The toilet looked ancient, and a very new, cushioned seat seemed to be the only concession to the times. The sink, richly fashioned with gold-plated faucets, seemed to be original with the mansion. The medicine cabinet served as the support for a plump cupid who smiled down on me benignly from atop the shaving mirror.

I unpacked my shaving kit, hurriedly lathered, and removed the stubble bristling my chin. I hung up my clothes in the roomy closet, exchanged my blue plaid sport coat and slate gray trousers for a midnight blue suit. I decided against a white turtleneck in favor of a necktie until I was able to gauge how formal an occasion Darmanian considered the evening meal. I am certain that I took no longer than twenty minutes before I joined Delores in the library.

"How nice you look!" she said and smiled as I entered the room. I was suprised at her compliment, and I'm afraid I accepted it without a great deal of poise.

"Thank you," I said. "I've had this suit for so long it is kind of like my security blanket."

Delores nodded as though she understood. She closed the book that she had been reading, and I saw that it was my biography of Swedenborg. "Darmanian will be down shortly," she said, setting the book on the end table beside the dark leather chair in which she sat.

The library was lined with bookshelves that extended from the floor to the ceiling. A bibliophile as well as an author, I was curious to examine the titles and determine Darmanian's reading taste. I wondered how many of the books . . .

"Some of them were hers . . . Esther's," Delores said.

I turned, startled. It was the second time that she had seemingly responded to an unspoken thought. Did she merely anticipate one's questions through keen observation and supposition? Earlier, when she told me that Darmanian was in meditation, it would be considered obvious that a newly arrived guest might wonder where his host was. Now she noticed my attention turning toward the hundreds of titles on the bookshelves. It was coincidence and nothing more.

"I'm certain that Worthington must have told you about Esther Woods," Delores said, a slight edge to her voice.

If she were telepathic, there was no use lying. "Yes." I admitted. "I heard that Darmanian inherited Woodlands."

"So many of the townspeople are filled with poison toward Darmanian," Delores said bitterly. "They simply cannot comprehend his genius. What is strange to small-minded people often becomes something to be feared."

"An age-old conflict," I remarked. "Those who innovate and create must often fight the retarded thinking of those whom they are trying most to help."

"I know that the book you write about Darmanian will help him share his thoughts and his goodness with the world," she said, smiling confidently.

"That's why I'm here," I said with a shrug, trying for humility but only managing to sound like a dullard. "How did you come to be Darmanian's assistant?" I asked, hoping to divert her attention from my conversational ineptitude.

"I'm originally from Saratoga Springs," she answered without hesitation. "After college I went to New York to seek my fortune as a model."

"Yes, of course," I agreed blandly. "I'm certain that you must have been very successful."

"Oh, I quickly became the toast of Manhattan," she said with a laugh, tossing her long brown hair against the back of the leather chair. "I soon recognized that modeling could become the briefest of careers. I went into fashion designing and managed to build up a modestly successful business."

"How marvelous!" I said, wishing desperately that I had something to drink that might loosen both my sluggish brain and my awkward tongue.

"Marvelous, indeed," Delores said, smiling. "I managed to develop both an ulcer and a spastic colon, two marks of success instantly recognized and respected by every hard-driving career person."

"The purple hearts of all those who have made it," I said.

"So, I came limping back home to Mama a nervous wreck," she went on. "That was in 1972, not too long after Darmanian had moved his clinic to Woodlands. I went to Darmanian for hypnotherapy because I felt I had nothing to lose. And, I soon discovered that I had everything to gain. Darmanian really put me back together again—but better than I had been before."

"I should have had my tape recorder going," I said. "I just heard a testimonial for Darmanian."

"I owe him so much," Delores said softly, her large brown eyes growing misty around their edges. "He's wonderful. I underwent such rapid improvement through hypnotherapy that I stayed on with Darmanian to study under him. Eventually, thanks to his tutelage, I became proficient enough so that I might help others. There are no words adequate to express the skill and love of this man, Eric. I certainly don't envy your job attempting to define him in a book."

I was envious of the man who could inspire such loyalty and devotion from the beautiful woman sitting here before me. "I'll do my best," I said.

"Of course you will," came the deep, resonant voice behind me. "That is why I summoned you here, Eric Storm."

I had mentally rehearsed a dozen different ways to conduct myself during the my first meeting with Darmanian. As I turned to face the man, I realized that it would have been impossible to prepare adequately for the charismatic impact of the brilliant hypnotist.

Chapter Four

Darmanian stood tall, authoritatively erect, a slender but powerful figure in a well-tailored black suit. As he crossed the room to grip my hand in a firm clasp of friendship, he walked with the smooth, catlike grace of a sinewy panther.

"Welcome to Woodlands and to the New Age," he said with a smile, exposing fine white teeth. In spite of slightly saturnine features, Darmanian was darkly handsome. A spattering of gray at his temples only added to his personal attractiveness and provided an immediate visual confirmation of his seriousness of purpose.

I told him how pleased I was to be at Woodlands and to meet him, but he seemed not to hear. He made a sweeping gesture toward the bookshelves and said, "There are many fine volumes that will hold your interest should you have a few hours to spare from our work."

I began to answer in regard to my passion for

books, but the expansive movement of his arm had caused his coat to fall open from his chest, and my attention was immediately seized by the striking medallion that he wore about his neck. The large silver face bore the imprint of two sinuous, winged serpents, or dragons, supporting a crystal ball on pointed snouts that nearly touched. Each dragon had a blood-red ruby eye fixed on the many corruscating facets of the brilliant crystal.

"A family crest?" I inquired, my gaze riveted by the object.

Darmanian seemed pleased by my fascination with the medallion. "It is an artifact of my own creation," he said. "I find it very useful in the induction of the hypnotic trance state. Not that such physical stimuli are necessary, but some people seem to believe that they are."

"So many of Darmanian's clients are at the 'look me in the eye' level of sophistication when they first come to him," Delores remarked.

"She's correct," Darmanian agreed. "When I hold my medallion chain between thumb and forefinger and set the face to move gently back and forth, many people are assured that now they truly are about to be hypnotized. It actually helps place them in a more receptive mental state."

I nodded my understanding. "I guess the media have conditioned our responses even to the experience of hypnosis."

Darmanian's heavy-lidded blue eyes grew sad. "Yes, that is so. And they have done so with so many unfortunate misconceptions."

There was a moment of somewhat awkward silence as Darmanian seemed suddenly distracted by some internal dialogue. Then his dark features once again became friendly and animated. "I hope your trip was not unpleasant and that Delores has made you comfortable."

"The flight was uneventful, thank you," I said. "And Delores has been a charming and helpful hostess."

"Your room is to your satisfaction?" he inquired. There was a slight trace of accent in Darmanian's speech and I could not help noticing the almost labored precision with which he spoke, as if English had been a carefully learned second language.

"It is comfortable," I answered, pausing slightly and wondering if I could jokingly complain about the gargoyle at my window. I decided I hardly knew the man well enough to gauge his sense of humor.

"And it is my sincere hope that Worthington did not bore you with his inane chatter when he drove you from the airport," Darmanian said. "Did he say anything that troubled you?"

"Not at all," I assured the hypnotist. "I'm used to talkative taxi drivers in New York City. They all seem to feel that they are philosophers."

"Did he speak to you of the local gossip?" Darmanian asked, pursuing the issue.

"He spoke of the sort of things that I would expect to hear from a very provincial and modestly educated man," I said, wishing the subject had never arisen. I had no desire to upset my host within moments of our initial meeting.

"Yes," Darmanian said, stroking his chin between thumb and forefinger. "I suppose one might assume that an author of your varied experience has long since learned to place the comments of critics and detractors in their proper perspective."

Darmanian seemed at last prepared to drop the matter, and he stepped before Delores and offered her his hand. "Come," he said, helping her to her feet. "Let us go to the dining room. Agnes has prepared us a delightful dinner. I do hope that you enjoy seafood, Eric."

"Certainly," I replied, following them into an adjoining room.

Although the aroma of the food was most inviting, I found the atmosphere of the dining room instantly unpleasant.

The ceiling was somewhat too high, and the tall, stained-glass windows set against one wall gave me the impression that I was dining in a chapel. There was a narrow, tiled fireplace that looked chill in spite of the logs blazing across the andirons. The candelabras provided the room with additional dancing illumination that should have made for an aura of softness and warmth. Instead, the convoluted patterns of the carpet seemed treacherous, as though one had to avoid hidden falls and staked pits to attain a place at the massive table. Above all, a marble gargoyle grimaced down on us from the mantel, as if begging scraps from our plates.

"You're right, Delores," I said with a smile, nodding toward the winged beast. The gargoyles definitely outnumber the cupids."

"Always," Delores said, smiling, as Darmanian helped her to a comfortable sitting position at the table.

"I hope you don't find them morbid or grotesque," Darmanian said. "I am amused by the carvings and the architecture of the place in general. It is so . . . What is the word?"

"Campy," Delores supplied.

"Yes," Darmanian said, laughing. "It is all so high camp."

"Do you often do that?" I asked Delores as I slid my own chair closer to the table. "Supply the missing words and the endings to people's unspoken questions, I mean."

"I propose a toast," Darmanian announced, hoisting his wine glass to arm's length. Delores made some reply to my question, but Darmanian's exuberance smothered the words. "To Eric Storm, a skillful biographer, who shall translate and transmit my concepts for the world."

"Hear, hear," Delores said, as she clinked the edge of her glass against ours. "And may the book become a best-seller."

"Hear, hear," I said, laughing. "And to my host, whose genius and international reputation could have summoned me to the very gates of Hell for the opportunity of writing his biography."

Darmanian's heavy-lidded eyes narrowed, and in the flickering light of the candelabra between us he appeared almost serpentine. I felt strangely uncomfortable, as if my toast had somehow offended him. Then the blue eyes widened, and his thin lips formed a slight smile.

"Thank you, Eric," he said softly.

"And now," Delores reminded us, "let us drink our wine before it turns to vinegar."

It was excellent wine. And whoever the invisible Agnes might have been, she was a superb cook. A marvelously blended clam chowder was followed by a crisp salad carefully dressed with oil and vinegar. Large and succulent Maine lobsters had been removed from their shells, and there was nothing left for us to do but to dip the steamed meat into bowls of deliciously seasoned butter. French beans and almonds, together with baked potato, provided a nourishing balance to the meal. A lemon soufflé brought the meal to a wonderfully tart close.

Darmanian made certain that my wine glass was full before he asked me if I would like an after-dinner cigar.

"I have my pipe," I said, fetching my pouch from a coat pocket. "If Delores does not mind . . ."

"Not at all," she said. "I like the smell of a good pipe and a fine cigar. I myself"—she smiled at Darmanian—"was cured of the habit through hypnosis."

"I smoke only after the evening meal," the hypnotist explained, as if Delores's comment required an apology. He reached for an inner coat pocket and removed an elegant, black leather cigar case. "Then," he said, slipping a long, thin, dark cigar between his lips, "I truly enjoy a good smoke."

Darmanian flashed an expensive-looking lighter into full flame, held it a proper three inches beneath his cigar, and drew the fire to the tobacco. He sat in polite silence until I had my pipe loaded, tamped, and lighted.

"I should tell you a few of my thoughts about the book project," he said by way of preamble.

"By all means," I said.

"First of all, Eric, I really would like this book to examine my techniques and to emphasize my work, rather than my life," Darmanian told me. "My life is really rather dull. My true life expression lies in my work."

"Certainly the reader will wish to learn of how you

have accomplished so many almost miraculous cures," I agreed. "I believe there should be lots of case histories in the book."

"My files will be completely open to you," Darmanian said. "And I will arrange to spend certain hours each day for interviewing regarding the project."

"You have mentioned that time is of the essence," I reminded him.

Darmanian took a long pull on his cigar before he answered. "Yes," he said. "I am about to launch an exciting new phase of my work and I wanted you here for the advent of a series of experiments."

"I see," I said around the stem of my pipe. "Then I had better learn as much about your previous work as I possibly can so that I have the proper background and the correct perspective in which to present your new area of research."

Darmanian seemed pleased with my response. "That is why I insisted that you be here before the eighteenth. Tomorrow night I shall make a rare public appearance at a gathering of police officers in Albany. Although no one is yet aware of it, I have quite a surprise for everyone who attends the demonstration."

"A surprise, Darmanian?" Delores leaned forward, her eyebrows arching expectantly. "Have you been keeping a secret from me?"

The hypnotist laughed quietly. "A surprise is good for you, too, my dear. I would not wish for you to become bored with me."

Delores shook her head emphatically. "That could never happen, Darmanian. To me, you are the essence of excitement and vitality."

"I am certainly pleased to be on the scene when you introduce a new phase of your career, Darmanian," I said. "But I know that the readers of the book will want to know something of your background. I am sure that you sell yourself very short when you say your life has been dull. I know that I have always thought of your work as fascinating."

Darmanian shrugged, took a reflective pull on his cigar.

"People are always interested in learning of the childhood of a great man or woman," I went on. "They want to learn what elements during those formative years combined to produce the successful product of today."

"My childhood is unimportant," Darmanian said firmly. "What is important is what I have become. What I have made of myself. All that I have brought with me from my childhood is a powerful sense of destiny."

"But that in itself is important," I pointed out. "Did you envision yourself as a master hypnotist as a young boy? When did you begin to study hypnosis?"

Darmanian seemed to be considering my questions. I wished that I had had my tape recorder with me, for I sensed that he was about to reveal something of importance.

"Since earliest childhood," he began, "I have felt that I was destined to do important work. I had an adolescent conviction that I should form a new religion, perhaps, or structure a new politics or create a new society free of mental confusion and traumas."

I could not help smiling in satisfaction. "You see?" I said. "It was that childhood conviction that helped shape the healer and the idealist of today."

"Yes," Delores agreed. "You are such a private person, Darmanian. You must open up to Eric if he is to do the best kind of job possible on the book."

Darmanian's eyes narrowed again, as if he were weighing both decisions and memories. "I was a very solitary child, but I learned at an early age how easy it was to exercise control of people. I suppose that I was practicing a primitive, but effective, form of hypnosis. No doubt this gave me a sense of power."

Darmanian paused, tapped the white ash of his cigar into an ebony tray. He sipped at his wine for a moment, then set the glass down and fixed me with such a penetrating gaze that it seemed as though I could feel it in the deepest coils of my brain.

"Do you believe that we have lived before, Eric?" he asked me.

I was taken aback at that question that seemed so apropos of nothing. "Do you mean reincarnation?" I asked tentatively.

Darmanian nodded soberly. "Since earliest childhood I have had this strong conviction that I have lived before."

Delores shook her head as if in disbelief. "You never told me this before," she said.

Darmanian smiled, took her hand in his. "There are many things I have not yet told you, my darling."

"And you feel that this . . . conviction sharpened your sense of destiny and helped make you the man of vision that you are today," I commented.

"Quite so," Darmanian answered. "I once was given several stripes with my father's belt for persisting in telling him that this was not the first time that I had walked this earth."

The hypnotist tapped the medallion on his chest

with a forefinger. "You expressed curiosity about my medallion, Eric. It, too, was part of my reincarnational . . . fantasies, if you will. I seemed to remember it."

"Tell me, Eric," he said, looking intensely at me, as if seeking any sign of betrayal from my eyes. "So many people have commented that the image on my medallion triggers impressions within them. Does it do that for you? Do you seem to remember anything when you look at it?"

"I must confess that I was instantly drawn to it," I told him. "And it does seem somewhat familiar. But to be honest I think it is because of those serpents. I mean, I guess I share the almost universal distaste for snakes."

"They are dragons," Darmanian said, a bit impatiently. "You will note the wings."

"Yes, of course," I conceded. "But dragons, too, appear to have some almost universal archetypal significance, do they not?"

Darmanian was going on, apparently uninterested in my individual response to his medallion. "I first drew and colored the image on a cardboard shirt backing, then cut it and hung it around my neck with a red ribbon. It wasn't until I had saved enough money from a part-time job in high school that I could afford to have a skilled jeweler custom-craft this medallion to my specifications."

Delores was about to speak when a door behind Darmanian opened and a smallish, pinch-faced woman in a dark dress and white apron entered and approached her in a very obsequious manner. "Yes, Agnes?" Delores asked, inclining her head toward the woman.

"May I clean up the table now, ma'am?" Her eyes seemed held by something on the floor, and her question had the whining tone of one who is begging.

"We'll be leaving the table in a moment, Agnes," Delores said. "Please wait in the kitchen until I summon you."

"The meal was excellent, Agnes," Darmanian pronounced in an expansive lord-of-the-manor gesture.

The gray-haired woman suddenly looked up, her features animated, her thin, reddish hands rubbing themselves together in unrestrained pleasure. "Oh, thank you sir," she said, grinning. "I'm so happy you found the food to your liking."

Without another word the woman clucked happily and went back to the kitchen. A prisoner condemned to death row who just had been granted a reprieve could not have undergone a more rapid transformation from baleful resignation to hopeful exuberance.

I took advantage of the distraction to make a point with Darmanian. "Stories like the one about your medallion are the kind of personal anecdotes that readers like," I said. "It is obvious that you are a private person. Judging from my background reading, it would seem that not even *Time* magazine was able to ferret out the details of your past. We've got to be more open in the book."

Darmanian tapped his cigar on the edge of the ebony tray. He glanced at Delores and smiled before he returned his attention to me. "I was born Lucius Adolphus Darmanian on October 30, 1931," he said softly. "My father was a pharmacist in Auburn, New York. My mother had been a schoolteacher."

Delores's laughter was background music of approval. "Eric, you are now one of a very select, very small company who know Darmanian's full name."

"And once we have noted it at the beginning of the book, we need never mention it again," I told her. "There is no reason why I should not refer to Darmanian in the manner he most prefers."

Darmanian nodded over his cigar, then continued: "My ancestry is Middle European. My mild, ineffectual father used to boast that the blood of the great Hungarian warriors who held the Turks from invading Europe coursed wildly through our veins."

My pipe rattled with spittle, and I removed it hastily from my mouth.

Darmanian sipped at his wine, stared reflectively for a moment into the deep, red liquid. "My parents were both obsessed with religion," he continued. "It seemed as though they were constantly switching from Roman Catholicism to Protestantism in a perpetual effort to be on the winning side when Judgment Day sounded its awesome trumpet."

It was difficult to envision Darmanian having been reared in a churched background. He seemed somehow aloof from matters of the spirit. I thought again how amazing it was that he seriously entertained the metaphysics of reincarnation.

"When I was a boy of about thirteen," the hypnotist went on, "my parents dragged me along to an old-fashioned, evangelistic tent meeting. The men and women were seated on wooden planks set on concrete blocks, and there was sawdust scattered on the ground.

"A tall, gaunt, full-bearded hellfire specialist, who looked for all the world like an Old Testament prophet, was shouting about how we must all be born again. Everyone there must come forward and be born again."

Darmanian interrupted himself with his own appreciative laughter as he visualized the memory. "I was suffused with adolescent fervor and misunderstanding," he told us. "I jumped to my feet in the midst of those sweating, fundamentalist fanatics and shouted out that I had been born again"

"You can imagine the excitement as people began shouting to hear my testimony," Darmanian said. "My father's eyes were rolling in his head as though he were in ecstasy. My mother was screaming her thanks to God.

"Dozens of hands pushed me toward the preacher on the coarse plank platform. I shall never forget that big, bearded face, dripping with sweat, pushing itself next to mine. 'Tell us, boy!' he demanded. 'Tell us!' "

Darmanian lifted his medallion in both hands, held it at arm's length. "I jerked my cardboard medallion from under my shirt. I suppose the frenzied Holy Rollers thought it at first to be a religious medal. Then I shouted: 'I have been born again. I lived before hundreds of years ago, and I have returned. This is my sign unto you!' "

Darmanian had begun to laugh so hard that he was forced to interrupt his anecdote for a few moments while he regained his composure. "That sweaty, bug-eyed servant of Jehovah grabbed my medallion from my neck and screamed at the chanting sinners in an incredibly high-pitched voice: 'He's got serpents around his neck! He's wearing the seal of Satan!' "

Delores placed a hand on Darmanian's forearm. "How terrible for you to have experienced such a thing as a young boy!" she said, her large brown eyes glowing with pity.

Darmanian patted her hand gently, but his lips had curled into a sneer. "I'm certain you can both imagine what happened next. That whole damn tent descended on me. I was prayed over, exhorted over, exorcised, and soundly thumped until I began to vomit. And my pitiful wretchings they took to be a sign that Satan had left me."

"What an incredible experience," I said, shaking my head sadly.

Darmanian had not finished: "When we got home, my father beat me with a belt to be quite certain that any residue of Satan would be thoroughly flayed from my body. He told me if he ever caught me wearing that medallion again, he would beat me until I was crippled. I took him at his word. I never let him catch me wearing it."

Delores frowned her distaste of the episode, then asked: "But what happened when you were in high school and you had the real medallion made?"

Darmanian seemed to become wistful for just a moment. "Oh, my father was dead by then. One night he choked on a piece of steak while he was ranting over some imagined sin of mine at the dinner table. You know, it's remarkable the number of people who die each year from choking on meat. I've considered becoming a vegetarian for that reason alone."

"And your mother?" I asked, suppressing a strange chill that had suddenly set my flesh to trembling. It seemed somehow inordinately cold in the dining room.

"She died within a month of Father," Darmanian answered, dropping his eyes once again to the wine glass. "Of a broken heart, I guess. I was on my own in this world of terror and chaos when I was but fourteen."

There seemed nothing relevant to say, but Darmanian himself broke the silence. "This," he said, stroking the medallion, "seemed the only real thing in my life. It seemed the only tangible anchor in a transitory world. I had only my medallion and my vision of assisting others to find themselves free of earthly torments."

"Blast it, Darmanian," I complained. "I do wish that I had recorded all of this."

Delores laughed. "I'll help you remember all of it, Eric."

"Ah ha." The hypnotist smiled. "It appears that you have gained a willing assistant in your reportorial endeavors."

Delores nodded her lovely head in affirmation. "You know that I will do anything to see that this book is a success, my darling," she said soberly. "Properly written, it can do so much to vindicate you in the nasty eyes of your critics."

Darmanian snuffed the cigar in the tray before him. "It is as it should be," he remarked. "The three of us working together. I feel very strongly that we have worked as one before."

"Do you mean," I asked, "in some previous lifetime?"

Darmanian's heavy-lidded blue eyes widened and held my own fast. "Yes," he answered without hesitation. "Do you find that so hard to believe?"

"I keep an open mind about such matters," I said.

"Good," he said, smiling. "I have the strongest conviction that we may have come together in this lifetime because we left something unfinished in another."

Delores stretched her hand across the table and entwined her fingers among those of my right hand. "Perhaps Eric left your biography incomplete in a previous lifetime," she said, smiling warmly.

"Perhaps," Darmanian said. "I know that something has been set in motion. I believe that it is our Karma that we should have met again."

"Karma," I echoed. "Is that the same as punishment?"

"Not at all," Darmanian explained. "It is divine compensation. Cosmic cause and effect. "What you sow, so shall you reap. It is a process of evolution and growth, not punishment; but we do pay our debts to one another so that our personal dramas may be completed and we may move on to a higher level of consciousness."

My brain was becoming a bit boggled, both from the wine and my continuing astonishment that this brilliant and resourceful innovator of hypnotherapies ascribed so firmly to the ancient doctrine of reincarnation. I was so involved in an internal dialogue assessing the significance of this peculiar eccentricity that Darmanian had to repeat his question to me. "I'm sorry," I apologized.

"I asked if you knew anyone in the area other than us," Darmanian said.

"Only by correspondence," I explained. "There is a man here in Saratoga Springs with whom I have been corresponding since the release of my book on Swedenborg. He seems to be a very accomplished scholar of the occult and metaphysics."

Darmanian arched a heavy, dark eyebrow. "Really? What is his name?"

"Vogel," I answered. "Edward Vogel. Do you know him? I am certain that he could speak to you at great length about such things as reincarnation."

Darmanian toyed with the stem of his wine glass. "And why should you correspond with a man with interests that seem so alien to your own?"

For some reason I was growing uneasy with Darmanian's questions. He seemed to be interrogating me for some purpose that I could not determine. "As you know, the biography of Swedenborg explored the life of a brilliant mystic," I replied. "Vogel has been encouraging me to turn my talents—however meager they might be—to write biographies of certain contemporary mystics and psychic sensitives."

The aura of tension seemed at last to have dissipated. Darmanian was once more the affable host, and I could feel the muscles in my back and neck begin to relax.

"Let us adjourn to the library," Darmanian said, pushing back his chair and rising.

"Only if you keep Salem away from me," Delores said, her lips forming a playful pout as Darmanian helped her with her chair. "That creature haunts the library this time of night."

"My God!" I exclaimed with a laugh. "I hope you're not speaking of one of those damned gargoyles come to life!"

"Not at all," Darmanian explained. "I obtained a beautiful black cat for Delores, but she claims not to like it."

"Darling," she protested. "I have never liked cats.

Besides, Salem loves you. She spends more time on your lap than I do!"

"I know that you will soon grow to love her," Darmanian said somewhat forcefully.

"That will be the day," Delores said, her lips crinkling into an expression of distaste.

"A very important day," Darmanian told her as he took her arm in his. "Come, Eric," he said, his face serious as his free hand firmly gripped my shoulder. "Let us talk for a bit in the library before we retire. It is good to be together . . . again."

I rose to follow them into the library. I convinced myself that the involuntary shudder that seized my body at the touch of Darmanian's hand on my shoulder was due to the April chill that had so thoroughly permeated the room. It was not, I silenced my inner voice, due to the sudden menace that I had seen in those magnetic blue eyes.

Chapter Five

Sleep seemed almost impossible to attain that first night in Woodlands. I was puzzled and, yes, disturbed by certain of Darmanian's comments, especially his preoccupation with reincarnation. He seemed determined to bring up the subject at every turn in our conversation. Would the average American man or woman seeking hypnotherapy have confidence in a practitioner who discussed their past lives with them? Surely, Darmanian kept his personal philosophy a secret from his patients.

I was disturbed in yet another, much more basic and primitive, area by the presence of Delores Touraine. I couldn't remember when I had encountered a woman more compelling, more captivating. I did not wish to create false hopes, but there were times when she had looked at me across the table that she had seemed an almost obtainable dream. Her attitude toward Darmanian seemed strangely ambivalent. She appeared to vacillate between an almost worshipful idolatry of his deeds and a cool, distant aloofness toward his words. It was as if his love had not managed to touch her innermost depths, and she was yet open to the promises of the right other man.

Then there was the ungodly chill and dampness of the room. Someone, in a desire to be thoughtful, no doubt, had opened my window before I returned, and the spring wind had borne a generous supply of April rain through the screen. Although I had quickly shut the window upon entering the room, I was certain the temperature must have dropped to sixty degrees.

My sheets and blankets seemed to be damp enough to wring, and my body heat was making little progress in making a nest of warmth under the covers.

To make matters worse, thunder and lightning had begun a violent atmospheric "show and tell." And the damn window glass was loose in the panes so that the wind that was ever growing in velocity had begun to rattle the individual plates in several discordant frequencies.

The only one who appeared to be enjoying the evening was the humped-back gargoyle outside my window, and in the explosion of the lightning flashes I once thought that he had looked at me over his shoulder.

There was the musty stench of old wood in the room as the humidity rose within its walls, and I did so wish that the ancient fireplace in a corner of the bedroom was still operable. A handsome marble mantel matched the marble-topped dresser, and its once serviceable mouth was now closed by an ornate wooden fan. I toyed with the notion of splintering the decoration into kindling and setting it ablaze across the old iron hearth. But no doubt Darmanian would steam at the inconsiderate action of his guest, and the room would probably be filled with smoke from a chimney clogged with birds' nests.

The wind had risen to a rushing speed that produced the inevitable howling wail as it moved across the roofs, turrets, towers, and chimneys of the sprawling old mansion. And even though Woodlands appeared as sound as a fortress of steel, it now began to creak and groan from a dozen different points of weakness. It was as if the keening wind provided the music for a chorus of protesting voices within the ancient, darkened corridors of the big house.

Feeling more than a little irritable from lack of sleep and rather frustrated over my mental replays of the evening's conversation, I sat up in bed. It truly seemed as though the window glass would be set free of their panes unless I once again raised the windows and eased some of the pressure from the wind. I cursed myself for not remembering my velvet bathrobe. Then, using the chill of the room as an excuse for my ill temper, I pulled the top blanket from the bed and draped it around my shoulders.

The damp April wind touched my flesh through the thin material of my pajamas as I opened the window the slightest crack. I wrapped my blanket tighter around me and paused for a moment to study the roiling black clouds as they churned over the wooded hills surrounding the estate.

That was when I noticed the light dancing eerily in the garden. It had suddenly become very dark, and I prayed for a flash of lightning to illuminate the area below so that I might have some clue as to the source of the strange glow. I frowned into the blackness, straining to see better any object that might be surrounding the light or that might be bearing it toward the thick stand of trees that bordered the lawn.

Somehow my attention was directed toward the hills again, and I was startled to see another light bobbing rather quickly through the trees. It seemed to twist and bounce as though it were tied to the back of some great, writhing, night-crawling serpent.

I stood before the window in total fascination. Perhaps I was observing some local phenomenon of the area. Perhaps I was witnessing some sort of foxfire or will-o'-the-wisp. Yet I realized that the concentration of light was too steady, and even though the rain smashing against the window glass was distorting my vision, I felt certain the globes of illumination were both man-made.

At last the two lights met at the very edge of the woods, and an obliging explosion of lightning revealed two men in dark raincoats carrying large flashlights. I felt certain that one of the men was Darmanian.

I remembered Worthington saying that the gates to Woodlands were locked promptly at five fifteen each afternoon. Darmanian's late night visitor had come from somewhere over the forested hill.

In the next dramatic flash of lightning I saw the figure I took to be Darmanian walking swiftly back toward the mansion bearing a rather large bundle or package in his arms. The other light was bobbing its way back along a forest trail.

A chill prickled my body, and I began suddenly to shiver. As if I were somehow bringing down the curtain on a drama far beyond my capacity to understand, I slammed the window against its sill—and to hell with the glass breaking in the wind!

The lightning erupted again, and I saw that Darmanian had stopped in the garden below and was looking up at my window. Could he have heard the slamming of the window above the night noises of rain and wind?

His flashlight beam turned upward, probing the darkness near my window. I found myself jumping backward, tripping over the blanket I had wrapped about me, and falling across the bed. I really had no idea why I had not wanted him to know that I had seen his mysterious midnight rendezvous. Yet I somehow felt that I had spied upon him and had witnessed something that was none of my business. And I was somehow convinced that that was precisely how Darmanian would view my presence at the window.

The searching beam of light must have remained at my window for at least fifteen or twenty seconds before it returned to the garden below. With a rush of self-awareness, I realized that I had been holding my breath.

"My God, man!" I cursed my weakness. "You act as if you are afraid of your distinguished host! Eccentricities are supposed to make for amusing or even insightful anecdotes if the writer is truly skilled. Go to sleep, you blithering idiot, and ask about the midnight expedition in the morning. You know that Darmanian will have a logical explanation for what appeared to be an extremely bizarre activity."

And amazingly, in spite of the chill, in spite of my confusion and bewilderment, I did crawl once again beneath the damp, musty-smelling blankets, and fall quickly asleep.

But the blessed arms of Morpheus were not to hold me for very long. I could not have slept for more than an hour when I awakened feeling unbearably warm. I took a deep breath, and heat seemed to fill my mouth like a thick, unpleasant liquid.

I sat up, shaking off the blanket that a short time ago I had been clutching to me to keep warm. Now the same blanket was sticking to the sweat that was coursing from my body.

Dazed, slightly nauseated, my head throbbing from the humid closeness of the room and from lack of sleep, I struggled with the question of how the bedroom that had been so chilly such a short time ago was now literally pulsating with warmth.

Before any possible solution could present itself, I heard the sound of muffled weeping. No sooner than I had been alerted to the sobbing than an anguished scream of a woman in severest travail split the night and rose above the wail of wind and the drumming of rain.

"I'm burning!" was the terrible cry that followed the dying echo of the scream. "Help me! Oh, help me! I'm burning!"

There was more, but unintelligible. There was a name—or so it seemed—of someone who was being asked to help. It seemed a Spanish name. Something like Diaz. Something-or-other Diaz. And other people were being called swine, bastards, and a variety of choice expletives.

At last I recognized the voice to be that of Delores Touraine. And as her sobs and cries lessened in intensity and volume, I heard Darmanian's deep tones attempting to calm her.

Both of their voices soon trailed off into a murmured dialogue, which was far below the range of my hearing. I could easily imagine Darmanian soothing her, and Delores describing the awfulness of her dream. Perhaps, she, too, had awakened in the uncomfortable warmth, and that aspect of the psyche that seeks to preserve the sleep state had incorporated the heat into a dream of fire, which had regrettably outgrown its perimeters and crossed the borders of nightmare.

"What Darmanian is dealing with," I said aloud as I lay back across the bed and yawned toward the ceiling, "is a stuck thermostat. The damn furnace kicked in against the chill of the rainstorm and just kept pumping out heat."

I placed the extra pillow over my upward ear as I turned over on my side. Although I could not make out individual words any longer, I could still hear the hypnotist attempting to calm Delores, and I sincerely wanted to have another go at sleeping. Tomorrow would begin the steady work of interviewing Darmanian and researching his case histories. And tomorrow night was Darmanian's demonstration before the area law enforcement officers. I did so want to get some rest.

I am not certain that I ever slept that night. A bizarre montage of grotesque images continuously flitted across my fatigued brain. A crouching, hideous night creature beat its wing outside my window. Two dancing lights raced madly toward each other in the blackness of a rainy night. As they touched, they were instantly transformed into two men, one of whom bore Darmanian's saturnine features. The men exchanged gifts and disappeared in a flash of lightning. The lightning struck a pile of oily rags and burst into flame. Delores came with a broom to sweep up the flaming mess, and she, too, caught fire.

In the theater of my dreams Delores was screaming for help when my eyes jerked wildly open—only to close to a tight squint against the early morning sun.

The scream, though, was really the soft squeal of my bedroom door as its rusty old hinges protested against their service. I turned to see the partially opened door in the process of being closed.

"Yes?" I called out to whoever had begun to enter my room unannounced.

But the door closed without my receiving an answer to my exceedingly polite response to someone invading my privacy.

I closed my eyes and sought vainly for at least a semblance of sleep, but I was too much on edge after the incident. I kept feeling that the moment I might fall asleep someone would sneak into the room. Who would do this and for what reason I could not imagine, but the absence of logic did nothing to lull me to sleep. Although it was difficult to conceive of Darmanian, Delores, or even the maid Agnes creeping into my room, the uncomfortable fact remained that someone had just attempted to enter my room and had not declared himself or herself when I indicated that I was awake.

I swung my feet over the edge of the bed, reached for my digital wristwatch on the nightstand, pressed the time button. It was early—seven fifty-one. The fresh light of dawn revealed that it had stopped raining.

I decided to walk to the window to verify that last night's overly dramatic April shower had ceased and that it had been an authentic ray of sunlight that had poured into my eyes. As I glanced down toward the garden and the grounds, I was astonished to see Darmanian digging with a long-handled shovel near the stone archway at the far end of the sidewalk leading toward what appeared to be a guest cottage.

"Does the man never sleep?" I asked myself aloud. I thought again of the strange, rain-drenched meeting that I had witnessed between Darmanian and an unknown man. Now what was he doing? Planting tulips?

Darmanian set the shovel aside, knelt beside a small mound of dirt, and appeared to shape it with his hands. Then he stood erect, thrust his arms toward the morning sun, and began to sound a deep, bass mantra, which he sustained far longer than I had thought possible without one's having to take a breath.

He offered me yet one more surprise before he picked up his shovel and returned to the house. He shouted the same Spanish-sounding name that I had heard Delores calling out in her terrible, fiery nightmare: *Ansemo Diaz!*

Chapter Six

I breakfasted alone that morning, for by the time I had showered and dressed, Darmanian and Delores were already meeting their first clients of the day in the offices that occupied the west wing of Woodlands. It was a few minutes before nine when I entered the dining room. The day was sunny, and the room did not seem nearly as chilly and unpleasant as it had the night before.

"They're early risers," Agnes explained as she served me an omelet, tea with cream, and dry toast. "Sometimes patients start arriving before eight."

I sliced at the omelet with the edge of my fork. Bits of mushrooms and ham had been skillfully mixed with a thick cheese, and the individual scents of the ingredients blended together in an aroma that set my tastebuds into anticipatory salivation. The omelet was superb.

"Agnes, you are a magnificent cook," I complimented her. "Darmanian must have stolen you away from a fine restaurant somewhere."

Agnes shook a strand of gray hair back in place, smiled broadly at my words of appreciation. She wiped her hands on her apron in a gesture of awkward satisfaction, then returned to the kitchen. For the first time I noticed that the small, thin woman walked with a bit of a limp.

Before I had finished my omelet, Agnes returned with a fresh pot of tea. As I looked up to smile at her and acknowledge her presence, I noticed that her features were set in an austere attitude of sobriety. "I came of my own accord," she said.

"I beg pardon," I said, frowning, momentarily at a loss for a reference point by which to make sense of her statement.

"Mr. Darmanian didn't steal me," she told me. "I came of my own accord. I would have left the restaurant by and by, and, besides, coming to work for him was small enough payment for what he did for me."

"I see," I replied. "You were actually a cook in an elegant restaurant somewhere."

"It wasn't so elegant," Agnes volunteered. "Just a little home-style place in Camden, New Jersey. Mr. Darmanian used to eat there when he was a boy. He used to come in after school. He'd look at me, half-crippled, almost a freak, slaving in that hot kitchen, and he'd tell me how someday he'd cure me and put me to work cooking for him. Well, he kept his promise. He came back one day and put me through his therapy. Now I barely limp at all."

"That's marvelous, Agnes," I said around a mouthful of toast. "I must interview you for the book. Would you like that?"

THE HYPNOTIST 63

"If it will help Mr. Darmanian," she said, pushing crumbs from the table with the edge of a small, leathery hand so that they landed in the net she had made with her apron.

Then a niggling thought surfaced. "Did you say Camden, New Jersey?"

"Yes, sir," she answered, her somber, pinched features now hovering over my left shoulder.

"I understood Mr. Darmanian to say that he grew up in Auburn, New York."

Agnes shook her head emphatically. "No, sir. Camden, New Jersey. I've known him since he was but a lad of twelve or so. Lost his parents at an early age, he did. He's been on his own most of his life."

"But his father was a pharmacist." I questioned her. "I do have that information correct, do I not?"

"Oh, no, sir," Agnes shook her head again. "His father was a common laborer. Just a common—"

"Ah, Eric," Darmanian's deep voice sounded behind us. "I see that you have arisen and that you have enjoyed one of Agnes's delicious omelets. Aren't they good?"

Before I could turn to greet my host, he had moved into the chair opposite me. "Agnes, please get me some black coffee," he said in that peculiarly accented voice. "From the fresh pot in the kitchen, please."

Darmanian was dressed in a black-and-white tweed sport coat with black turtleneck and gray trousers. The medallion clanked against the edge of the table as he moved his chair closer. He touched it gingerly with his fingers, turned it face upward as if to inspect it for damage. Satisfied that neither serpent had lost a ruby eye to the table's edge, he turned his attention to me.

"How did you sleep?" he asked. "I do hope the bed was comfortable and that the sounds of the storm did not disturb you."

I looped a forefinger through the stem of my cup so that I might better receive the fresh brew Darmanian was offering me from the pot Agnes had brought to the table. "I often have difficulty adjusting to a strange bed," I said honestly. "I regretfully am not one of those who can go immediately to sleep in new surroundings."

Darmanian's blue eyes narrowed slightly, and they seemed to be probing my own with such intensity that I at last lowered my gaze to the remnants of my omelet. I reached for the fork and began to find a bit of ham in order to mask my discomfort.

"Agnes's omelets are very good," I said, wishing to break the peculiar silence that had settled between us. "You are lucky to have such a good cook."

Then I decided to continue my verbal maneuvers with a direct question. "Is it true that Agnes has known you since you were a boy?"

"No," Darmanian said sharply. "That is not true. I met Agnes when she came to Saratoga Springs for therapy. From our first meeting she had been convinced that I am the boy who used to promise her that he would one day heal her."

"She is certainly convinced in her own mind that such is the case," I said, lifting my eyes once again to meet those piercing blue orbs that had hypnotized thousands of men and women.

Darmanian smiled, his eyes now lidded, tranquil. "In her own mind," he said, "such may be the case."

"Well, if I could find a cook like that," I offered, hoping to divert the subject at least momentarily, "I wouldn't care if she believed that I was her Uncle Harry."

I returned my attention to the last bites of omelet on my plate. I could literally feel Darmanian's eyes on my face. "The more material we include of a personal nature, the more people will relate to you as a human being," I told him. "Readers simply need those basic reference points of when you were born, who your parents were, whether or not you might have some famous ancestors."

"Each man is his own ancestor," Darmanian said, his voice barely more than a whisper. "And each man is his own heir. The man who is truly in balance creates his own future and inherits his own past."

"That is beautifully stated," I conceded. "And I'm willing to forego a lot of the standard background data in favor of the here and now and the dramatic results of your therapy. But people still need to place you in some kind of precise time context, even though they know you are contemporaneous with them in a general sense."

Darmanian glanced up at Agnes as she reentered the room with a tray of coffee and fruit juices. "I thought you'd be wanting your juices now, sir." she said to her employer, a tiny smile playing with her thin lips. She seemed hungry for any crumb of affection that might fall from her master's lap.

"You are very thoughtful, Agnes," he nodded.

"Thank you, sir," she said, her full smile indicating that Darmanian's words had reassured her. Her limp was barely perceptible as she walked proudly from the dining room, bearing my dirty breakfast dishes on a tray.

"As regards one's birth," Darmanian said. "It was Richard Whately, Archbishop of Dublin, who once remarked that the happiest lot for a man, as far as his birth is concerned, is that it should give him as little occasion as possible to think about it at all."

"Well stated," I smiled. "And certainly true as far as it goes. But as a biographer, I must take as my standard the words of the poet Longfellow, who observed that a life worth writing about at all is worth writing about minutely and truthfully."

Darmanian's eyes held my own for several moments. "It will be good having you about the place, Eric," he said at last, just the slightest indication of a smile tugging at one side of his mouth. Then, rising to his feet, he asked me: "Are you ready to begin work?"

"Certainly," I said, wiping my mouth with a fine linen napkin Agnes had provided. "Just a moment, and I'll get my tape recorder from my room."

"I have not time for interviews today," Darmanian said firmly. "I must prepare for tonight's presentation. I will now merely show you the office we have set aside for you and acquaint you with my files and records."

As we walked from the dining room, Darmanian suddenly stopped, turned to face me. "Did it puzzle you to see me out in the garden in the rain last night?" he asked, as if he had divined the unspoken question that had been bobbing about inside my brain ever since I had seen Darmanian, flashlight in hand, meeting the stranger at the edge of the woods.

Small beadlets of sweat dotted my upper lip. My stomach felt as though I were standing in an elevator that had just dropped two floors. I had only my intuition to guide me. I decided to lie.

"I guess I must have slept through that," I said, trying for a straight wide-eyed bluff.

Darmanian studied me for several seconds as if his eyes were small but relentless blue inquisitors. He nodded slowly, as if accepting my denial of having witnessed the mysterious transaction in the rain. Then, without another word, he resumed our exodus from the dining room.

As we walked to the west wing, we passed a room in which I could see a grand piano. Sensing both my hesitation and my interest, Darmanian paused to inform me that that was the music room. He stepped inside and bade me to do the same.

"I do hope that I shall have the pleasure of hearing you play the piano very soon," I said.

Darmanian made a slight bow. "I should consider it a pleasure to play for you."

The piano now stood tightly shut, a rich golden candelabra above the music rest. A marble-topped table held a fresh bouquet of yellow roses. Here and there about the room were a number of elegant chairs, some stuffed and warm, others with legs as thin as twigs and seats barely cushioned. The brilliant morning sun streamed through a large stained-glass window and scattered fragments of blue, orange, yellow, green, and red on the dark wood of the wall.

The far end of the room was dominated by a large work of marble statuary, which set against the purple stripes of the wallpaper and the flowered carpet, appeared commanding and forceful. At first the piece seemed to have caught the final death struggles of some unfortunate wretch set upon by grotesque monsters, so I could do nothing else than to approach the marble work for a closer look.

As I drew nearer, I could perceive a warrior with breast plate and sword just beginning to rise from a kneeling position. The double-edged blade had severed the head of an ugly, dog-faced creature and was now pointed at the breast of a cadaverous man with a pointed head. A hulking brute seemed held at bay behind the smaller menace, and the large club he held in a massive paw seemed ineffectual against the knight's sword. Sprawled in his death throes behind the hulk was a hideous, toad-faced monster whose mace and chain would smash and bite no new victims.

Although the work appeared to be of great antiquity, I was astonished to see that the conquering warrior bore Darmanian's medallion about his neck.

"One of my early patients sculpted it," the hypnotist explained. "I'm afraid that he had a very idealistic conception of his therapist. As you can see, the statuary represents me triumphing over the forces of ignorance, prejudice, greed, and the small-minded guardians of the Establishment, whose conventional restraints and regulations inhibit progress."

"It is certainly . . . impressive," I offered after several moments' reflection.

"It is really quite terrible," Darmanian said. "But somehow it inspires me when the going gets a bit rough. And the poor artisan who did it worked so long and so damn hard chipping it all out of marble that I felt I must show at least enough gratitude to display the piece."

Without any additional discussion Darmanian led me from the music room into the west wing, where the clinic was located. He pushed open two large double doors, and we walked down a green-carpeted hallway that brought us to a beaming, white-haired woman in her early sixties. The white-smocked lady sat at a large walnut desk, and she seemed fully capable of dealing with the two punch-button telephones and the Executive model IBM typewriter that barricaded her from the clients who entered the clinic through the door to her left.

"Miss Lundby," Darmanian told the woman, who reminded me of a perpetually smiling elementary school teacher I had once had, "this is Eric Storm, the writer about whom I have told you."

"Oh, how nice to meet you, Mr. Storm," she said in such an old-fashioned sweet tone that I nearly expected her to rise to her feet, step away from the desk, and curtsy.

I told Miss Lundby that it was a pleasure to meet her and that she should call me Eric.

"Miss Lundby will assist you in any way that she can," Darmanian assured me, and Miss Lundby nodded vigorously in agreement.

"Over here"—the hypnotist indicated a room with a gesture of his right hand—"is a small office we have set aside for your use while you are exploring the various files. The rest of the time I expect that you will wish to use your room, where it will be much quieter for writing."

Darmanian glanced at his watch, and Miss Lundby immediately picked up the cue.

"You have five minutes, Mr. Darmanian. Mrs. Van Raessler is coming for her weekly weight control reinforcement." Miss Lundby unconsciously drew in her rather plump midsection as she read from the appointment book.

"You will, of course, excuse me, Eric," Darmanian said. "I must have a few minutes to myself before my client arrives. You will find a number of folders that I have sorted and placed upon a desk in your office."

With those words of dismissal, the hypnotist turned and walked into a room I took to be his own office.

"Would you like some coffee?" Miss Lundby asked, true to what would appear to have been a lifetime training as an efficient secretary.

I thanked her, told that I had just finished breakfast, and entered my office. As Darmanian had promised, a medium-sized desk held several file folders in addition to a Selectric IBM typewriter, a number of pencils and ballpoint pens, and a fresh ream of paper. No one could fault my host for consideration.

I spent the next two hours reading accounts of how Darmanian had salvaged the lives of men and women who had been mentally maimed by the ravages of war horrors, the traumas of adjusting to a Space Age world, the neuroses of adapting to marital or job situations. In each instance the genius of Darmanian's approach to hypnotherapy had restructured the lives once nearly destroyed.

It was ten minutes to twelve when I heard a slight tapping on the frame of the door, which I had left open. I was delighted to see Delores standing there, smiling quizzically at me.

"Are you finding anything of interest?" she asked. "Anything that will be useful to you?"

She was dressed in a beige-colored dress that reached just below the knee. A cream-colored cardigan sweater and attractive, low-heeled shoes completed her sensible work ensemble. As before, Delores transmitted the aura of sensual vulnerability strangely blended with studied aloofness.

"I am certain that there will be a great deal of material here that I can follow up on," I said. "At this point, of course, I am merely reading and gaining an overview of Darmanian's work. I can't begin to get a solid fix on how the book will evolve until I have read many more cases and until I have spent some time interviewing Darmanian."

Delores nodded her understanding of the biographical process. "I know that he plans to spend a great deal of time with you, Eric. But you understand about the normal routine of seeing clients. And, of course, the major demonstration that he is presenting tonight for the area police officers."

"Yes," I said. "I realize that I must adjust to Darmanian's busy schedule, and I am very much looking forward to tonight."

I withdrew my tobacco pouch from a coat pocket and got out my pipe.

"Your pipe gives off a very pleasant aroma," Delores commented.

"Thank you," I responded. "It's my own mixture. I'm glad it doesn't offend you."

"Not at all," she said as I began packing the smooth briar bowl. "I like it. My father used to smoke a pipe, as a matter of fact."

I chuckled. "Am I becoming a father image for you?"

Delores smiled. "No, but Daddy was thoughtful and scholarly, the way you are."

"Thank you again," I said. "I will take that as a compliment."

I flicked the spark of my lighter. Somehow the adjustment had been altered, and the flame shot upward in an explosive tongue more than eight inches long. I was startled, but Delores screamed in horror.

I released the pressure on the spark and apologized for the unexpected conversion of my pipe lighter to a flame thrower. But Delores continued to register shock by shuddering. She sat meekly on the edge of the desk, her eyes still wide with a nameless terror.

Then I recalled her muffled cries of the night before, and I heard an echo of the panic in her voice as she screamed that she was being burned alive.

Her large brown eyes looked deep into my own, as if plumbing them for sympathy and concern. "Did—did you hear me last night?" she asked in a quiet voice that seemed both ashamed of the incident, yet pleading for an understanding ear.

I told her that I had been awakened by the extreme warmth that had permeated my room and that I had happened to overhear her distress over what I assumed to have been a nightmare provoked by the stifling heat.

"We have been having trouble with the furnace sometimes heating up at night," she said. "But my nightmares began in my childhood. I wish I could blame them on external triggers, such as a room becoming too warm, but I cannot. I don't know what causes them."

"I'm sorry, Delores," I said. "Could the nightmares be prompted by any sort of nervous tension?"

Delores's teeth pulled thoughtfully at her lower lip. "Sometimes when I was a little girl, I would run a fever and become ill within a day or two after one of the nightmares."

"I think a lot of people have such triggering

dreams," I said, attempting to reassure her. "When I was a kid back in Minnesota, I would dream that I was chewing big wads of soggy cardboard. Whenever I had that dream, I would awaken with mumps, measles, flu, or whatever damn bug was going around."

Delores nodded. "When I was younger, I would most often have the dream when I was fatigued or under stress. I had the dream a lot when I was in college, more often than when I was a kid in elementary school or high school."

"What images do you see in the dreams?" I asked.

"Always the same," Delores answered. "I'm surrounded by a lot of angry men and women who are screaming at me. Some rough men—soldiers, I think—pull me to a stake in the middle of high piles of wood. Then someone throws a torch on the pyre and I start to scream that I am burning."

"That's a decidedly unpleasant dream," I conceded.

Delores nodded. "And lately I have been having the dream a couple of times a week."

I shook my head slowly in commiseration. "By lately you mean how long?"

"Probably the last three months."

"My God, that's terrible! And have you had any fevers or illnesses?"

"None," Delores answered in a hoarse whisper. "But I've begun to feel nervous, strung out, jumpy."

"I should think so." I grimaced. "Can't Darmanian do anything to help you?"

Delores's brown eyes brimmed with tears. "He . . . he seems to become upset whenever I ask him for help with my nightmares. He almost seems pleased that I am having the dreams. He says . . . to let them come. That I'm working something out in my psyche.

That I'm approaching an emotional breakthrough that will more completely integrate my entire personality."

I considered this for several moments, tapping my unlighted pipe stem softly against my teeth. "Well," I ventured. "Darmanian is the expert on such bizzare mental states." I gestured toward the large pile of folders on the desk. "There's the evidence to support the fact that he seems to know what he is doing when it comes to the dark corners of the human mind."

A tear broke loose and coursed over a beautifully high cheekbone. "I've ceased even asking Darmanian for help with the dream," she told me, her voice quavering. "He says that I must be strong and permit my psyche to purge itself."

"Purge itself of what?" I wondered.

Delores lowered her eyes, and her palms nervously outlined her hips in tight, rapid movements. "Darmanian says that there are certain residues of thoughts, feelings, and emotions from my past that I must release."

Her voice was soft, childlike, frightened when she added: "But I don't like having the dreams, Eric."

"It is nonsense to suffer unduly," I told her emphatically. "Insist that Darmanian help you. Or seek professional help on your own."

Delores's tear-puddled brown eyes widened as if I had uttered something very shocking. There was an awkward moment as I realized that I had committed an inadvertent *faux pas*. I had intruded too deeply into their personal relationship, and now I must say something to set the matter right.

"I'm certain that if you really let Darmanian know how much these dreams are distressing you, he would help you," I said, cautiously, feeling my way.

"But he always becomes very angry when I am weak," Delores said, her voice no more than a whisper. "I cannot endure Darmanian being angry with me."

Her hand reached out to touch my arm and her eyes held me in earnest focus. "I hope, Eric, that you never see Darmanian when he becomes angry."

"It is hard to imagine Darmanian angry," I said. "He seems so in control of himself."

"He is," she admitted. "It is only when that control is threatened that he becomes angry. And he becomes enraged when it appears that he is not fully in control of others."

I smiled confidently. "I can foresee no reason why we should have any disagreements. We share the common goal of producing a successful book about his work."

"If you sincerely wish to continue getting along with Darmanian," Delores advised me, "you must be prepared to bend your will to his. Sooner or later, he will demand this of you. And you will find—as I quickly discovered—that it is impossible to resist him."

Chapter Seven

Although Darmanian was quoted in the interview for *Human Behavior* as stating that he considered stage hypnotists to be crass, commercial befoulers of the art of mesmerism, Delores told me that there were none better than he at holding an audience in absolute thralldom. I saw no reason to doubt her statement, biased though it might have been.

On that Tuesday night, April 18, 1978, Darmanian's audience was composed almost solely of hard-nosed police officers and detectives. This fact appeared to stimulate rather than intimidate him.

"He does this once a year for the policemen and their wives," Delores told me as we found our seats near the front of the high school auditorium that had been appropriated for the evening so that the wives and the husbands of the law enforcement officers might be able to attend the hypnotist's demonstration. "Darmanian has often cooperated with the authorities in the area. He has an excellent working relationship with them."

We settled in two seats on the aisle. I noted that some pubescent lover had carved "E.K. loves M.W." on the back of the seat in front of me. "It would appear that high school kids in Albany are no different from the kids in Rochester, Minnesota."

"Is that where you're from?" Delores smiled. "Minnesota? The land of sky-blue waters."

"Hmm," I said, nodding. "I would like to impress you by saying that my father was a brilliant neurosurgeon at the Mayo Clinic in Rochester, but I can tell you without fear of contradiction that we had an excellent herd of Holsteins."

Delores laughed delightfully and melodically. Darmanian had jokingly asked me to keep a close eye on her to protect her from some cop who might wish to make an unauthorized "pinch." It was the most agreeable assignment I had ever received. She was wearing a pale, rose-colored suit, a loose-flowing brown neck scarf. She looked very neat, very feminine. She also appeared much more at ease, as if the memory of last night's bad dream had at last been dissipated.

She had been glancing over her shoulder from time to time as the police officers and their guests steadily filled up the seats in the auditorium. "Eric," she said. "I hope that you are not really an international jewel thief or something."

I laughed. "Actually, I am a cat burglar. Gave it up, though. My fence couldn't get rid of any more hot cats."

"Well, joke if you want," Delores said, frowning. "There is a very mean-looking, very big policeman scowling at you. And he is walking toward you very rapidly down the aisle."

Before I could turn to follow her gaze, a hand the size of a catcher's mitt dropped onto my shoulder. "My God, it *is* you, Eric."

The voice boomed from behind me, startling me, puzzling me, until the broad face bent nearer my own so that I might identify the owner of the fingers gripping my left deltoid.

"Sergeant Burton Kandowski, the pride of New York's crime busters," I said, offering my hand to be squeezed in the huge paw that was reaching for it. "It has got to be ten years. What are you doing in Albany?"

The big man knelt beside my aisle seat, grinned expansively. "I'm on the force here, kid," he explained. "I got tired of those concrete canyons, and I decided to move upstate, where a cop doesn't get shot at every day."

He glanced at Delores, gave my hand an extra squeeze. "And you?" he wanted to know. "What brings you here? Or should I say 'who'?"

"Yes, you should say 'who,'" I said, smiling. "I'm here because I am going to do a book on Darmanian This is Delores Touraine, Darmanian's assistant."

Delores greeted Kandowski, extended a hand toward his. I admired her courage, although I knew that the husky cop could be as gentle as a gardener caressing the petals of his miniature roses. Kandowski mumbled a "pleased-to-meetcha" and redirected his attention to me.

"That's terrific, kid! You ought to get a best-seller out of Darmanian. You still do anything for *True Detective*? I got some more good stuff."

"I haven't written any crime material for a long time, Burt," I said. Then turning to Delores, I explained: "Burt used to help me research cases."

"Eric even did a couple of articles about me." Kandowski smiled proudly. "Man, I bought a dozen copies of those magazines and I was the envy of the precinct."

The house lights dimmed as a signal that the demonstration was about to begin. While we had been talking to Burt, the auditorium had filled to capacity. All around us mumbled conversations trailed off, and chair seats slammed down in preparation for the performance.

"I better get back to the missus," Burt said. "Hey, Eric, let's get together and bend the elbows for old times' sake, okay?"

"I'll give you a call when I get a chance," I agreed.

Burt waved good-bye, and I had a fleeting image of his bulk moving down a row of shifting and scowling men and women. Then the house lights went out.

The spotlight on stage suddenly illuminated a blinking, ill-at-ease lieutenant, who appeared as though he must have lost the coin toss that determined which officer would get up in front of his peers to introduce their guest demonstrator. The lieutenant nervously tapped the microphone.

"Is this on?" he wondered.

A chorus of "yes" and "affirmative" answered his query. The lieutenant grinned sheepishly, removed a small stack of note cards from an inner breast pocket. He cleared his throat preemptorily and then, occasionally glancing at his notes, began the introduction.

"Fellow officers, wives, husbands. It is once again our pleasure to have with us this evening the brilliant and entertaining hypnotist Darmanian, who will provide us with a demonstration on the potential value of hypnosis in police work. Darmanian, by way of brief introduction, maintains the Woodlands Clinic of Hypnotherapy in Saratoga Springs. And we police officers have enjoyed his cooperation on several occasions. Darmanian has used his hypnotic skills to enable us to question both victims and accused criminals and thereby to gain details that became instrumental in solving cases that might otherwise have gone unclosed. Without further adieu, I wish now to present Darmanian, master hypnotist, responsible citizen. *Darmanian!*"

Darmanian smoothly pushed aside the purple curtain and moved gracefully into the spotlight. He shook the lieutenant's hand, waited a moment or two while the officer left the stage, then stood before the audience—tall, assertive, a commanding figure in black. About his neck, catching the light from the carefully placed spotlights anchored on a balcony railing, was the ever-present medallion. The police officers and their guests were instantly stilled by Darmanian's presence on stage, as if they were already under his spell.

His voice was soft, crushed velvet, yet authoritative, magnetic. He swiftly dealt with the amenities, then told his audience that there really existed little agreement about precisely what went on when an individual was hypnotized.

"Some researchers explain away hypnosis as a kind of role playing in which the hypnotist assumes the position of a parent and regresses the subject to a flexible childlike state," Darmanian said. "Other authorities insist that there actually *is* such a state as hypnotic trance, but they concede that we do not presently possess the technology to measure or to identify its full therapeutic usefulness. Still other experts have called hypnosis a dissociative mental state in which certain psychological functions may conduct themselves autonomously, away from the censure of conscious control."

Darmanian paused for a moment, as though he were giving his audience an opportunity to permit the initial information to be absorbed by their individual mental processes. From behind me I heard a woman whisper: "I don't know for sure what he said, but I could sit here all night and listen to him say it!"

Her companion agreed: "He's so handsome."

Two male throats cleared themselves noisily, and the female voices were again absorbed by the silence.

"Hypnosis is not something that a hypnotist *does* to anyone," Darmanian continued. "Hypnosis is something the subject does to himself.

"In just a few minutes, I will ask for volunteer subjects from among you. I will induce a trance state within those of you who will join me here on the stage. I will create the conditions under which the volunteers will permit themselves to enter a trance state. But the trance state will be a product of their own inclinations, not my will."

Darmanian told the audience that a subject in the trance state reduces his peripheral awareness and increases his focal attention.

"Such hypnotic phenomena occur spontaneously within many individuals several times a day without any kind of induction procedure," the hypnotist told them.

"Think of Saturday afternoons—if you are ever fortunate enough to have them off!" Darmanian began his illustration, then paused for the obligatory bursts of scattered laughter and applause for his recognition of a police officer's long workweek.

"If you are a sports enthusiast, you may spend some time before your television set, watching your favorite team locked in desperate combat with its arch foe. For the next several minutes you will have your attention fully focused. Your conscious mind will be deeply absorbed. You will be oblivious to what is happening around you.

"Your wife comes into the room and asks you to take out the trash. You do not hear her.

"Your little son yanks the cat's tail. You hear nothing of the yowls of pain and protest.

"You are intensely alert to every motion and sound emanating from your television set, yet you are unaware of your wife calling you to dinner. You may not even be fully aware of your own body sitting in the easy chair."

There were mumbles and squeals of recognition as men and women in the audience identified with the situation that Darmanian was describing.

"I could hit Harry with a frying pan when the Mets are playing," some woman commented, "and he'd never know it."

"Let us take a more noble example." Darmanian's voice rose a bit in volume, his subtle way of regaining the audience's complete attention.

"As a police officer, you are locked into a case. Solution seems near at last. You are totally involved in going over your notes and integrating them with the new facts and clues that have just become available to you. As you more completely focus your attention, all other sounds in the squad room become an unintelligible hum.

"The sergeant asks if anyone wants to send out for coffee. You don't hear him.

"The telephone rings repeatedly at the desk next to yours. It could just as well be ringing in a room across the street. Your conscious mind is fully absorbed in solving that stubborn case."

Darmanian concluded with the example of how one spontaneously induces a hypnotic state within himself as he watches telephone poles whiz by when someone else is at the wheel of the automobile. Then he began to lead into the actual demonstration.

"If you possess these three traits, you are potentially a good hypnotic subject," Darmanian said. "One: You must have the ability to focus attention and to concentrate. Two: You must have an openness to new experience. Three: You must have a willingness to comply with suggestions."

"I know that in this particular audience—perhaps more so than in most—we will find dozens of men and women who exhibit these three traits," Darmanian told them. "Indeed, such traits are among the attributes of every good law enforcement officer."

Darmanian brought three officers, two men and one woman, forward from the audience and asked them to be seated on straight-backed chairs that had been arranged on the stage. As the officers sat facing their peers, there was a minimum of laughter or shouts of encouragement. There was no question that this was a very serious-minded audience.

"I want you three volunteers to relax," Darmanian said in an authoritative yet friendly voice. The officer farthest to the left appeared as though relaxation did not come easily to him. He was a slender, nervous man whose fingers drummed his thigh in rapid bursts of energy. Next to him was a husky officer, whose amiable, smiling features seemed more suited to a used-car salesman than a cop. The lady officer on the right was an attractive redhead who seemed the very model of sobriety.

"Please do not cross your arms or legs," Darmanian told them. The nervous officer started slightly, for he had just crossed his legs in an effort to relax.

"Please do not move once you have made yourselves comfortable. Feel yourself relaxing. Relax. Let yourself go."

Darmanian's voice assumed a slight sing-song pattern. He named individual muscle groups, from the ankles and calves on up to the necks and shoulders and told the subjects to relax these muscles totally.

"Your eyelids are becoming heavy. Your muscles are getting more and more relaxed. Just float away and become totally at peace," Darmanian urged his subjects. "Your unconscious mind is listening to me. It is altering your blood pressure. It is slowing your heartbeat. It is slowing your respiration rate. It is allowing you to feel total comfort. Close your eyes and enjoy that comfort. Let yourself enjoy a deep sleep. Deeper . . . deeper . . . deeper."

I touched Delores's hand, and she bent her head closer to mine. "What happens if I succumb to trance?" I asked her.

She smiled, squeezed my forearm in a friendly gesture. "I'll stop you from revealing any intimate secrets," she promised.

I heard a stifled snore behind me and to my left. A man shifted noisily in his chair, coughed to cover his wife's embarrassed, scolding hiss. If the sleeping officer had been on stage, she might have felt pleased that he was demonstrating his ability to concentrate. In the audience, though, he was the same clod who fell asleep in front of the television set when she wanted him to watch the Bette Davis late movie with her.

There was no question that Darmanian had the full attention of every member of the audience assembled in that high school auditorium in Albany that night. It would have been a relatively simple matter to have hypnotized over half of them in the next few minutes.

"You are now accompanying me to a movie theater," Darmanian was telling his entranced subjects. "I want you to be my guests and enjoy yourselves."

The three subjects smiled as if they were small children being treated by their daddies to an afternoon matinee.

Darmanian began to stage-laugh. "Isn't the movie funny? You are watching the funniest movie that you have ever seen. It's the Marx Brothers, Abbott and Costello, Laurel and Hardy, and *your* favorite comedian all in one movie!" Darmanian laughed again. "Oh, look at that! It is the funniest scene that you have ever seen!"

The three officers were laughing loudly and unchecked at the funny movie, which only they were seeing in their individual theaters-of-the-mind. The hefty policeman had a laugh to match his size. He bellowed out his merriment as if he were attempting to drown out his fellow subjects, as well as the audience, who had now begun to laugh at their colleagues' entranced, mirthful hysteria.

Darmanian commanded the three to stop laughing,

to fall back asleep. "Deeper and deeper sleep. Deeper, deeper, deeper, Down, down, down."

Delores touched my forearm again. "Now comes the sad movie," she whispered.

Obviously this part of the demonstration was quite familiar to Delores, but I wondered if she were as curious as I was about the surprise that Darmanian had promised to reveal during tonight's performance.

"When do you think Darmanian will spring his big surprise?" I asked her, cupping my left hand beside my mouth to block the sound from reaching any of our neighbors. "Have you any idea what it is?"

Delores smiled, her eyes crinkling in wonder. "I have no idea what it is or when he'll pop it on us," she whispered.

The three subjects on stage were weeping noisily as Darmanian presented them with a tearjerker as a change of program from the comedy. The audience could only guess what sorrowful movie their fellow officers were viewing in their private mental machinery.

Darmanian had a magnificent sense of pacing, and he knew that he must not overmilk this particular demonstration. He undoubtedly had even more impressive situations planned for the police officers, and he did not wish to drive the initial experience to the point of boredom. He silenced their tears and left the subjects for a moment or two with their heads hanging limply toward their chests.

"People such as our three subjects, who have been hypnotized for the first time, may sometimes feel disappointed," Darmanian explained. "They may feel that they have experienced nothing.

"In the trance state most people feel mildly relaxed, but they are astonished when they remain in touch with reality, their conscious minds, and their thoughts. They may feel quite capable of resisting the hypnotist's suggestions. They may feel alert and awake, convinced that they have not even been hypnotized. Let us hear from our three subjects, and I think you'll see exactly what I mean."

Darmanian did a backward count from three, brought the subjects to full, responsive consciousness. He stepped to his left and directed his first questions to the pretty but still sober redhead.

"Did you feel as though you were in a deep sleep?" he asked her.

"No, I did not, Mr. Darmanian," she answered seriously. "In fact, I even thought I was resisting a couple of your suggestions."

"Did you feel in control of your actions?" Darmanian wondered.

"Completely," she replied. "That is what seemed so weird. I kept thinking, how can I be hypnotized? I can hear him clearly. I am certain that I am thinking clearly. Why am I doing these crazy things?"

Darmanian moved his attention to the husky officer in the middle. "Did you feel hypnotized?"

"No, sir, I did not."

"What did you see when you were laughing so hard at the comedy?"

The officer grinned and emitted another of his hearty belly laughs. "Well, sir, at first I thought that you were going to try to get us to laugh. I got stubborn and said to myself that I didn't feel like laughing and I wasn't going to do so. But then I saw Harpo Marx jump in this go-cart, see? And he took out after Lucille Ball. She threw a pie at him and smacked him right in the face. Then Laurel and Hardy and the

Three Stooges were throwing pies at everyone on the golf course. I just couldn't keep from laughing!"

Darmanian pointed the mike toward the slender officer on the end and indicated that he should lean forward to give his response. "What did you see that was so funny and so sad, officer?"

The man smiled. "Well, first I got more relaxed than I have been in about six months. I want to thank you for that. But to be truthful, I saw nothing. Yet, I couldn't keep from laughing and from crying when you told us to do so."

"Apparently you wished to resist me on the conscious level of thought," Darmanian said. "But your unconscious and I had managed to become good friends during the trance state. It wanted to obey my suggestions. Someone once said that hypnosis is like a kind of psychic kung fu, in that a hypnotist can actually use your resistance against you."

Darmanian went on to explain that even though none of the subjects might feel comfortable sitting before their fellow officers, laughing like zanies and weeping like soap opera freaks, he did not transform them into different people.

"I only shaped your experience," he said. "No hypnotist can evoke something within a subject that is not already within him or her.

"Remember: The trance state of hypnosis reduces peripheral awareness and increases focal awareness. What I enabled these three subjects to do was to focus their attention on the tasks to which I assigned them. They shut out the peripheral distractions of audience laughter and personal feelings of embarrassment."

The husky police officer had become quite serious

again. He folded his arms across his chest, cleared his throat. "A question, sir."

Darmanian turned away from the audience, held the microphone to the man's mouth. "I am certain you have researched this question, Mr. Darmanian, but I am also certain we want to hear your answer. Can a good hypnotist make someone do something against his or her will? By that I mean, something that that person would not normally do."

Darmanian paused to give full effect to his answer. "Some individuals are more hypnotizable than others. Some men and women have a greater trance capacity than others.

"Those who have such a deep capacity could quite easily be made to kill, steal, and commit antisocial acts that they would not normally perform."

The big officer frowned his concern. "What of those who do not enter such a deep hypnotic state?"

"Those men and women would take longer to condition," Darmanian said. "But given time for conditioning, a skillful hypnotist could devise means by which he might make anyone commit an act of treason, murder, or any deed that he might so desire."

The audience of law enforcement officers broke their discipline and began to whisper and gesture among themselves like school children reacting to teacher's outrageous statement.

"Yes," Darmanian recaptured their attention by raising his voice into the microphone. "The implications of mind control through hypnosis are many.

"And what of the trance state that might be induced by the flickering of television sets or neon lights?

"What of the man or woman unknowingly maneuvered into a spontaneous trance state who receives a violent suggestion prompted by an angry passerby?

"What of the oppressed, the disenchanted, the volatile dissidents who can literally be hypnotized en masse by street-corner demagogues or aspiring dictators?"

Darmanian had them now. He was working his own mass hypnosis on the audience of men and women who had sworn to uphold the law. What began as an evening of entertainment for them was about to become a channel of learning, a time of enlightenment, a tool of utmost usefulness. Darmanian dismissed the three subjects on stage and called for new volunteers.

He next demonstrated how hypnosis might be used in obtaining more accurate information from accident and rape victims.

Skillfully, he arranged hypothetical situations based on actual crime cases undergoing investigation by the Albany Police Department and carefully manipulated police officers into assuming the roles of the victims or perpetrators of the criminal acts. He showed how the memory could be mined, how the traumas might be soothed, how the unconscious could always be made the ally of an astute hypnotist.

Darmanian continued his program of demonstrations for nearly two hours, and his audience was betraying not the slightest clue of boredom or restlessness. But it was now time for his surprise. Within a few minutes the police officers would see one of their number sent to death and brought back to life on the stage of that high school auditorium in Albany, New York.

Chapter Eight

Darmanian removed a white pocket handkerchief and dabbed at his forehead and upper lip. I had noticed the slight sheen of perspiration on the hypnotist's features, but I knew it was due to the labors of his exertions on the warm stage. Darmanian betrayed not the slightest sign of nervousness or tension. He appeared thoroughly confident, totally in control, completely calm.

"What I wish to present in this next demonstration is an indication of the borderless perimeters of the human mind," Darmanian announced. "What are the limits of the human psyche? What, indeed, is the human psyche?"

It was readily apparent that the hypnotist was about to provide his audience with the climax of the evening, and an expectant silence seemed to have struck everyone mute. I glanced at the audience members in my radius of vision. I could detect no physical indications of restlessness or lack of interest. It was as if Darmanian were about to provide each man and woman with a revelation that, on some level of consciousness, each individual soul knew had been lacking in its present construct of reality.

Darmanian called the name of the stocky police officer who had participated in the initial demonstration of the evening. "Officer Singer," he said softly, persuasively into the microphone, "would you please rejoin me on stage?"

The big policeman rose to his feet. "It would be my pleasure, sir," he said, grinning with a kind of pride in accomplishment for an action he did not thoroughly understand.

"I assure you, Officer Singer," Darmanian declared as the man was approaching the stage, "that this demonstration will offer much more food for thought and deliberation than your laughter or your tears as you viewed the imaginary movie."

I felt Delores tugging at my coat sleeve. "I think we are about to witness Darmanian's surprise." She smiled, her brown eyes wide with anticipation.

"Do you think so?" I asked her in a whisper.

Delores nodded, returning her attention to the stage.

My admiration for the master hypnotist was growing by the moment. Darmanian had seized my curiosity and attention in much the same manner as he had captured his audience. It was becoming increasingly difficult to retain my writer's detachment, which had been continually analyzing and evaluating Darmanian's techniques and stage presence. I, too, was falling under the spell of his mental magic. The sinuous, crystal-bearing serpents on Darmanian's medallion had begun to seduce and place me in as deep a servitude to his mesmerism as it had any other member of the audience.

Darmanian quickly placed Officer Singer in trance, then he turned to face the audience, his voice that of an impassioned friend.

"An individual's past is very much like a vast stretch of a dark and lonely seashore," Darmanian said, offering his students a poetic simile. "One's life can so often be nothing more than undistinguished bits and pieces of sand and rock. But every now and then, there appears a lovely seashell, a crumpled beer can, a bit of driftwood. These objects break the monotony of the beach. In each of our lives, that seashell or beer can is a memorable moment—a childhood Christmas, a broken leg, a victory on the athletic field, the death of a loved one.

"Hypnosis permits us to walk through the darkness and the dull stretches of the beaches of memory and to pick up whichever seashell or bit of driftwood that we wish. A skillfull hypnotist can regress his subject to his first day on the job, his first day of school, his first day of life!"

"Officer Singer was sitting slumped somewhat awkwardly on the hard metal chair. His full chin was bobbing just an inch from his barrel chest.

Darmanian asked him his name.

"Sergeant William Singer." The man's answer was prompt, self-assured, almost a challenge for disputation.

Darmanian regressed the officer to his high school days, asked him the same question.

"Bill Singer," came the reply quickly. The man's rigidity seemed to flow out of him. The square set to his broad shoulders slumped. He crossed his legs in an attitude of relaxed informality. "My old man is Joe Singer. You know, the guy who took over old man McGuire's tavern."

The count of three, another hypnotic suggestion, and the sergeant was back in first grade, faced with what appeared to be a stuttering problem: "B-bi-Billy S-s-singer."

There were a few incredulous and sympathetic whispers and chuckles from the enraptured audience.

Another countdown, and the burly police officer was regressed to the consciousness of his three-year-old self: "Bil-lee."

"And what is your last name, Billy?"

Embarrassed, squirming, desperate locking together of the fingers, a thickened tongue curled nervously against a cheek. "I dunno."

The audience was both intrigued by the ostensible transformation taking place before their eyes and amused by the infantile postures and baby-voiced responses of the stocky police officer who sat on the stage before them.

Darmanian's voice became strongly authoritative. "Now, Billy, William Singer, I want you to go back to the first day that your soul and life essence became William Singer in this lifetime. You have that ability. Your higher self knows and has recorded all your experiences. You will remember everything that happened on that first day in this life expression, but you will be able to talk and to describe everything that is happening to you and to those around you. Now, on the count of three . . ."

The audience was astonished as the big man graphically related the trauma of the birth experience. He

THE HYPNOTIST 95

began to weep when he felt that he had caused his mother pain.

Delores's hand was again at my coat sleeve. I bent closer to her mouth, for the auditorium had become as still as a chapel. "You don't suppose," she asked me, "that he is going to attempt to take Sergeant Singer back before the birth experience, do you?"

I crinkled my forehead in an unspoken question of my own: What lay before the birth experience? I had, of course, read about the hypnotist Morey Bernstein and his famous "Bridey Murphy," but that was a one-in-a-million kind of case. And to my understanding, "Bridey" had been discredited as an unconscious hoax. I had been made dramatically aware of Darmanian's belief in reincarnation, but surely there was no way that he could demonstrate such a philosophical position to an audience such as the one presently assembled.

Darmanian permitted the audience to deal individually with the implications that each adult man and woman had within him or her the tendrils of memory of the birth experience. Once each person had had time to savor those thoughts and fit them in a personal reality, he moved the personality of Sergeant Singer even farther back in consciousness.

"Go into the womb," Darmanian commanded. "And before."

All around us men and women shifted noisily in their seats. I could see mouths dropping incredulously. Perhaps in certain cases, the owners of those suddenly gaping mouths were offended. This was a conservative area of New York State—that I knew. And police officers do tend to be somewhat conservative in their general points of view toward new ideas and unconventional concepts.

For the first time that evening, I noticed that Darmanian's voice was betraying a slight trace of accent suggestive of his Middle European forebears. Since his diction was normally so precise and clean, I wondered if even he were feeling just a slight amount of tension.

"I want you to go back to a time *before* you were William Singer," the hypnotist said. "I want you to keep moving backward in time until you have a conscious memory of being someone else. I want you to select the past-life experience that has had the most significance, the most correlation, the greatest connection to your present-life expression.

"You will find yourself spinning as if in a vortex. Float along with the sensation. *One.* Moving back in time. *Two.* Farther and farther back. *Three.* You will remember a time and a life before you became William Singer. It will be a lifetime that was—and *is*—connected to your present life experience. You will see yourself doing something that will be importantly linked to your present life. You will tell me everything that I ask you. Who are you?"

There was a collective and highly audible gasp from many men and women when the bull of a man whom they knew as Sergeant William Singer answered Darmanian's query in soft, measured, feminine tones: "My name, good sir, is Patience Prescott."

Delores and I exchanged wide-eyed glances. "I can't believe this is really happening," she said, slowly shaking her head. "He's taking a terrible chance of running his reputation in the area."

Under Darmanian's skillful questioning, the rather

prissy Patience described her life in Boston, Massachusetts, circa 1840. Her portraits of her stern-faced sea captain father and her unfaithful mother were both poignant and sharply etched. Her knowledge of the city streets was sparse, since she was a gentle, indoor creature; but her observations of city government and civic strivings were extremely keen.

The audience of law enforcement officers and their mates conducted itself very well. There were a few nervous throat clearings, a smattering of outraged whispers, but I saw no one leave their seats.

One woman, directly in front of us, asked her husband what Father Riley would think of such a demonstration, but she seemed pacified with his explanation that the whole thing was a put-on.

It was perhaps fortunate for Darmanian that the majority of men and women appeared to accept the demonstration in the familiar vein of hypnotized subjects laughing and crying at imaginary movies. If they had interpreted the transformation of Sergeant Singer into the alleged entity of Patience Prescott as an assault against their belief structures, the evening might have ended quite differently. Rather, they chose to believe that Darmanian was helping Sergeant Singer imagine that he was another person in a previous lifetime. Darmanian was entertaining them.

At times, the answers of Patience were totally smothered by outbursts of laughter. To see the solid bulk of Bill Singer assuming the mannerisms and gestures of a genteel young woman who was so easily shocked by the daily traffic of life set some of his fellow officers into paroxysms of unrestrained laughter.

But the howls of glee left the throats of those same men and women to be supplanted by uncertain coughs when Patience began to weep and to describe her death at the hands of one of the vicious street gangs that had prowled Boston at that time.

The crude men had not been satisfied with looting her purse. They had sensed virginal flesh beneath her billowing skirts. They had stripped her, debased her, taken her one after the other, then beaten her to death with a wagon wheel spoke.

"I . . . I'm dying," Patience said in a voice so weak that the microphone barely shared it with the stilled audience.

"Are you still in pain, Patience?" Darmanian asked sympathetically.

"I . . . I was, but it doesn't hurt . . . any . . . more. Oh, oh, ohh. . . ."

Patience emitted a long death sigh, and the big man in the straight-backed chair slumped forward. Darmanian allowed Singer to remain in awful silence until he seemed to know intuitively that some members of the audience—especially Singer's wife and closest friends—were about to leap to their feet and scream the unspoken questions on everyone's mind.

"What are you doing, Patience?" Darmanian asked, finally breaking the silence.

"I'm floating," the voice replied, in childlike wonder.

"Can you see your body?"

"My . . . my body? *My body!*"

Question. Realization. Then a terrible scream:

"*I'm dead!*"

That awful cry, amplified by the public address system, must have echoed for hours in the psyche of every member of the audience.

Darmanian quickly regained control, soothed the

entity. "Yes, you are dead. But you no longer feel pain. You like to float. Look beneath you and tell me what you see."

"My . . . my body is lying there. Oh, it looks so terrible. They did wretched things to me. My poor face is all smashed in."

"Move along in time," Darmanian instructed. "Tell us what you see."

"Birds peck at my eyes. Rats nibble at my toes and fingers."

All around us came sighs and gasps of disgust and distaste. Delores reached for my hand and laced her fingers through mine. I glanced over at her, but her attention was riveted on the stage.

"Does it bother you that this is happening to you, Patience?" Darmanian continued with his questioning.

"Not anymore. I'm not in that body anymore. Oh, look there!"

"What?"

"A policeman is coming. He chases the rats away. He covers me with his coat. He prays for me. I can hear his prayer."

There were tears streaming down the full cheeks of Sergeant Singer. "Oh, that is too bad. He is blaming himself. He says that he should have been there to stop what happened to me. He stopped to help a wealthy man get his carriage out of a chuckhole. He says that he should have let the man sit there. He should have continued on patrol. He cries. He . . . he is a good man."

Darmanian chose that remarkably touching moment to move the entity ahead through time and space. "Float, float onward, Patience," he commanded. "Float forward in time until you are no longer Patience Prescott. Move forward until you once again inhabit a physical body. At the count of three, you will be there. One . . . two . . . *three!*"

"Oooo!" The man's mouth made a round *o* of delight. "There's a baby down there! Oooo, I'm spinning faster and faster. Down. Down. Down."

Sergeant Singer's heavy body jerked spasmodically. Then after several convulsive seconds, he sat quietly, but his eyes were wide and staring with innocent wonder. His mouth was opening and closing, but no sound issued forth.

"You can speak," Darmanian told him. "Tell us who you are. It is the first day of your new life."

"Baby, came the clipped response. "Baby boy Singer."

"That is your name?" Darmanian asked. "Baby boy?"

"They can't decide," the choppy voice explained. "Mama-Girl want David. Papa-Boy want William."

With the sense of a master showman, Darmanian sent Singer into a deep sleep, then moved him forward to the present hour and his present consciousness. He instructed the big policeman that when he awakened he would feel better than he had felt in months. He would awaken totally refreshed in body and mind.

Singer came awake, rubbing his eyes and yawning. Then, remembering where he was, he dropped his hands into his lap and sat smiling at his fellow officers and their guests. He seemed contented to remain sitting on the stage.

"What have you witnessed, my friends?" Darmanian asked. "Could it be possible that the man, husband, friend, police officer whom you know as William

Singer was once a young woman in the Boston of 1840 who was named Patience Prescott?"

Sergeant Singer's relaxed smile tightened, and his forehead wrinkled into a puzzled scowl. It was obvious that he was the rare somnambulistic subject who went deep into an amnesiac sleep. He had no memory of his dramatic portrayal of Patience Prescott.

"And is it something more than coincidence," Darmanian challenged his audience, "that a young woman who was once so terribly murdered by street thugs is today a police officer who has sworn to exercise his duty so that other young women might not meet similar fates?"

Darmanian's eyes narrowed, as if he were personally asking his question of each individual member of the audience.

"Have you, ladies and gentlemen," he went on, "just witnessed an incredible bit of fantasy? Possession, perhaps? Some remarkable psychic psychodrama? Or might we be bold enough to suggest that the entity, the soul, that once lived in Patience Prescott's body now exists in the physical structure of William Singer, sergeant of police, Albany, New York?

"I leave you with the thought that the human psyche is truly eternal. And that the boundaries of that same marvelous spiritual essence may virtually be without limits.

"If it should seem strange to you that you have lived before and that you will live again, is it any less strange that you should have lived at all? Your very existence is a miracle. Accept your eternality as a natural process that follows your having come into being.

"Thank you for being such a receptive audience,"

Darmanian said, bowing slightly at the waist. "Good night."

Applause was scattered. Few people rose to leave. It seemed as though the audience was stunned, baffled, awaiting some further sign to reassure them that the world they had left outside the auditorium was still there.

A compact, medium-sized man in his early fifties was walking heavily across the stage. His face was red, and it seemed as though he were either puffing or muttering to himself as he strode purposefully toward Darmanian.

Delores squeezed my hand. "Oh, my God!" she gasped. "It's Chief Weyerhaus. He's a strong Roman Catholic, and he looks furious!"

The police chief snatched the microphone away from Darmanian's hands, glowered at the hypnotist. "Let me have your attention!" He said it as a command, not a request, and the public address system made certain that everyone heard it.

Then it seemed to me that a very strange thing took place. From the moment Chief Weyerhaus had begun to approach him, Darmanian had faced him squarely and had begun to swing his medallion from its chain. The spotlights had corruscated brilliantly from the crystal borne by the two feathered serpents.

Chief Weyerhaus cleared his throat, his eyes moving from Darmanian to the large, swaying medallion. "I just want to say," he began, "that . . . that . . . Darmanian is a good man. A fine man. And . . . and . . . I personally want to thank him for a most provocative and challenging presentation. I . . . I . . . that's all I have to say. Good night."

Almost without exception the audience now responded as if they had become one single, collective entity. The applause was thunderous now that their chief had given Darmanian his personal seal of approval. It appeared as though Darmanian had once again demonstrated his mastery of his subject matter and his compelling control of any audience—regardless of how daring his presentation.

But I wondered if right before the oblivious eyes of the entire police force Darmanian had also demonstrated his control over Chief Weyerhaus.

Chapter Nine

"I must say, Darmanian, that I was very much impressed with your eloquence this evening," I said as we were driving back to Woodlands after the lecture and demonstration.

Delores was driving the Oldsmobile Cutlass. Darmanian sat beside her. I was in the backseat. After the brilliance of his performance and the great number of individual accolades and compliments that he received, the hypnotist had been nearly mute since he had got into the car. Delores had said no more than three or four words. And I, not wishing to intrude on what may have been a required period of quiet during which Darmanian replenished himself after a particularly taxing demonstration, had taken my cue from their silent behavior. But now that we were no more than a few miles from the estate, I could no longer retain what might be considered a rude silence on my part.

Darmanian turned to face me, his dark features illuminated only by the light issuing from the dashboard.

"Rochefoucauld once remarked that true eloquence consits in saying all that is proper, and nothing more," he said softly. "I'm afraid that I might have said more than was proper."

Approaching headlights briefly lighted the interior of the Oldsmobile and I could see a slight, wry smile on Darmanian's lips. "Darling," he said to Delores, "you've not given me your impressions of tonight's demonstration."

"I'm still attempting to evaluate tonight," she said without hesitation. "I think you took an awful chance of ruining your reputation and everything that you've worked so hard to establish."

Darmanian reached for the back of Delores's neck, and I saw him give her a gentle squeeze of reassurance. "It is time, darling," he said. "I feel a profound responsibility to show people what a mistake it is to think that everything has been discovered and that the horizon one sees is the boundary of the world. I must show them that the actual boundaries lie far beyond the false ones that they have placed around themselves."

"But, Darmanian," Delores pointed out, "some people feel secure behind their boundary lines. Wasn't it a bit risky to burst through those boundaries in one blast by giving those conservative men and women a massive dosage of reincarnation?"

Darmanian shook his head. "The gods never help the man who will not act," he said. "It is time to act. I have developed a whole new therapy around the memory of past lives."

"Then this is the new direction in your work of which you spoke?" I inquired.

"Precisely," Darmanian answered. "Tell me, Eric,

now that you have witnessed a demonstration of hypnotic regression to a possible past life with its correlations to the present life, what do you feel about reincarnation?"

"I guess I would have to say that I am still an agnostic toward the concept," I answered honestly.

Darmanian laughed. "An agnostic is a man who doesn't know whether or not a deity exists, doesn't know whether or not he has a soul, doesn't know whether or not there is a life beyond the grave. Furthermore, an agnostic doesn't believe that anyone else knows any more about such matters than he does, and he thinks it is a waste of time to try to find out."

I considered Darmanian's response a bit caustic, but I attempted a soft answer so that I might turn away any potential wrath. "I surely do not believe it is a waste of time to seek the answers to the Big Questions of life, death, and immortality," I told him. "I do, most certainly, believe in God. And I have faith that there is life after physical death. I simply am not certain that reincarnation is the form that life after death assumes."

Delores slowed to accommodate the sharp bend in the road that preceded one's first glimpse of Woodlands. "Really, Darmanian," she said rather sharply, "you must know that reincarnation has never been a popular theory in the Western world. I think Eric is expressing a very open-minded attitude."

Darmanian was fumbling in his coat pocket for the key to the gate chain as we approached the driveway. "It won't really matter for the success of my new therapy whether or not one believes in the validity of reincarnation."

He pushed open the door of the Oldsmobile, got out, walked briskly to the gate.

Delores turned to look at me over the back of the seat. "Eric, I am so happy that you are here. I don't know what happened to Darmanian tonight. He seems so changed, so different."

"He is obviously a man possessed by a new insight, a new direction in his work," I said, attempting to mollify her.

"One thing I've always told you, Delores," Darmanian said as he slid back into his seat and slammed the car door, "is that I believe that the clinical hypnotist must be like an artist—free to follow his creative urges. I must be permitted to use whatever method is most effective in order to best serve my patients."

"And you feel that your new past-lives therapy will be able to serve your patients in the best possible way?" I wanted to know.

Delores had driven the car through the gate, and Darmanian opened his door so that he might get out and lock the chain behind us. He paused with his hand on the door as he stood outside the car.

"I learned long ago that I must be allowed to enter into mental rapport with my patients so that we might cooperatively devise the kind of individual therapy to which the patient will most readily respond," he told us. "In my initial experiments with past-life therapy, I have found that I have been able to enter the closest kind of rapport and that I have been able to increase the rate of response by incredible leaps forward."

Darmanian locked the chain, rejoined us once again. In the light from the dashboard, I could see his left hand pulling at the medallion around his neck, as if it served as his physical stimulus for focusing his thoughts. Delores braked the car in front of the mansion, began to reach for the handle to her door, but the hypnotist reached across the steering wheel and placed a restraining hand on her wrist.

"Whether one believes that reincarnation is all delusion, fantasy, or actual past lives coming forth as memory, I have found that many men and women can obtain a definite and profound release of present-life pains and phobias by reliving the origin of the trauma in an alleged former existence," he told us.

Delores looked away from him, but my curiosity was becoming piqued. "How does this therapy work?" I asked.

Darmanian seemed pleased by my interest. "I suggest that the subject follow a number of self-destructive patterns through several supposed past lives," he said. "Soon repetitious elements in either the life patterns or the death patterns of the subject's prior existences begin to manifest. I have also discovered that the envisioning of traumatic deaths prove to provide carryover elements that are being expressed in the subject's current life experience."

Delores began to drum her fingers softly on the steering wheel. "I can envision our clients beginning to stay away from Woodlands by the droves," she said, still avoiding his eyes.

Darmanian would not be daunted. "Look at it this way, Delores: We know that diseases have emotional as well as physical origins and aspects. By our suggesting that a subject relive a past life, he will be able to release fully his emotions, and he will be able to accept responsibility for an action that he will see has already been performed and done in a prior existence. Therefore, we, as therapists, can encourage the subject to make the transfer of responsibility to the present life, since the fault lies in a time far removed from current concerns, embarrassments, and shame."

"But it is all fantasy play, isn't it?" Delores questioned, at last facing the hypnotist to confront him directly.

"If that is your feeling, my dear," Darmanian replied, "then you may regard the past-life material just as you would any fantasy material from the present-life experience. After all, isn't it true that any fantasy, be it from this life or a supposed previous one, will influence the individual who indulges in it? For all we know at our present stage of mental exploration, fantasy and memory may be essentially the same thing."

I spoke again from my position in the backseat. "It seems to me, Darmanian," I remarked, "that you are still the eternal pragmatist."

"Exactly," Darmanian said, readily accepting my categorization. "Men and women in altered states of consciousness are extremely suggestible. If the therapist permits them to structure a past-life experience to showcase their present problems, then they will be likely to see their fantasy as a safe manner of dealing with an immediate trauma.

"Integral to this system of past-life therapy," Darmanian added, "is the fact that the physical body conducts itself according to the beliefs of the mind. If a subject believes that his headaches are due to his being struck on the head by a tomahawk in 1850, then, at least on some level of consciousness, he will act as though it is so."

"All right, Darmanian," Delores said politely. "What

if a subject has repeated dreams of being burned alive?"

The hypnotist sat quietly for several moments. I could almost feel the tension between them. Delores had told me how Darmanian had seemingly ignored her traumatic nightmares. Now, in a very real sense, she was challenging him to prove that he was as concerned with her problems as he was with those of his patients.

"My darling," Darmanian answered her at last, "since you have brought up those troublesome dreams of yours and since you are undoubtedly prepared to make an issue of them, would you permit me to demonstrate my new therapy on you?"

"What do I have to lose?" she asked. "Other than those damn dreams."

"You are an excellent hypnotic subject," Darmanian said. "You are thoroughly conditioned to go under quickly and deeply. I believe that I can yet prove my points to both of you tonight."

"Tonight?" Delores echoed, just the slightest touch of apprehension in her voice.

"It is at night when you dream, is it not?" Darmanian asked her as he opened his car door. "Come. Let us go into the house and begin."

"Why not?" Delores wondered rhetorically, sliding out of her car seat. "Maybe I was Joan of Arc."

Chapter Ten

Darmanian had but to touch Delores lightly on the forehead, command "Deep sleep," and pause a moment to permit the state of attentive, responsive concentration to permeate various levels of consciousness.

We had chosen the library for the experiment. Delores lay on a couch near a marble-topped fireplace. A comfortable fire kept back the April night's chill, for although the evening was much more pleasant than the previous day's rain and cold, there was still a bite to the air. Darmanian had given me permission to record the demonstration, and I sat in an overstuffed chair just to Delores's left.

"Delores has previously been regressed to the birth experience," Darmanian told me, as the lovely lady lay somewhere in psychic limbo. "Therefore, I shall cheat you of the experience of hearing her babble baby talk and move her directly back to a previous lifetime."

The hypnotist rubbed his forehead with the thumb and forefinger of his right hand, as if he were engaging in a brief mental struggle prior to some decision making. "Delores," he said, "I want you to move far, far back in time. I want you to move back to a time before you were Delores Touraine. I want you to move back to a time when you were someone else. I want you to move back to a lifetime that has influenced the life you are living today.

"This is important, Delores," he emphasized. "As you move back in time, I want you to move toward a life pattern in which your experiences had great significance for your spiritual evolution.

"At the count of three, Delores, you will awake in another time and place. You will be able to speak to us. You will tell us of a day that is very important to you. You will be a child in that life, but you will be old enough to tell us what you see, hear, and think."

"*One.* Moving farther and farther back, going deeper and deeper asleep.

"*Two.* Deeper and deeper asleep, farther and farther back.

"*Three.* What do you see?"

Delores's answer came in a flurry of excited chatter, which after my first confused moments, I recognized to be French. Her brown eyes widened to their ultimate stretch, and she seemed upset by our inability to answer her.

"I only know schoolboy French," I told Darmanian, "but I am certain that she is speaking in that language."

Darmanian nodded, smiled, as if he were immensely satisfied about something not at all evident to my sphere of understanding. "It is an archaic Parisian dialect," he said.

Delores had become frustrated to the point of tears

and her hands were mussing her hair in what seemed to be both fear and anguish.

"Deep sleep!" Darmanian commanded, and Delores's head rolled weakly to one side. Her breathing returned to a normal rate.

"I am close enough to you to speak directly to your unconscious," Darmanian said, each syllable resounding with the touch of authority. "Your unconscious understands that all language is but verbal representation of symbols and thought patterns. When I remove you from your deep sleep, you will be able to speak to us in the language that we understand best, American English. You may think in French, but you will speak in English."

Darmanian counted again to three, and Delores responded by taking a deep breath. Her eyes remained closed, but I could almost hear the mental computer banks reprogramming themselves for instant translation.

"I am Catherine," she answered in response to Darmanian's next question. There remained a not unpleasant trace of French accent. "Would you like me to tell your fortune?"

Darmanian straightened to his full height, and his chest expanded several inches. I nearly expected him to crow, he seemed so exuberantly pleased with himself. At this point in the experiment, I could see nothing about which he should be so elated.

"How old are you, Catherine?" he asked.

"I am twelve, sir," responded the soft, musical voice.

"So young a girl tells fortunes?"

"Oh, yes," she replied in earnest tones. "I am very talented. I have God-given powers. You may ask anyone."

Darmanian nodded his head in obvious relish. "What year is it, Catherine."

"It is 1650, sir. That is not a fortune, m'lord, but if you keep asking me questions, I must charge you for my time." The lilting voice had become firm, businesslike.

"Of course," Darmanian agreed. "That goes without saying. Can you see me?"

The little-girl voice snorted impatiently. "Do you take me for a blind beggar girl? Of course I can see you. You are elegantly dressed, like a gentleman. I have many of the royalty among my clientele."

"What is your full name, child, and where do you live?"

A petulant sigh escaped from Delores's lips. "I am Catherine Deshayes. The streets of Paris are my home. But I am a prophetess. I have been telling fortunes here in the streets since I was but nine. I have God-given powers!"

Darmanian commanded another deep sleep, then he moved the entity ahead in time to the age of twenty-one.

Delores's supine body stiffened as if it had been suffused with electricity. Then she became supple, sensuous. "Yes, m'lord? What is it you wish of La Voisin? You wish a potion for your mistress so that she might better satisfy your desires?"

Darmanian had poured us each a glass of red wine, and now he strode quickly to my chair and clinked the rim of my glass with his own, as if in celebration. "We are having a great success this night." He smiled, his blue eyes glinting in fierce pleasure.

I managed a weak smile and nodded my confused agreement.

"Your name has changed, Catherine," Darmanian challenged the personality that was speaking through Delores. Or was it the personality that Delores had assumed in the trance state? I was in no position to be dogmatic about either interpretation. Perhaps, after all, it was a memory of one of Delores's past lives speaking. If such things are possible.

"Have you married?" the hypnotist suggested by way of providing his own solution to the problem.

A resigned sigh. "Yes, to Antoine Montvoisin. He does not beat me, as other men might have done, but he is a loafer." Then brightening: "Do you like my shop?"

Delores's arm rose and broadly swept the space before her. "Here are the herbs and bromides. Over there is where I prepare m'lady's hair. And everyone knows that I am among the best midwives in all of Paris."

Darmanian congratulated her. "You have become most enterprising."

"Thank you, m'lord. In addition, I interpret the stars, read palms, and use my God-given powers to help all. All who pay my price, that is."

Darmanian decided to move Delores's trance personality ahead another ten years.

A powerful laugh issued from Delores's throat. "Tell you how I have prospered? Paris is mine! Ask anyone about La Voisin. I even have the ear of King Louis."

Darmanian interrupted. "Forgive me, La Voisin. Is that King Louis the Fourteenth?"

"None else," came the impatient reply. "With what other King Louis have you acquaintance? Know you that the Madame de Montespan herself participates in the services in my secret chamber!"

"And who is Madame de Montespan?"

Coarse laughter shook the slender frame of the reclining, entranced Delores. "I think that you have been exiled to a far-off land, m'lord. Madame de Montespan is the king's mistress."

"How have you gained so much power, La Voisin? Is it, too, God-given?"

The voice assumed a reverential tone. "Yes, it has been given to me by the true Lord of the Earth. But I have bought it from him with the blood of a thousand babies!"

I squinted my distaste at Darmanian. What mental quagmire had his hypnotic probing discovered within Delores's interior geography?

A thin trickle of laughter issued from Delores's full, sensuous lips. "But, m'lord, you were there, weren't you? You saw the blood gush from their torn throats. You heard their flesh crackle, their tiny bones pop in the roaring ovens. You, too, made your obeisance at the living altars of our Holy Satan!"

"Satan!" I started at the sound of my own voice echoing that of the trance personality.

Darmanian placed Delores into a deep sleep. "She has quite obviously incorporated me into her past-life imagery," he said to me. Then, before I could ask any questions, he moved Delores ahead another ten years.

Neither of us was prepared for the terrible scream that was torn loose from Delores's throat. Her body began to writhe on the couch as if she were suffering insane torments and violent pain.

Darmanian quickly recovered his professionalism as a clinical hypnotist and told her that she need feel no pain, that she would be completely relaxed, that she could view whatever was happening to her in a dissociated, dispassionate manner.

"Those swine," she hissed through clenched teeth. "How they were hurting me!"

"What is happening to you?" Darmanian asked.

The voice was angry, defiant, yet coarse and ragged. "It is my second period of torture. They are trying to make me tell who belongs to our circle. Don't—don't worry, my love. I will not betray you! The priests and other pigs who serve the Chambre Ardente will never break me!"

Darmanian's voice was soft, compassionate. "You need not tell us any more about those things. I want you to move along until it is your last day as Catherine Deshayes, La Voisin. You will be able to tell us exactly what is happening; but remember, you will feel no pain! It will be as if it is all happening to someone else."

Delores's head tossed fitfully from side to side, then she became very still. When she spoke, it was in a voice almost totally devoid of emotion. "They are leading me to the stake. I look so terrible. My body is black from the branding irons. My left breast has been seared away. Most of my beautiful hair has been singed to nothing but ugly strands. My eyes are clotted with blood.

"A slimy worm of a priest comes to me as they prepare to bind me to the stake. He asks to hear my final confession. I am strong enough yet to push him away. The crowd laughs and applauds. They knew they could count on La Voisin to give them a good show."

"Tell me what the date is!" Darmanian was suddenly insistent. "Do you know?"

Bitter laughter. "Yes, the inquisitor always announces the day before the torture begins. I have kept count. It is February twenty-third, 1680."

"Has not Satan betrayed you?" Darmanian asked politely. "You are going to the stake. He did not deliver you from your enemies."

"You seek to test me?" the voice answered in a low murmur. "Will the questions and testing never end? You know that our Holy Satan has explained the Great Plan to us. When the fullness of time has passed, we shall again have our day. And in that day, we shall succeed. All power, glory, and majesty will be ours forevermore."

Delores's body began to twitch and jerk, as if she were trying to escape some invisible horror.

"What is happening now?"

Delores's voice was urgent. Her breath was coming in short, quick gasps. "The swine are lighting the straw and the wood. Some men and women move closer to the stake. They are screaming that I murdered their babies! With the bare feet I kick the burning straw into their faces. The soldiers push the crowd back with their pikes."

Delores began to cough, as if unable to breathe properly.

"You will feel no pain," the hypnotist reinforced. "Nor will the smoke bother you. You will continue talking to us. You will feel no concern for the physical body of Catherine."

Delores gritted her teeth, whimpered only once. "There is still some pain, but I can bear it. The smoke stings my eyes. I see my mother. *But she is dead!* She is beckoning to me. Oh, now I understand. I am dying."

She emitted a long sigh, then her head rolled to one

side. "I am floating. Floating high above the crowd. I can see the poor body being eaten by the flames. The men and women are cheering as the flesh falls away in blackened lumps. But I am floating up to the clouds. Floating . . . floating . . ."

Darmanian instructed the personality to move forward through time until it had arrived at the present.

"You will once again be Delores Touraine," he told her. "None of the things that you have heard and seen will trouble you in any way. When you awaken, you will feel refreshed. You will feel better than you have felt in months. All pains and irritations will have left you."

At the count of three Delores blinked open her eyes and began to cough. Darmanian poured a glass of water from the carafe on a stand near the fireplace and set it in her trembling hands.

"What," she gasped after a number of deep swallows, "was all that?"

Darmanian returned the question with one of his own. "What do you think it was, my dear? And, Eric?"—his narrowed blue eyes stabbed at me—"what do you think it was?"

I had removed my pipe from a coat pocket and was stuffing the bowl with my favorite mixture. I waited for Delores to respond, but since she only lay on the couch in reflective silence, I offered my opinion.

"We may have witnessed an example of the incredible creative capacity of the human mind," I said. "Whatever it was, it was most interesting."

Delores spoke up from her reverie. "I'll want to hear your tape later, Eric, because I don't really know how much I'm remembering from the trance and how much is flooding in on me now. But I felt that I knew Catherine in some very intimate way."

I paused in lighting the tobacco. "Couldn't that be because your unconscious created her?"

"But," Darmanian said as he helped Delores to a sitting position, "now we have a hook to work with, regardless of the role of her unconscious in creating it. Delores, who dreams of being burned alive, has, under hypnotic regression, revealed a past life as a woman who was literally burned at the stake."

I drew deeply of the fragrant tobacco, issued my protest with clouds of smoke. "But isn't that a bit obvious? I mean, creating a fantasy of having been executed at the stake to explain the burning dreams."

Darmanian met my opposition. "That is the way the unconscious often works, Eric, especially in a trance state. It is so desirous of pleasing the hypnotist. It may reveal much in symbols, but it seldom hides the truth from a skillful seeker.

"From the viewpoint of a therapist," he continued to explain, "now that we have regressed Delores to a former lifetime when she was burned at the stake, we may be able to carry those memories into her present lifetime, deal with them for what they are—symbols of her current fears—and dissipate them once and for all. Her past-life recall will cure the phobias of the present lifetime."

"It is all very fascinating, I will admit," I agreed. "But unless I could find evidence that there really was a nasty little Parisienne named La Voisin who cooked babies in an oven, it is really all beyond my comprehension."

Darmanian scowled his impatience. "It has been said that he who believes only what he can fully comprehend has either a very long head or a very short creed."

I smiled around my pipe stem. "It has also been said, by Terence, I believe, that one believes easily what he hopes for earnestly."

Delores called a halt to our wordplay. "All this is academic unless the regression experience has helped me with my nightmares," she said.

"Exactly," Darmanian nodded. "My point exactly!"

I shrugged my shoulders. "I, too, am a pragmatist. If past-lives therapy works, for God's sake, use it!"

Darmanian was thoughtfully stroking his medallion. "It is good that you keep an open mind, Eric. And that you are so practical."

"And"—I smiled, glancing at my wristwatch—"I am also practical enough to know it is time to go to bed at two thirty in the morning."

"My God, Darmanian!" Delores gasped. "We have a full day of patients tomorrow. And the first one arrives at nine!"

I excused myself to retire to my room. But as I climbed the stairs alone, I seemed to sense a presence near me. It was almost as if I felt a palpable energy swirling about me. There seemed to be another intelligence intent upon impressing upon my own that Catherine Deshayes was much more than a creation of Delores Touraine's unconscious. Somehow I knew that La Voisin, like a persistent succubus, would be my bedmate that night.

Chapter Eleven

In addition to the Oldsmobile Cutlass, which was a 1978 model, Woodlands Clinic owned two other cars, a 1975 Chevrolet station wagon and a 1977 Lincoln Continental. The Lincoln was apparently Darmanian's concession to status, and I imagine that he only drove it on special occasions. I asked permission to borrow the Chevy, since the hypnotist told me that he and Delores had a full schedule until late afternoon. I wanted to see some of the countryside, and I wanted some time to myself apart from Woodlands to evaluate what had occurred the night before.

I also wanted to take advantage of the time away from Woodlands to attempt making contact with Ed Vogel, the ambitious letter writer from Saratoga Springs who had been in touch with me since the release of my book on Swedenborg. Vogel was apparently an authority of sorts on the occult and the paranormal and he had been trying his best to persuade me to write a series of biographies of great mediums, clairvoyants, and such.

It had occurred to me that morning as I was eating breakfast that Vogel might be able to give me an intelligent and scholarly response to the whole matter of La Voisin and past-life regressions. It might be good to bring Vogel and Darmanian together before the hypnotist extended himself any further in his past-lives experiments.

Ever since I had moved to an apartment in Manhattan five years before, I had heard Saratoga Springs mentioned synonymously with mineral waters and horse racing. Although I had never had occasion to visit the picturesque little city, I knew that August was the thoroughbred racing season and that gamblers, tourists, and prominent social figures flocked to the tracks. The mineral-water baths and springs were open all year, and I had seen them advertised as providing relief for arthritis, rheumatism, and circulatory disorders.

In the Victorian era, Saratoga Springs was known as the "queen of the spas." Even then it was famous for its horse racing, mineral waters, and extravagant social life. Luxurious casinos had remained open in the city until the 1940s, even though gambling had been declared illegal in other parts of the state.

It made great sense for Darmanian to have established his prestigious clinic in the greenery and the graciousness of Saratoga Springs. The famous and the wealthy could become his patrons and celebrate their cures at the race track—or they could supplement their therapy with a couple of treatments at the famous baths. And it could all take place in beautiful natural surroundings, rather than the grit, grime, and menace of the Big Apple, New York City.

As I drove through the streets of Saratoga Springs, I

saw evidence everywhere that its residents were ambitiously striving to transform its facilities into a year-round resort. Several old buildings were in the process of receiving dramatic face lifts. The old Canfield Casino had been completely restored, according to a poster on its entryway, and it now housed two historic museums.

I continued to weave absently through the streets of Saratoga Springs, sifting my thoughts, sorting my impressions.

Then, I pulled into a gas station where I saw an outdoor pay telephone. Within minutes, I had dialed Vogel's number and was listening to the call ringing through.

"It's your dime," came a gruff response when the receiver was lifted. "Talk."

"Ed Vogel?" I wanted to be certain.

"Speaking." He acknowledged his identity.

"It's Eric Storm, the author with whom you have been corresponding."

"You're kidding," Vogel roared. "Where are you, Eric? Are you calling from New York? I'm flattered, believe me."

It was a beautifully warm April noon. After the rains of the previous days, one could almost hear things growing. I loosened my tie and opened my collar. "I'm here in your fair city, Ed," I told him. "I'm talking to you from a pay phone at an Exxon gas station on Huron Street and Thirty-fourth."

His voice became excited. "Can we get together? Or are you just passing through?"

"I'm here for a few days, Ed. I would very much like to get together. I need to ask a favor."

He nearly shouted into the receiver. "Anything I can do, Eric, you ask. Okay?"

Ed gave me explicit directions on how to find his home. By the time he had completed his street-by-street delineations, my graphics covered an entire notebook page. Within fifteen minutes I was presenting myself at the Vogels' door.

"Hi, Mr. Storm," the woman who opened the front door gretted me. "I'm Paula, Ed's wife."

She was a tall, rangy woman with broad shoulders and wide hips. With her sandy-colored hair and the irregular rows of freckles dotting the bridge of her nose and spreading out across her cheekbones, Paula could have served as an artist's model for the pioneer woman trudging beside her man and a Conestoga wagon.

"It's such a pleasure to have you visit our home," she said, smiling broadly.

"It is a pleasure to have you receive me so graciously," I replied, shaking the hand she offered me. Her grip was strong and confident.

Ed Vogel had written some of the most intelligent letters that I had ever received. I had told him early in our correspondence that he could himself be a writer of considerable skill. Although I warmed to him instantly, I must admit that I was taken off guard by Ed's appearance. I had visualized him differently, I quite readily concede.

He had been standing in a doorway of the smallish home, respectfully permitting Paula and I to exchange greetings. He was attired in a faded red bathrobe, belted over patched green work trousers. A yellow daisy-strewn pajama top was visible wherever the robe did not quite overlap, Shabby, lace-up workshoes completed Ed Vogel's sartorial suicide.

"Beautiful day, huh?" he asked around a panatela cigar tucked firmly against a ruddy cheek. "I'm so grateful that you called on a day when I wasn't working at the lumberyard."

"What a happy conincidence," I agreed, wishing that his handshake was less emphatic. His fingers, while rather short and stubby, were possessed of great strength.

"There are no coincidences in God's world," Vogel pronounced with an element of almost clerical solemnity. "Everything happens for a reason."

"I can accept that," I said. "It was our destiny to meet."

Vogel searched my face to see if I were being flippant or friendly. I had made the remark about destiny in a somewhat jocular vein, but I had not intended to be caustic. If I had not learned as much from his letters, I had now to accept the fact that Ed Vogel was an intensely spiritual man.

He smiled, released my hand, and stepped aside so I might enter a room that was lined from floor to ceiling with books about the paranormal, the occult, the unknown. "Not too many guys at the lumberyard know about my hobby." He laughed. "Oh, they know that I'm weird. They just don't realize how weird I really am."

Ed Vogel was a big man, who must have been formidable in his day. But now that he was in his mid-fifties, his physique looked like a bag of laundry under his ill-fitting robe. Not that those thick forearms had not retained an impressive musculature. I also sensed powerful thighs and bulky calves that were capable of walking men half his age into the ground.

"Sit down, please." Ed indicated a thread-bare easy chair near a leaning tower of books stacked on the floor. "Words cannot express my delight in welcoming you to my home. You are a scholar as well as a writer. That is why I keep writing to urge you to turn your generous intellect toward contemporary mysticism. You should do for some of our modern psychics that which you did for Swedenborg and Quimby."

Paula entered the room with a tray of glasses, sandwiches, and two pitchers.

"Please join me in my lunch of juices and vegetable sandwiches," Ed said. "There's cucumber and tomato. And what else, Paula?"

"Peanut butter and banana," she smiled, offering me a tray.

"Thank you," I returned her smile. "I'll take the peanut butter and banana."

"Grape or pineapple juice?"

"Ah, pineapple, please," I decided.

Ed had produced two chipped and battered television food trays from a closet behind his cluttered desk. Paula spread a dish towel over each, and lunch was served.

"Very considerate," I said. It was natural peanut butter, and it stuck to the roof of my mouth. I washed it down with my juice, and received a refill from the attentive Paula.

"Paula was a waitress for many years," Ed explained. "She still works part time at Howard Johnson's during their busy period."

"She's very accomplished," I said. I was surprised when Paula very noticeably blushed at my compliment.

"But you said you came here to ask a favor of me?" Ed inquired. He rolled his eyes toward the ceiling as if his brain could not comprehend what he could possibly offer to anyone.

I wiped my mouth on the yellow paper napkin that Paula had thoughtfully set beside my plate. "Ed," I began, "does your expertise extend to witchcraft or Satanism?"

"My God," Paula interjected. "He's more than likely got two hundred books on witchcraft alone."

"Three hundred and sixty-two," Ed corrected her with a small gesture of impatience. "There's three shelves of them in the back room, besides what's in here and in the living room."

I raised my eyebrows to indicate that I was impressed. Then I proceeded with my question. "Have you ever read of a high priestess who allegedly lived about the time of Louis the Fourteenth named Catherine Deshayes, or La Voisin?"

Ed emitted a good-natured, mocking snort, which sent ashes from his cigar swirling toward the soiled yellow carpet. It was apparent from Paula's anguished sob and her dash for a larger ashtray that Vogel had a few mannerisms that had evaded domestication.

"I'll assume that you are not pulling my leg." Ed grinned around the panatela. "Yes, I have certainly heard of La Voisin."

An icy, feathery finger tickled my stomach. "You mean there actually was such a person?"

Ed nodded slowly, his eyes studying my face for any hint of a test or a taunt. "Yes, there certainly was such a person," he agreed cautiously.

"Well," I prompted, "can you tell me something about her?"

Vogel shifted his bulk in the easy chair, tossed the last bite of his cucumber-and-tomato sandwich in his mouth. He chewed laboriously for several seconds before he spoke again. "Eric, La Voisin is one of the biggies in the history of demonology and devil worship. She was a Satanist, not a witch. There's quite a difference, take my word for it."

"Witchcraft, as I understand it, is the old, pre-Christian religion of Europe," I ventured, not wanting to appear totally uneducated in the field of magic and mysticism. "Satanism is the antithesis of both witchcraft and Christianity. A perversion of Christianity, actually. The opposite side of the coin, so to speak."

Vogel released a large cloud of tobacco smoke. "That's correct, Eric," he said. His twinkling blue eyes were crouched behind his thick brows. He was suspicious once again. "But you've *never* heard of La Voisin?"

"My God, Ed!" I answered a bit impatiently. "I've never researched either witchcraft or Satanism to any degree. And hers is hardly a household name, you know. At least not"—I indicated the row of books with an emphatic sweep of my arm—"in the average household."

Vogel blinked, rubbed the stubble on his broad chin. He seemed satisfied at last. "Well, La Voisin probably sacrificed damn near two thousand babies to Satan, and she was so skilled in the art of brewing poisons that half the population of Paris would have been eliminated if someone had ever dumped those fatal fluids in the Seine."

The chill finger was now at my spine, moving up and down its length, raising the hairs on the back of my neck. "She spoke of sacrifices," I said, transmitting my thoughts into words. "She said that she was an herbalist."

Paula was making a face of profound distaste. After a few seconds of facial protest she managed to come up with an "ick" to match. "This is terrible talk. Sacrificing babies and poisoning people. Let's talk about something nice," she said. "Ed, talk about Stewart Edward White's Betty books. I like to hear about nice spooks who give good advice."

"I'm sorry, Paula," I told her. "I really need to know about La Voisin, nasty character though she might have been."

Ed scowled his curiosity. "You gonna write a book about her?"

"Nothing like that," I replied. "Ed, I'm in Saratoga Springs because I'm writing a book about Darmanian."

Vogel's eyes widened in surprise. "No shit," he hissed, shaking his head slowly from side to side. "You're going to write a book about Mister Evil Eyes? How in hell did you get sucked in to do such a thing?"

I could not help being defensive. "I cannot imagine your reacting in such a manner, Ed," I said. "Darmanian has an international reputation as a clinical hypnotist. He has accomplished some of the most—"

"Yeah, yeah." Ed closed his eyes, waved me silent. It appeared as though he were suddenly suffering from an intense migraine headache. "I know all those wonderful public-relations things that he does. But there's another side of him, a darker side, that scares me."

"What could Darmanian do that could frighten you?" I persisted. "And what do you mean by a darker side?"

"I just pick up things about him, Eric," Ed said, his eyes still tightly closed. "Bad things."

"By 'pick up,' I would suppose that you mean you have gained this information through psychic or intuitive sense," I suggested.

"Ed is a very good psychic," Paula spoke up, rushing to her husband's defense. "He knows about lots of things a long time before they happen. I've seldom known him to be wrong when he really tunes in on things."

Ed took a long breath, opened his eyes, and studied me as if he were seeing me for the first time. "What," he wanted to know, "do your questions about La Voisin have to do with Darmanian?"

"Darmanian is enterting a totally new phase of his work," I answered. "And last night, by chance or some incredible design, he regressed his assistant, Delores Touraine, back to an alleged lifetime as this La Voisin."

Vogel's eyes widened again. He rolled the cigar around in his mouth as if it were a baton. "Darmanian is into regression? The great master hypnotist, who makes a big thing of working only with bona fide medical doctors and psychiatrists, is into past lives?"

"I won't go into the details of how it all came about, right now," I told him. "But I had no idea that La Voisin was an actual historical personage, and I am quite certain that Delores had no prior knowledge of the woman's existence."

"Do you think that she might have come up with a lot of verifiable data?" Vogel asked, pouring us each another shot of pineapple juice.

"I think now that she might have," I said. "I mean, judging by the little that you have said. I would like you to come to Woodlands tonight to serve as an expert witness and to evaluate whether or not we might actually have tapped into something."

Vogel laughed. "How would you smuggle me into Woodlands after dark? Have you a key to the great iron gates?"

"You know about how the place is locked after five fifteen?"

"Sure," he said. "Everyone knows about the thick chains on the gate. And everyone has a half dozen legends of his own about Darmanian and what goes on at Woodlands behind those gates."

"But a man of your knowledge—" I started to protest, but Ed raised a thick palm to silence my argument.

"I believe little of what others say about Darmanian," Ed told me. "But I know him to be something other than what he represents himself."

"And what is that 'something other'?" I wanted to know.

Ed shrugged his heavy shoulders. "I don't have a name for it yet."

I raised an eyebrow in arch disapproval. Ed Vogel had disappointed me, but I would quickly give him a chance to redeem himself. "Will you return to Woodlands with me?" I asked.

"I'll come," Vogel answered after he had chomped down heavily on his cigar. "If Darmanian will let me in."

I asked to use their telephone. It was nearly three. Darmanian and Delores would still be at the clinic. Darmanian was expecting to spend the evening with me, locked into the interviewing process for the book. Since he was entering this bold and controversial phase of his career, it seemed to me that he would welcome verification of an actual past life. Especially with his bias toward reincarnation.

Mrs. Lundby answered the telephone. I identified myself, brushed aside the amenities, asked if it were possible to speak immediately to Darmanian.

In about twenty seconds Darmanian came on the line. He was friendly, but brusque. I had probably interrupted his work with a patient.

I got directly to the point of my call. "I'm at a friend's house, Darmanian. You may recall that I mentioned that I had been corresponding with a man who is an authority on the mystical and the occult."

"Oh, yes," the hypnotist responded. "I do recall that, Eric."

"Well, my friend, Ed Vogel, has just told me that Catherine Deshayes, La Voisin, was an actual historical personage."

"Really?" Darmanian said. "Is he quite certain? But then I suppose he is if he is an authority of sorts."

"Yes," I replied. "He's certain. He has hundreds of reference books here in his home."

"This is most remarkable," Darmanian agreed. "This is very exciting. How do you feel about this discovery, Eric?"

"I want to investigate further," I said firmly. "I would like you to regress Delores again with Ed present as an expert witness. If Delores has read about this person in a reference book and forgotten about it, then she will not be able to come up with enough data from her memory banks to satisfy a scholar in the field that she was actually La Voisin."

Darmanian chuckled into the receiver. "Always the skeptic, aren't you, Eric?"

"Always the researcher," I corrected him. "Unless Delores is a secret scholar of Satanism, there is no way that she could know one tenth of the facts about La Voisin that Ed Vogel knows."

"And if the regressed personality satisfies your friend?" Darmanian asked.

"Then we might have two books to work on," I told him. "We just might produce two best-sellers behind Woodlands' walls."

"Be here," Darmanian told me, "before I chain the gates."

Chapter Twelve

By seven o'clock that evening, Darmanian had placed Delores in a state of deep hypnotic sleep. Her lithe body was swathed in a pale blue caftan, and its sheerness hugged her as she lay once again on the couch in the library.

"I want you to move, down, down down, deeper, deeper down," Darmanian commanded. "I want you to reach a deeper level than you have ever before attained in hypnosis. When you have reached that level, I want the middle finger of your left hand to raise as a signal to me. Do you understand?"

A feeble hissing sound came from Delores' lips.

"Louder, please," Darmanian instructed.

"*Yesss,*" Delores repeated. She lay quietly for several seconds, then, slowly, the middle finger of her left hand began to raise until it was quivering to achieve perpendicular status. Her eyes were tightly closed, but her mouth had become slack.

Darmanian told her that she could lower her finger. "Now that you are at such a deep level," he said, "I want you to travel back in time and space. At the count of three, it will once again be the country of France in the year 1650. You will again be able to remember the most minute details of your life as Catherine Deshayes, La Voisin."

Ed Vogel had positioned himself in a black leather reclining chair. He had a yellow legal pad propped across a rounded thigh. At Paula's urging, he had managed to wedge himself into an old black flannel suit. I know that he had left their house with a necktie neatly wrapped about his neck, but somehow, in transit to Woodlands, it had disappeared. Curly strands of black hair bristled at the "v" dip of the shirt that was now open at the collar.

Darmanian sat before Delores on a large black footstool made of elegantly polished leather. He slouched forward, his elbows resting comfortably on his knees, his fingers laced together beneath his chin. His brilliant blue eyes were narrowed, as if they were somehow probing Delores's entranced psyche. He was dressed casually in black trousers and a white turtleneck sweater. The ever-present medallion lay across his chest as if it were monitoring the scene before it.

I had taken a chair to the right of Delores. My tape recorder sat on my lap, and I held the microphone so that I might aim it in sweeping, ping-pong motions from Darmanian to Delores.

Darmanian was extending his hypnotic suggestion: "Because you are at such a deep level of the soul, where the normal limitations of time and space do not exist, I want you to be able to retain a certain detatchment," he said to Delores. "I want you to be able to see everything through Catherine's eyes, but I want you to remain aloof from the pain and the suffering so that you will be able to share everything with me."

The hypnotist moved Delores back at the count of three, asked her to tell him what she was seeing.

"Heaps of garbage," came the soft, musical child's voice. "The garbage piles of Paris. I am hungry. I am searching for food to eat."

Darmanian's dark brows dipped low over his narrow eyes. The thumb and forefinger of his right hand reflectively stroked his medallion. The movement was not lost on Ed Vogel, who had seemed from their first moment of meeting inordinately fascinated by the winged dragons and their flashing crystal ball.

The gently accented voice of Catherine—and I shall now call her by that name rather than Delores—told us that her mama had died three years before of the coughing sickness. She was uncertain who her father might have been.

"I live with old Juliette," Catherine said. "She is good to me. She teaches me how to tell fortunes in the streets. She shows me how to burn candles and how to make the elves and spirits help me. She knows all about the old religion before Jesus and Mary."

Old Juliette provided the girl with a crude roof over her head and food when it was available. Although their lodgings were squalid, we heard how each night the old woman spun tales of magic for the girl.

"Now when I go to the streets and the marketplaces, I can hear my little elf brushing up against my skirt and speaking soft words of love to me," the girlish voice said. "When I am reading fortunes, he whispers in my ear and tells me things about people."

Catherine told us how she could walk anywhere in Paris without fear. Her elf was always ready to protect her. Once two thugs had grabbed her to steal the coins that she had earned that day. Little Catherine had glared at them malevolently and called a curse upon their heads. Both men were suddenly seized with severe stomach cramps and fouled themselves with the spewing from their own loosened bowels.

I glanced at Ed Vogel. He was furiously scribbling notes to himself. Darmanian sat quietly, listening to the trance personality, stroking the dragons on the medallion as if they were living pets.

We heard a bit more of the prowess of Catherine's elf, and we learned how the demand for the little witch-woman's street-corner prophecies kept her busy from sunrise to sunset.

On the count of three, Darmanian moved Catherine ahead in her moment of time in seventeenth-century Paris. He told her that she was now twenty years old.

"I am now Catherine Montvoisin," she said. "I am married to Antoine. He never beats me, as some men might, but he seldom contributes to the welfare of our family. He is a good-natured oaf."

"Have you children?" Darmanian asked her.

"Marguerite, our daughter, shall be as beautiful as I!"

"If Antoine is not a good provider," Darmanian suggested, "you must be."

There was a strong pride of accomplishment that flavored Catherine's response: "When I married Antoine, all of Paris knew of Catherine Deshayes as one who talks to the spirits, who reads the stars, who sees the future. I make a very good living for us with my God-given powers."

Darmanian moved Catherine ahead two years. This

time when she spoke, she was frightened, devoid of her bravado.

"The cell," she whimpered. "It is so damp and filthy. Here I must await the first questions by the priests. Oh, I do not want to be tortured!"

Darmanian reminded her that even though she was remembering everything as it was then, she would feel no pain.

"Oh, help me!" she gasped. "Here *they* come again. I know what they want. I know what they are going to do to me!"

We learned that *they* were three jailers, visiting her in the wretched cell.

"Pah!" Catherine spat. "They speak about me as if I were an animal, not human."

"They say I am pretty. They say they should enjoy my charms before the inquisitors . . . destroy . . . my beauty . . . forever. I am not a member of the aristocracy. They know that they need show no respect for my body."

Catherine's scream rang with rage and indignation. "Get out of my cell!" Her breath was coming in short, rasping gasps. The lovely body on the couch began to writhe as if in hideous torment.

Forcefully, authoritatively, Darmanian reminded her of her detachment from the scene being relived by her soul's memory.

"The ragged man across the way begins to rattle his chains. His eyes are crazy. 'Mount her for me, too, lads!' he screams. They have driven him mad with torture. I know he would not say such a thing if he were not crazy in pain. In cells all around us, men and women are shouting: 'Mount the bitch! Mount the fortune teller!'"

Delores's breasts were heaving as she twisted in pantomine of the terrible ordeal.

"I try to . . . fight. Scratch. Claw," Catherine grimaced. "They slap me. Push me roughly between them."

She gasped, gritted her teeth. "One of them twists my arm behind my back. I scream in pain, and they shove a filthy rag in my mouth."

Darmanian soothed her, reassured her once again that she would feel no pain, but he permitted the memory to be played out:

"God, they are so ugly!" Catherine swallowed hard. "One is fat, covered with hair across his shoulders like an ape. Another is like a giant, with big hands that are gnarled with scars and old burns. He is the torturer. The third has a face that looks as though it was kicked in by a horse. He has only one eye, but he does not bother to wear a patch to cover the hole in his skull."

Delores's breathing was becoming more regular as a result of Darmanian's repeated suggestions that the trance personality could be totally objective about the debasement and humiliation.

"The short, fat one has both my arms behind my neck. One-eye . . . rips off my lovely, purple velvet dress. All around me men and women are calling for my degradation. They are jealous of me. They hate me. They wish to see me brought to my knees. A woman shouts for my dress so that she can wipe her ass with it."

"Where is my elf!" Catherine screamed in desperation. "Attend me, wee one. I need you!"

She became very silent for several moments. Then the voice was little more than a whisper. "The giant is sucking my naked breasts as if he is some hideous babe. His jagged teeth tear at my nipples . . . until . . . they . . . bleed . . ."

Darmanian was working his jaw as if moving it against some invisible bit. Ed Vogel had stopped his note taking, and even the movement of his cigar in his mouth stilled.

But the hypnotist permitted Catherine to continue the narrative of hurt and horror.

In the most graphic minutiae imaginable, we heard the details of how the three jailers stripped her, pawed her, slobbered over her flesh. How they had taken turns mounting her while the others pinned her flailing arms and thrashing legs.

When the clerical and civil inquisitors arrived, they found Catherine sprawled in a dazed condition, dabbing at a bloody mouth with an end of her torn velvet dress. She was ordered to be lightly flogged in order to sharpen her wits for a morning appearance before the tribunal.

After a few more minutes of explicit descriptions of maltreatment at the hands of the inquisitors, Darmanian at last moved the trance personality ahead to her hearing before the tribunal.

At this point, we were astonished to hear a new Catherine Montvoisin. She was no longer a frightened, defeated, degraded young woman. She was confident, almost aggressive. She seemed eager to engage the learned judges in ecclesiastical debate.

For the next ten minutes we heard a woman gifted with oratory argue that her gifts were truly God-sent and that her approach to the arts of divination were wholly acceptable to Church doctrine. Darmanian's eyes seemed almost to glow in the reflected light from the fireplace. Ed Vogel's mouth hung open in astonishment, his cigar dead between two fingers. I was careful to see that I had the whole thing on tape.

I glanced at my watch as Catherine was telling us how she had returned to her shop to become highly sought after by the wealthy and the powerful. Delores had been in hypnotic trance for nearly two hours.

Darmanian moved the trance personality ahead to the various life's milestones which we had established during the initial regression. The hypnotist had said that he would do this so that Ed Vogel could hear the facility with which the entity progressed from event to event and determine whether or not the names used were those of actual historical personages.

Within another fifteen minutes we had been presented with a verbal montage of babies having their throats cut, of roaring furnaces consuming the tiny bodies, of men and women dancing nude, debauching one another, writhing across naked flesh like bundles of groping, fornicating serpents. We paused for detailed descriptions of the arrests, court politics, the Chambre Ardente; but we moved rapidly through the terrible images of La Voisin on the rack, being branded, being lashed, being cruelly burned with torches, and being dragged to the stake.

Darmanian had coffee ready for Delores when he at last brought her back to full consciousness. But first she waved away the cup, blew her nose in a tissue that she plucked from her purse on the floor beside the couch.

"Did I say anything that made any sense, Mr. Vogel?" she wanted to know at once. "And Darmanian," she protested, "you took me so deep that I don't remember anything!"

"I felt that it was best that you not recall the details

of this session," Darmanian said firmly. "Eric has made a recording which you may hear at a later time."

Delores seemed unhappy with Darmanian's decision, but Ed's analysis of the session appeared to be the next best thing to having her own memory of the past two and a half hours.

"Please, Mr. Vogel," she coaxed. "How did I do?"

Ed looked from Delores to Darmanian to me. He grinned nervously, wiped a moist open palm on the trouser leg of his black suit. He noisily flipped the pages of the legal pad in which he had been taking notes.

"Miz Touraine," Vogel said quietly, yet with deep feeling. "You did remarkably well."

Chapter Thirteen

Ed Vogel cleared his throat in three short, staccato rasps, then he began: "Catherine Deshayes, according to the reference works, was born about 1638. She became La Voisin when she married Antoine Montvoisin at the age of twenty. And she did begin her career in the occult by telling fortunes in the streets when she was just a kid of nine or so."

Ed paused, looked at each of us as if he were a teacher calling for questions from the classroom. Darmanian sat, arms folded across his chest, on the couch next to Delores, who now sat upright, sipping her coffee. I still sat to the right of the couch with my back to the fireplace. When Vogel saw that he had an attentive audience, he continued.

"La Voisin was in her early twenties when she incurred the wrath of the Church for making claims that she had spirits at her beck and call. One of the greatest miracles the woman ever accomplished was being released by the Inquisition. Somehow she managed to convince a learned tribunal composed of the vicars-general and several doctors of theology from the Sorbonne that her fortune telling was totally in keeping with Church doctrine. Just like we heard her say, they let her return to practice astrology, palmistry, prophecy, and all the rest with what appeared to be the Church's blessing."

"How did she manage that neat trick?" Delores asked, holding her cup out to be refilled by Darmanian.

Vogel pushed forward from the reclining chair in which he had been sitting, got to his feet. His only vanity appeared to be his scholarship, and he was warming to the occasion of being questioned about his favorite subject.

"It's a mystery," Vogel answered her. "Catherine Deshayes came out of the Inquisition wealthier and more powerful than when she went in. That just didn't happen in those days. When someone got fingered for heresy, they usually had all their property confiscated, and they ended up broken in torture and being burned at the stake."

"There must be some reason given for her escape," Darmanian persisted. "Surely, one of your many reference books gives us a clue."

Vogel cleared his throat once again, glanced down at his shoes as if the answer might be somehow woven into their laces. After a moment or two of silence Ed lifted his head once again and met Darmanian's questioning gaze.

"According to the more esoteric reference books," Vogel said, "La Voisin made her pact with Satan while she lay in the dungeon awaiting her appearance before the tribunal."

"A pact with Satan," Delores echoed. "People really did things like that?"

No sooner had she uttered her incredulity than she became suddenly very still, very contemplative. "Yes," she said softly after a few moments silence. "I guess they did."

It was as if memories from that alleged past-life experience were still filtering through her present consciousness. "And it must have worked, too," she said solemnly. "She got out of prison and escaped an almost certain death."

"Yeah." Vogal nodded grimly. "And that's where the story gets a bit gory. La Voisin became an incredibly powerful figure in the Paris of the mid-seventeenth century. She received her coven members and aristocratic thrill seekers in an underground chamber. It was said that she put on an ermine-lined robe with two hundred eagles embroidered in gold on it in order to sacrifice the babies."

Vogel hesitated, glanced at Delores and Darmanian as if expecting one of them to interrupt and make some comment. The hypnotist smiled at him benignly, and Delores sipped at her coffee. Vogel briefly examined his notes, then went on speaking.

"La Voisin had plenty of palace connections. Madame de Montespan, the mistress of Louis the Fourteenth, often participated in La Voisin's ritual celebration of the satanic mass. Some accounts say that she even served as the living altar."

Delores apparently could not resist showing her colors as a fallen-away Roman Catholic. "They really had the *body* and the blood at their celebration of the Mass!"

"Yes," Vogel agreed. "But the blood came from a sacrificed infant."

"Yecch!" Delores crinkled her nose in distaste. "Why not chickens or some animal?"

"Because, there's more power in human blood, human sacrifices," Vogel explained.

"Disgusting," Delores pronounced, unable to check a slight shudder from visibly hunching her shoulders.

"But we heard some very graphic descriptions of such ritual sacrifices from your very own lips," Darmanian said.

"I don't know how such scenes could have got into my brain," Delores said. "I can't imagine that I could have done such a thing in any lifetime!"

Darmanian was unrelenting. "We are each of us capable of perversion and murder under the right set of circumstances. Even the mind of a saintly nun or priest could be programmed to unleash the most monstrous acts upon their fellow creatures."

"La Voisin managed to do something like that," Vogel spoke up. "She was always assisted in her cruel corruption of the Mass by maverick priests. Her favorite was a fat libertine named Abbé Guilborg."

Darmanian had laced his fingers together under his chin, and he seemed almost smug when he said: "And together with her renegade priests, La Voisin claims to have sacrificed more than twenty-five hundred babies to Satan."

"Or so she was accused at her trial," Vogel commented.

Delores slumped back against the couch. "How could La Voisin have murdered so many babies? Wouldn't that have depleted the infant population of Paris?"

Vogel shook his head in sad commiseration of Delores's horror. "Then, as now," he told her, "the streets were full of young girls who have the burden of unplanned pregnancies. La Voisin would take these poor street girls into her home, see them through their maternities, then relieve them of the problems of caring for a child. In this way, she always had a stockpile of babies for the sacrifices."

Darmanian laughed in what I thought to be a cruel manner at Delores's obvious squeamish discomfort: "Ha, Delores! You certainly were a bloodthirsty hag!"

Vogel was quick to correct the hypnotist. "La Voisin was far from a hag, Mr. Darmanian. All the reference works agree that Catherine Deshayes was a woman of considerable beauty, who never lacked for lovers."

Delores stuck the tip of a pink tongue at Darmanian. "See?" She smiled and fluttered her eyelashes in a parody of a coquette. "At least one factor has remained the same down through the centuries."

"All those lovers were a bit rough on her long-suffering husband, Antoine, though," Ed commented. "One of them almost bit off his nose. Another tried out his own mixture of poison on him. Still another resorted to fists and nearly beat him to death. That rather vicious individual was said to have been the Marquis Jean de Sainte-Croix. The marquis was a member of the aristocracy who was a long time lover of La Voisin and a kind of wizard in his own right."

Vogel flipped a sheet of his notepad, his eyes squinting as they followed one of his thick forefingers moving across the page. "Here's something interesting," he said. "King Louis was really put into an awkward position when the Chambre Ardente brought him evidence that several court favorites, including his mistress, Madame de Montespan, were involved with La Voisin.

"His advisors warned him that such an exposure of decadent court life could lead to revolution. They also suggested that foreign powers might attempt invasion if they thought France to be morally weak."

I chuckled appreciatively at the king's chaos. "Louis had set up a secret service that turned out to be too efficient."

"Exactly," Ed beamed, pleased that I had given evidence that I was following his presentation and apparently understanding it. "So, incredible as it may seem, Louis set about the sabotage of his own judicial system. He ordered that while La Voisin must be tortured, the interrogators need not apply undue pressure."

"In other words," Darmanian interjected, "he didn't want La Voisin to break under torture and implicate others."

"That's right," Ed agreed. "So while La Voisin was sitting it out in relative comfort in the dungeon, the Satan-worshipping aristocrats, tipped off by the king, left France for extended visits abroad. While they were out of the country, Louis's most trusted agents set about suppressing evidence that might be brought against highborn court personalities. The king himself ordered burned all incriminations against Madame de Montespan. And, although scholars debate the charge, it appears that Louis himself might even have ordered the attempted assassination of his relentless interrogator, de la Reynie."

Delores shook her head slowly in awe. "She really turned the country upside down, didn't she?"

"Indeed," Ed said, chomping down on the fresh cigar he had not yet bothered to light. "It was nearly a year before King Louis could breathe easier. By then all incriminating evidence and all troublesome witnesses had been summarily disposed of. Now that she had no living collaborators of any testimony which she might cry out, La Voisin could be put to the torture and tried."

"How terrible!" Delores protested. "Why would they have had to torture her at this point?"

Vogel shrugged. "Accepted procedure, I guess. Between February nineteenth and the twenty-first, 1680, La Voisin is reported to have suffered four six-hour ordeals. She was terribly disfigured with branding irons and sulfur."

"Sulfur?" Delores questioned weakly. Her eyes brimmed with tears.

"Ah, yes," Vogel said, his mouth opening and closing a couple of times as he searched his mental resources for the proper words. "The torturers stuffed sulfur up women's . . . ah. What I mean is, they pushed sulfur up . . . any opening they would find. Then they ignited it."

"Oh, my God!" Delores winced, her eyelids clamped tightly closed.

"Really, now, Vogel," Darmanian reprimanded him. "Is it necessary to speak so graphically?"

Ed shuffled his shoes together awkwardly and hunched his thick shoulders, as if attempting to diminish his great bulk to a smaller target for disapproval. "I'm sorry if I offended. But that's what they did," he offered by way of defense.

Delores opened her eyes, smiled feebly. "That's all right, Mr. Vogel. Please continue."

"There's really little more to tell," Vogel said. "She

went to the stake on February twenty-third. She went singing hymns to Satan, ribald songs, and roughly shoving aside the priests who asked to hear her final confession."

"Game to the end, eh?" Darmanian smiled, but his eyes were still hard on Vogel.

"Sure was," Vogel said. "She died kicking burning straw into the faces of the crowd that screamed for her death."

His report completed, Vogel dropped back heavily into the leather recliner.

Darmanian sat quietly, his fingers thoughtfully stroking the curves of the dragons on his medallion. "We are indebted to you, Mr. Vogel, for your willingness to share your expertise with us," he said. "There is no question in my mind that, if not true rebirth, a preternatural phenomenon of great importance has occurred during our regression sessions with Delores. I am greatly inspired to push on boldly with my new therapy."

Ed Vogel shifted in his chair, chewed on his cigar as he marshaled his thoughts. Just before he spoke, he nervously rubbed the stubble on his chin with thick fingers and produced a sound not unlike a cricket's rasping night call.

"You know, Mr. Darmanian," he said, "in my belief structure, recincarnation and a knowledge of past lives is another form of awareness. Your intention of using this awareness in a practical way is not in itself wrong, but I am cautioning you to continue your work with respect."

Darmanian glowered at Vogel in tight-lipped silence. It was readily apparent that the hypnotist did not graciously receive unsolicited advice.

Vogel was not intimidated, however, and he seemed intent on having his say. Once again he got out of the chair, as if standing to his full height gave him leverage. "I believe that each incarnation is for the purpose of learning so that we might transcend to higher levels of awareness," he said. "If we do not learn a particular lesson in one lifetime, we must start all over again in a subsequent lifetime."

Darmanian's impatience found expression. "I am a metaphysician as well as clinician," he snapped. "I'm quite aware of these concepts you seem determined to reiterate for us."

Vogel nodded, held up a beefy paw as if in a salutation of peace. "But don't forget about Karma," he came back at the hypnotist. "You should be cautious about interfering in the divine justice of the cause and effect."

"Mr. Vogel"—Darmanian's voice had acquired a fine cutting edge—"I firmly believe that if one sets out to accomplish a goal with integrity and strength of purpose, allowing nothing internal or external to get in his way, then he can conquer anything and bend all things to his will—even the illusory finality of the grave and the immutable laws of Karma."

Vogel's arms flapped helplessly at his sides. His mouth opened and closed, but he seemed disoriented. He was not at all accustomed to impromptu speech making, especially in the face of a hostile audience.

"I—I've enjoyed being a part of this experiment tonight," Vogel mumbled softly, his hands seeking refuge in his coat pockets. "I'm glad I was able to help in some small way. Eric, would you please take me home now?"

"Certainly," I said, glancing from Ed to Darmanian.

The hypnotist seemed no longer poised to attack. Rather he seemed lost in thought.

"Eric," Darmanian called to me as I got to my feet. He held the key to the gate chain at arm's length. "Don't forget to lock it as you leave and again when you return." He seemed to have nothing more to say to Vogel, and I left Delores and him sitting there in peculiar silence.

Silence had become the order of the evening, for Vogel, too, sat hunched against his car door in total quiet. I simply puffed at my pipe, busy with my own thoughts and with the negotiation of unfamiliar roads after dark.

Ed did not break his mute behavior until I pulled up in front of his small, two-bedroom home. "Eric," he said, one of his big hands closing about my right wrist. "Stay here with us. You've got to move out of Woodlands."

The light from the station wagon's dashboard illuminated the distress and anxiety that had contorted Ed's features. His hand had become a vise in his urgency.

"But why?" I asked him, shaking his hand from my wrist. "Why should you say such a thing? Just because you and Darmanian had a bit of an argument, that's—"

"I saw him!" Vogel nearly shouted at me. "I saw him for the evil thing that he is!"

"What are you talking about, Ed?" I demanded. "You aren't making any sense."

"Eric," he sighed, settling his bulk back against the seat. "I really do see things. I don't mean hallucinations, I mean visions. Clairvoyant flashes and things.

You know, the kinds of things that Swedenborg used to experience."

"Yes," I conceded. "I can understand that such things are possible. But what can you possibly see evil about Darmanian, a man who has only used his life for good."

Vogel's voice became very low, almost pontifical in tone. "He who does evil that good may come pays a toll to the devil to let him into heaven."

I was later sorry for my response, but I could not help laughing. "What does that bit of grandiosity mean?" I asked.

Vogel's eyes were sad in the soft light of the dashboard. "Darmanian is something other than he appears," he said. He pushed open his car door, touched his feet to the curb. Then he turned to place a hand on my shoulder. "I'll do what I can for you, Eric. Please call me if you need help. And I can promise you, you will need all the help you can get."

Chapter Fourteen

I do not know how long I had been asleep when I felt a hand at my shoulder shaking me awake.

"Eric, please! Please wake up!"

"Delores?" My brain was fuzzy. I thought that I would be all night falling asleep, considering the bizarre revelations of the evening; but I had drifted off within minutes of having returned from taking Ed Vogel home. "Delores?"

"Yes, yes," she answered. "Are you awake?"

I reached for the lamp on my nightstand. I had been lying on my right arm and had cut off the circulation. My hand was "asleep," and I found it impossible to make my fingers work the switch. Finally, sensing my drowsy awkwardness, Delores reached across me and snapped on the lamp.

We both blinked at each other in the sudden transformation from darkness to light. Delores was wearing a white nightgown of a satinlike material. She also wore a robe, but had not bothered to draw it closed.

The shiny fabric of her nightgown caught the light from the lamp and emphasized her shadowy contours. The neckline dipped low enough to reveal inviting breasts, but it was readily apparent from her frightened trembling that she had not come to my room to seduce me.

"I've had a terrible dream, Eric," she said. Her brown eyes were blurred by tears and her lower lip was quivering.

"The one about being burned?" I asked her. I raised myself up on my elbows. Because this evening was mild, I had disregarded my pajama tops. I was wearing my bottoms, but I was in a mental quandary whether or not I should remain beneath the covers. I expected Darmanian to materialize at any moment, so I decided that it would appear more circumspect if I remained discreetly enveloped by the blankets.

"No, no," she said, shaking her head emphatically, setting her long hair swinging in wispy auras. "Well," she reconsidered. "Yes, that, too. But something so very much more."

I indicated that she should feel free to tell me about the disturbing nightmare. She smiled her gratitude, but she began by telling me of certain important bits of conversation that had taken place between her and Darmanian after Ed Vogel and I had left the library.

"Salem, that ugly cat Darmanian bought for me, came into the room," Delores said between clenched teeth. "I made some nasty remark about it and asked Darmanian to get it away from me. He laughed and told me that there was a whole new world beginning, and that I would have to get used to many new things."

"Did he explain what he meant?" I asked.

Delores's teeth caught at her lower lip. "Partially," she said. "He told me that we are going to begin a series of experiments in group regression beginning tomorrow night."

I whistled my surprise. "Darmanian certainly plunges right into things, doesn't he? I'm still trying to sort out what I'm going to do about the book I came here to write."

"Darmanian has become very concerned with the new direction in his research," Delores said, her eyes lowering to the blanket covering my body from the waist down. It seemed to occur to her for the first time that she was half-sitting, half-reclining across my bed.

"And he seems to want me here to record the experiments in hypnotic regression more than he wants me to write his biography," I agreed.

"I told him that I no longer wished to participate in any sort of regression studies," Delores said, the lower lip still quivering. "I told him that I was . . . frightened."

"And he said?" I prompted her.

"Darmanian told me that I was behaving as a foolish child," Delores said, a tear breaking free and coursing down her cheek. "He said that he had already contacted a number of former patients who had been particularly good somnambulistic subjects and that they would be arriving tomorrow night. He told me that I was an integral part of the experiments and that he would not permit me to drop out."

I frowned my concern. "Surely Darmanian would not force you to participate in something that is causing you such obvious distress," I said.

Delores touched a crumbled tissue to her nose.

"Darmanian is determined to launch a new phase of his career," she said. "No one or nothing stands in his way when he selects a course of action."

"Delores," I said, gently placing my hands on her shoulders. "Darmanian doesn't own you."

Tears moved unchecked from the corners of her eyes. Her voice was uneven as she spoke again: "I wish Darmanian had never played your recording of my regression for me. Oh, Eric, what *does* own me?"

So she had heard the tape. I shook my head questioningly. "I don't understand," I told her.

Delores took a deep breath, as if steeling herself for an unpleasant ordeal. "In my dream," she began, "I was back in the dungeon. I had been raped, abused, flogged, degraded."

I lifted a hand to interrupt her. "*You* were back in the dungeon?"

"In the dream, Eric, it was me," she answered. "I was Catherine Montvoisin. I lay crumpled on a pile of filthy straw. I recoiled when I heard a rustling in the corner. I thought that now the rats were going to have their way with me. But then—oh, God, Eric—then I recognized what was in the corner crawling toward me!"

Delores hesitated, unable to suppress a shudder that made her hands tremble.

I placed my own hand reassuringly over her cold fingers. "Go on," I said.

Delores's voice was a hoarse whisper. "I saw the tiny, sharp features of . . . my elf. But it was grotesque, ugly, misshapen. It looked like a demon, a gargoyle."

She turned her head away from me. "Oh, Eric, it

sounds so fantastic to be saying these things out loud!"

I squeezed her hand. "I'm listening. Let it out."

Delores bent her head and continued: "I cursed the thing for having deserted me in my time of greatest need. I said that I wanted a big, powerful spirit to protect me from such abuse and to take revenge on those foul swine who had molested me. I told it that I had only contempt for a wee elf that could stand idly by while I was being raped and flogged."

Delores put a hand over her eyes, and tears dripped on my arm. "Eric, I heard a thin, reedy voice screeching at me. God, it was only a dream, but I'll hear that voice forever."

"What did it say?" I asked.

"It . . . it told me that it was my own fault that it was so small," Delores went on. "It said that if it appeared to me as large as it could be, that I would have driven it off with priests and holy water. And Antoine would have been jealous when it lay beside me at night."

I sat up, slipped an arm around Delores's trembling shoulders. I urged her to go on with the account of the peculiar dream.

"It told me that it would free me from the dungeon if I would first give it a gift," Delores said. "It said that it wanted my pledge that I would serve the same master it served."

"It said that it was but the wee soul within me that spoke to my larger soul. It told me that it had once belonged to my grandmother and to all women in my line for more than a thousand years. It said that my line was a very special one that was entitled to receive special communion with the spirits."

I shook my head in amazement. "What an incredible dream," I admitted.

"Dream?" Delores questioned. "Or memory?"

I smiled. "I'm not convinced that you are the reincarnation of La Voisin," I said. "But I'm open to the fact that some remarkable things are occurring here at Woodlands."

Delores's teeth pulled gently at her lower lip, and fresh tears reddened her brown eyes. "I wish I could tell you how funny that sounds to me, Eric. 'Some remarkable things are occurring here at Woodlands.'"

Delores took another deep breath, continued her narrative of her dream experience. "The entity told me that God could not be everywhere. God must leave the Earth largely to the lower spirits and to their master, Satan. It falls to the lower spirits to correct the many miscarriages of justice which exist on Earth. Such is their labor while God keeps busy running the cosmos. My elf told me that I could not expect God to answer my prayers and come to such a miserable dungeon to help me. I must entrust my deliverance to one of Satan's servant spirits."

Delores stopped, her eyes wide with horror that remained invisible to me. "Eric," she said in that same hoarse whisper, "I learned how Catherine Montvoisin managed to escape the tribunal and was permitted to return to her occult practices. She . . . I . . . sold *our* soul to Satan!"

I gave her what I hoped was a comforting hug across her trembling shoulders. "Delores, listen to me. You realize that your dream is just burgeoning with all kinds of revealing symbolism. And in view of what has occurred the past two nights—"

"Wait!" she warned me. "Don't be so eager to tie

this up with a Freudian bow. From that point on, the dream was like some mad merry-go-round of crazy images. I saw myself gifted with the brilliant oratory that convinced the tribunal to set me free. I became wealthy, powerful.

"The pictures spun faster and faster, making me confused, fearful. From time to time there would be images of babies with slashed throats. Then there would be the terrible flashes of myself on the rack, being branded, being burned, being lashed! But always being burned, being burned, *being burned!*"

Delores's voice caught in a sob, and her hand seized my arm in a grip that I found amazingly strong. "Eric, please believe me. This next part . . ."

"Go on," I said.

"Well," she said, avoiding eye contact. "Whatever you think of it, it is true.

"The dream had been frightening me, sickening me. I must have whimpered because Darmanian put his arms around me as if to comfort me," Delores said.

She sat quietly, blinking back the tears, then she went on. "It felt so good to feel male strength lying beside me. I wanted to blend into it. His lips brushed against my cheeks."

I started to speak, but Delores placed her fingers on my lips to keep me silent. Her eyes were wide, desperate.

"Eric," she said in a voice that was little more than an extended sobbing. "That was when I woke up and remembered that I was *alone* in bed!"

"Darmanian?"

"He had stayed in the library to read," Delores blurted out in a rush of words. "I went up to bed. I had been angry, upset with him over the experiments.

I had locked the door in a pique. I was alone with *something* embracing me and kissing my cheek!"

"Jesus," I gasped in a kind of exclamatory prayer against evil. I felt the hard claws of atavistic fear pinching on my own stomach.

"I sat up screaming," Delores said, trembling against my arm. "I could still feel a firm male shape lying next to me. I reached for the lamp, but it would not come on. All about me there seemed to be a strange, metallic, buzzing sound.

"When I made myself look back to my side, the dark shape that I had seen was gone. But, Eric, I heard this voice, this deep male voice whisper right beside my ear: *'Once again, dearest Catherine, you are mine!'* "

Delores chewed on her doubled forefinger as if she were biting down on a bullet. "This time," she said, "the lamp worked. There was no one in the room.

"But, Eric," she exclaimed, gripping my forearm until I felt circulation being numbed, "on the bed there was the definite impression of where a body had lain."

Her eyes caught mine and held them. "I will swear to what I have told you tonight until my dying day," she told me.

The deep male voice from the open doorway startled both of us.

"Why, darling," Darmanian said, his eyes narrowed, his voice clipped. "You've never made such vows to me."

Delores straightened away from me as if a whip had snaked out and stung her back. Darmanian had seemed too confident to be a jealous man, and he did not seem at all interested in learning the reason why Delores was in my room.

"I had a bad dream," Delores said. "I was telling Eric."

Darmanian opened his arms, and Delores ran from the bed to be enclosed by them. His hands squeezed, then caressed her slender shoulders.

"I'm sorry you were troubled, Eric," the hypnotist apologized. "But I am here now and I will take care of all of Delores's needs."

"It's quite all right," I said by way of feeble response. "I was pleased that I might serve as a good listener."

"Yes." Darmanian nodded, his probing blue eyes searching my face and my bed for any indication that I might have served Delores in any other capacity. "Thank you, Eric."

He led Delores from my room, and just before he closed the door, I heard Darmanian say: "And now, my darling, you must tell me the dream. Every last bit of it. It may be very important to a greater understanding of my new therapy. You must keep nothing from me . . ."

Perhaps half an hour later, when I was finally drifting back to sleep, my eyes suddenly snapped open with the explosion of memory. In that final second of sound before Darmanian closed the door to my room and separated the two of them from me for the night, *I heard him call her Catherine.*

Chapter Fifteen

That next day, Thursday, April 20, Darmanian seemed to awaken as bright as the sun. I was up early, about seven thirty; but as I had my morning tea, I could hear Darmanian playing the piano in the music room.

"It's not often he's at the piano so early," Agnes said, smiling, as she methodically scooped scrambled eggs and bacon bits on my plate. "He's happy about something today, that's for sure."

The piece Darmanian was utilizing as an expression of his good spirits seemed familiar to me, but I could not quite place it. I doubted that Agnes was an aficionado of classical piano music, but, by way of conversation, I asked her if she recognized the selection.

"Oh, I do, indeed." She nodded emphatically as she brought me my dry toast. "It is one of his own compositions. He calls it 'Paradise Reborn.' He always plays it when he is happy about something. Kinda pretty, isn't it?"

"Very pretty," I agreed. "And once again you have

surpassed yourself with these eggs. Just the way I like them."

Agnes preened. "You're very kind, sir."

The playing stopped, and it was not more than two or three minutes before Darmanian joined me for another cup of coffee. I was pleased to find that he bore me no grudge or ill feeling for the night before. It was obvious that Delores had explained that she had sought me out only to serve as a temporary ear for her troubled dream.

"Eric"—he smiled at me over the rim of his cup—"I've cleared the morning for you today. Delores will be able to handle two or three people who will be coming for reinforcement of hypnotic suggestion. I'm yours to do with what you will."

"That's great," I replied, matching his enthusiasm for the work at hand. "I have a dozen or so questions to ask you in regard to certain case studies."

"Then you must ask them," Darmanian agreed.

"And I will want to discuss certain aspects of your new therapy so that I can trace its proper evolution in the book."

Darmanian's eyes were on mine with the fervor of a jungle cat that has found its prey. "Ah, yes, Eric," he said softly. "That is very important. I am so happy that you are beginning to take a greater interest in the new directions in which my work is taking me. I knew that I had made a correct decision in appointing you as my public relations officer to the world."

I wiped my mouth with the linen napkin in a gesture inspired more by nervousness than cleanliness. "Well, I want the book to be more than a public relations tool for Woodlands Clinic," I said.

Darmanian smiled. "Oh, it will be more. Much

more. I can assure you that it will. You will provide a bible for the New Age. And you will be communications officer for a whole new movement."

I was reminded of Montaigne's observation that ambition is not a vice of little people. I wanted the book to be a success, and, more importantly, I wanted to do justice to the unselfish healing work of a dedicated therapist. Although I could sympathize with Darmanian's enthusiasm for the new dimension that he had added to his work—and I could certainly overlook the occasional manifestations of exuberant ego—I could not conceive of the book precipitating a revolution within the mass consciousness.

Darmanian, apparently, had no difficulty in making this leap of faith. "I have been totally committed to one vision since I was a boy," he told me. "I want to fashion a world in which mental and physical illnesses will no longer exist. I want to help make the Earth a paradise, just as it was before mankind's fall from a state of perfection."

"This is one hell of a vision and one hell of a goal," I whistled softly. "How many lifetimes do you think it will take you?"

Darmanian sobered and his blue eyes became slits. The jungle cat was ready to pounce. "It has already taken me several lifetimes," he said. "I pray that all is in readiness so that my present existence will see the establishment of a new paradise on Earth."

"Darmanian," I sighed. "It would take a full-scale miracle to accomplish such a goal in one lifetime."

"Then how exciting for you." He smiled. "For you are fortunate enough to be on the scene to witness that miracle firsthand. You will be able to see this epoch-making event from what will amount to a ringside seat."

I arched an eyebrow in baffled disbelief. As a writer, I can appreciate the inner fires and convictions that provoke a zealot into speaking in dramatic hyperbole. But Darmanian had begun to speak of his new therapy with the almost irritating ego demands of the fanatic. However, I reminded myself in my internal dialogue, the fanaticisms of today become the fashionable creeds of tomorrow, and as trite as the multiplication table the week after.

So, in my external dialogue with Darmanian, I told him how pleased I was to have been invited for the advent of a technique in hypnotherapy that would so accelerate the awareness of the group mind.

Darmanian sensed tolerant skepticism. "Believe me, Eric," he said. "In nothing do men approach so nearly to the gods as in doing good to man. I seek only to do good. Please share my vision with me."

"I share your aspirations, and I hope that such a worthy goal might someday be reached," I told him. "Perhaps one day soon you will be able to convince me that yours is truly a vision that can be shared. Perhaps you will work a miracle that may have far-reaching implications for all of mankind."

Darmanian placed his hand on my own in a surprising gesture of warmth and acceptance. "Believe me, Eric," he repeated his promise. "You will see that miracle with your own eyes."

"I understand that I am going to see an additional demonstration of your past-lives therapy tonight," I said, intensely desirous of altering the conversation from what I considered a course moving close to delusions of grandeur.

"Yes," Darmanian said, responding to the suggestion. "Permit me to tell you who will be participating in the experiment."

"Please do," I replied. "I would appreciate knowing something about each of them in advance."

Darmanian extended his cup so that Agnes might pour him a refill. "Senator Tom Harrington from Albany will be in attendance," he said, as he set the cup down to cool for a moment. "Bishop David De Shazo, whom you may have seen defending the faith on several important television talk shows, will participate. Then we will have Shelley Eberhart, the fashion model of the hour, whom I know you've seen smiling back at you from a dozen different magazine covers. And if you follow football at all—and even if you don't—I'm certain you have heard of Don Gruber of the New York Jets. And let us not forget our own Viki Chung, a dynamic nurse who serves her fellow sisters by managing a home for unwed mothers in Schenectady."

I hoped my mouth wasn't gaping. "You're bringing a United States senator, a bishop, a leading model, a professional football player, and a registered nurse here to Woodlands tonight to assist you in an experiment?"

"And why not?" Darmanian wanted to know after he blew a cooling breath over the edge of the coffee cup.

"I'm impressed," I confessed with an awkward grin. "I'm really impressed. I had no idea that you had that much influence with so many influential people."

Darmanian shrugged. "I could have brought in a young woman who is currently starring in a popular series on television. Or the governor of a midwestern state, or one of the leading publishers. Or any number of men and women with celebrity status if my intention were solely to impress you, Eric.

"No," the hypnotist continued, somewhat waspishly, "I selected these individuals because they are excellent hypnotic subjects, because they each owe me a great deal, and because they are uniquely important to me in a special way."

"Well," I ventured, pushing my chair back from the table. "It should prove to be quite an evening."

"I can promise you that it will." Darmanian smiled. "Oh," he added, "by the way, I am certain that you will wish to interview each of them while they are staying here at Woodlands for the brief series of experiments. They all have success stories that are directly attributable to hypnotherapy."

"I see." I nodded in sudden insight. "That was what you meant when you said that each of them owed you something."

"Yes," Darmanian said. "And they will be happy to speak to you of their triumphant results. Senator Harrington, for example, had a sleazy law practice in Albany. He would have starved to death if he hadn't had a somewhat prosperous younger brother who managed a supermarket. I worked with Tom diligently, taught him some techniques of self-hypnosis to build his confidence, and his comet soared."

My writer's instinct had brought me to full alert. "That's excellent material for the book, Darmanian. What about Bishop De Shazo? I have seen him on a number of talk shows, discussing his inspirational books and championing Roman Catholicism. It is difficult to imagine him in need of hypnotherapy."

Darmanian presented me with an exceedingly smug

grin. "David came to me a hopeless stutterer. His problem was totally psychological, of course, since he had not been afflicted as a youth. He was uptight about being passed over year after year for advancement, and he had developed the stuttering as a device that would automatically eliminate him from any consideration, and, therefore, from any resultant tension. I soon restructured him into such a bombastic personality that the Church hierarchy could no more overlook him than the Coast Guard could overlook a hurricane."

I laughed at Darmanian's colorful analogy and in gleeful anticipation over the inclusion of the kind of celebrity anecdotes that made for best-seller books. "And what of the Jets' Don Gruber?" I asked, eager for more revelatory material.

Darmanian scowled at me in mock indignation. "Why should I do your work for you?" he said. "They will all be at your disposal over the next few days. You will have plenty of time to play journalist."

"I do hope that they won't be offended by my interrogating them," I said. "After all, they may consider it enough to ask of them that they have manipulated their schedules to participate in your initial experiments in past-life therapy."

"They will be pleased to make themselves available to you," Darmanian said, his voice firm. "They owe me that much, at least."

Chapter Sixteen

That evening at precisely eight forty-seven Darmanian had but to tap Delores's forehead lightly, and she was moving back through time and space to the niche in seventeenth-century Paris where we had first found Catherine Deshayes. The hypnotist had arranged the group in a circle in the library. Delores sat in the middle of an open end, as if positioned in a strategic power place in order to serve as example and prototype.

Her head dropped, then jerked erect, her brown eyes wide and inquisitive. I had a sudden, eerie sensation that those familiar brown eyes had been somehow replaced by those of another. It was as if Delores's face had become a mask for a stranger.

"Good evening, m'lord," she spoke in that somewhat saucy voice, lightly tinged with a French accent. She was dressed in a simple, delicate hostess gown. She looked elegant.

At the sound of her transformed voice, there were a

number of gasps and a chorus of excited whispers from the men and women whom Darmanian had assembled. The hypnotist held up an impatient hand for silence, but it was a few moments in coming.

"Good evening, Catherine," Darmanian answered the trance personality at last. "Tell me, what year is it?"

"Why, m'lord," she said, laughing, " 'tis 1666."

I glanced at the excited faces in the circle. I was sitting in the black leather recliner, my tape recorder on my lap, my attention unwavering from the scene before me. I had been surprised when, after dinner, Darmanian had explained to them very briefly and succinctly what he hoped to demonstrate. He had answered a few obligatory questions, but none of those he had summoned to Woodlands that evening had seemed at all upset by the suggestion that they might be regressed to a prior lifetime. In fact, most of them appeared to regard the proposal with some degree of enthusiasm. Even Bishop De Shazo seemed untroubled by the specter of reincarnation.

"What are you doing?" Darmanian asked the entranced Delores.

"Awaiting the others. We celebrate the Mass tonight for the Countess Montague, who has tired of her boorish husband. She is young and pretty, and she will make a lovely living altar."

"A living altar?" Darmanian asked.

Delores—I think it would be more correct to call her *Catherine* in the trance state—laughed again. "Are you teasing me with your feigned ignorance, or are you playing Sir Echo?"

It was at this point that I noticed that Bishop De Shazo's head was beginning to nod. He was a large, rotund man, perhaps a bit less than six feet tall, but well over two hundred and fifty pounds. I had nearly expected him to arrive in full ecclesiastical regalia, but he wore only the clerical collar and a black business suit. Now, I noted incredulously, he appeared as though he were entering hypnotic trance.

Darmanian had told me that the group had been selected for their suggestibility and their ease in attaining the deep trance state, but it seemed remarkable to me that Bishop De Shazo should begin to drift off during the initial demonstration with Delores. I wondered how the hypnotist would handle two subjects in trance at the same time.

The regressed personality "Catherine" was explaining something to Darmanian, when she stopped in mid-sentence, turned her head quickly to one side. "Ah, look who has arrived," she said. "It is the Abbé Guilborg. How fare you, you lecherous sot?"

I was startled to hear Bishop De Shazo's great voice boom forth in his best pulpit bass: "By the great horned god, La Voisin! Why must you hold the Sabbat on such a wretched night? It is raining pitchforks and demons out there!"

I could only gape in stunned amazement. If Bishop De Shazo had somehow slipped into hypnotic trance, it seemed to me that he should have remained asleep, waiting to respond to Darmanian's suggestions. And, according to my understanding, it was impossible for Bishop De Shazo and Delores to be sharing the same alleged prior lifetime. And it seemed odious that the pious Bishop should be enacting a former existence as a Satanist.

"Hah!" Catherine snapped at Bishop De Shazo, whom I shall now identify as Abbé Guilborg. "And would you rather stay the night in the monastery and play with your new choir boys?"

A muscle was twitching just above Darmanian's clamped jaw.

"What are you going to do?" I whispered.

His eyes narrowed as if he were trying better to focus on the strange scene being played out before him, but he did not seem at all distressed. He was completely absorbed in the bizarre psychodrama playing itself out in the library of Woodlands mansion. The faces of the other members of the group were as enraptured as that of Darmanian.

"It is when you speak like that," Abbé Guilborg retorted to Catherine, "that I am reminded of your guttersnipe beginnings. To others you may appear a rather elegant lady—the great and lovely La Voisin. But I remember you for the little street trash you were when I took you under my wing."

Catherine snorted contemptuously. "You only wanted to get under *my* dress!"

"Perish!" snorted Abbé Guilborg. "God only knows what diseases I would have caught from your scabrous little body. Nay, woman, I only pitied you. That was why I taught you all that I know about the skillful blending of herbs. You, in turn, taught me how to become even more deceitful!"

"And," Catherine reminded him, "how to become even richer than you were!"

Guilborg laughed deeply. "Ah, yes, there was that!"

Darmanian at last seemed prepared to enter the fray and reassert his control. He stood before Bishop De Shazo, whose large head was bobbing over his corpulent body like a demented dreamer's. I was disappointed, though, when all the hypnotist uttered was a greeting: "Good evening, Abbé!"

Bishop De Shazo's eyes widened, and he sat bolt upright, nearly losing his balance on the large chair in which he had slumped. "Oh, m'lord!" he gasped. "You gave me a fright. I did not see you there in the shadows!"

The trance personality of Catherine laughed heartily and shook her head. "The marquis is in a playful mood tonight, Abbé Guilborg."

Again I risked irritating the hypnotist by whispering a question: "Why do they keep referring to you as 'm' lord' and the 'marquis'?"

Darmanian answered with a minimum of annoyance showing in his dark features. "They have somehow incorporated me as a character in their regression. It is not an uncommon occurrence."

"And"—I took a chance on another question—"how is it that they appear to be sharing the same regressive experience?"

"Neither is that an uncommon occurrence," he answered, then returned his attention to the group in a manner that clearly indicated dismissal of my queries.

"Abbé Guilborg," Catherine demanded. "Did you bring a baby for tonight's sacrifice?"

"Father Louis is bringing a plump bastard but four months old," he answered.

"And did it issue from your own fat loins?" she teased him.

Abbé Guilborg erupted in raucous laughter. "No, but I have a cow that soon will calf. She is a young barmaid whose confession I heard some months before."

"Nine months before!" Catherine was specific.

My attention was now drawn to yet another voice speaking from the group. To my astonishment I saw Senator Tom Harrigan slumped in trance. Somehow his unconscious had also become activated by the psychodrama that was seemingly generating its own independent life force. I would have thought that Darmanian's ego would have been affected at his apparent lack of control over the group, but he conducted himself as though he were totally satisfied with the spontaneous blendings of the various personalities.

Senator Harrigan, a compactly built man with a politician's assertive voice, had begun to speak in shrill, piping tones. "Come, come! Somebody take this thing before it pisses on my new cloak."

"Aha!" Abbé Guilborg snickered. "It is Father Louis with the baby I spoke of. He spends too much time dabbling in court politics. He has lost his common touch."

"Marguerite!" Catherine shouted. "Where is that child! When I was her age, I had been making my way in the streets for six years! Antoine objects to her helping me in the rituals, but I say that a butcher's child helps her parents. Besides, she has yet to wield the blade. I only have her catch the blood in the bowl."

Catherine's eyes appeared to view the object of her impatience. "Marguerite, I expect you to come at once when I call you!" she scolded some invisible child. "Take the brat from Father Louis."

"Yes, please do so at once," Harrigan, now transformed into Father Louis, said in a mincing cadence.

Abbé Guilborg shook his head sadly. "Father Louis, your involvement in court life has made you a very vain priest indeed. Shall I hear your confession before the night has ended?"

"Guilborg!" came the shrill response. "Before the night has ended, you'll have strength enough only to carry your empty wine flagon in one hand and your empty cock in the other."

I looked at the remainder of the assembled group. The beautiful model, Shelley Eberhart, slumped forward in her chair, her long auburn tresses surrounding carefully maintained features that had never felt too much summer's sun or winter's cold. The kittenish, crinkled-nosed bundle of Oriental femininity that was Viki Chung, registered nurse, sat with her eyes glazed. Don Gruber's head bobbed up and down above the broad chest he had clothed in an expensive coat and vest.

Within moments, the whole damn group was going to be pulled back to seventeenth-century France. How and why, I could not guess. But it was happening. And Darmanian seemed content to permit it to happen.

"Are you Father Louis?" Darmanian asked the personality whom Senator Harrigan was impersonating—or housing.

"No, my lord," came the caustic reply. "I am the lord mayor of London traveling in disguise. I come to Paris only to sleep with whores. There are no whores in England, you see. The women there grow no holes between their legs until they have been blessed by the marriage vow for five years."

Catherine found no humor in the response. "Keep a respectful tongue in your head, Louis! How dare you talk to the marquis in that way?"

"Well!" Father Louis pouted. "Forgive me! I thought only to return his jest in kind."

"Yes"—Catherine turned to face the hypnotist—"the marquis has been playing the joker tonight. Tell me, m'lord. Why do you sport with us so?"

"I want," Darmanian began slowly. "I want to hear from your own lips who I am."

Catherine sighed, then smiled coyly. "Then will you behave?"

"Yes," Darmanian said. "Then I will stop sporting with you."

Catherine shifted her body coquettishly; her voice assumed a plaintive, little-girl tone. "First of all, you are a wizard of the highest order, an alchemist, a master of true magic of the purest degree. And," she added in a musical pealing of laughter, "you are my lover, the Marquis Jean de Sainte-Croix!"

I seemed to reverberate with intense surprise in a tiny segment of time and space that was separated from the alternate reality of the experimental circle by three hundred years. The Marquis Jean de Sainte-Croix! How had Ed Vogel described that historical personage the night before? A member of the aristocracy, a wizard in his own right, a longtime lover of La Voisin, and a particularly vicious man who had beaten Catherine's husband, Antoine, nearly to death. And it was as the Marquis de Sainte-Croix that the entranced group saw Darmanian.

The hypnotist seemed pleased with the first session's progress. The evening appeared to have reached an area at which he was satisfied to terminate the experiment.

"At the count of three," he began, "you will all begin to move forward—"

Catherine frowned her anger. "What game play you now? What is this, 'At the count of three'? You promised that the sporting was over. We have serious business to attend to tonight."

"M'lady," Abbé Guilborg shouted, panting as though he'd just run a flight of stairs. "The others are assembling. The guests among them. All the coven awaits you in the chamber."

"Ah, all my beauties," Catherine sighed, as if she were a great mother welcoming her brood come home to celebrate a holiday. "All my servants of the master."

She turned to her left, extended her hand. "Coco!"

In my peripheral vision I saw Shelley Eberhart snap to attention, a dutiful soldier in the ranks of Satan.

"Coco, my gentle little whore," Catherine said. "Neither you nor our lady Madame de Montespan will serve as altar tonight."

"As you wish, my lady," Shelley said in a subservient whisper.

"Sister Marie," Catherine spoke to the now alerted Viki Chung. "Did you have to drug the mother superior again?"

"Only with a bit of cognac in her evening bowl of milk," came the merry response.

"Did you bring the special herbs tonight?"

"Yes, my high priestess," Viki said. "They are potent enough in excess to kill a regiment. In the proper dosage, the studs shall be able to service their mares until the cock crows thrice!"

"Father Jacques," Catherine called, causing Dan Gruber's head to bolt upright. "If you have not worked on those chants, you cannot participate in tonight's Sabbat."

The husky quarterback answered with smooth assurance. "I have them letter perfect, my lady."

Darmanian had stopped in his countdown to the present, and I could not blame him. I, too, had become curious as to the claimed identities of the other members of the experimental circle. But now the hypnotist was ready to assert his mastery of the group.

"On the count of three," he commanded, "I want you to—"

Once again the hypnotist's enforcement of his control was interrupted, this time by shouts, hisses, and mumbled threats. It seemed to me as though I could feel an electric tension crackling the very atmosphere of the room.

Darmanian's confidence was not at all shaken by the regressed personalities' defiance. "When I count to three," he began again, "I want you to move forward in time. You will listen to me. You will—"

"No!" Catherine shouted. "I will not listen to you. Leave us alone!"

"Deep sleep!" Darmanian commanded, touching her lightly on the forehead. "All of you! Deep sleep! You have all been subject to my will. You have all obeyed my commands before. You will obey my commands now. You will go deeper and deeper, deeper and deeper asleep."

The battle of wills between Catherine and Darmanian continued for perhaps another three or four minutes before she succumbed to a deep sleep. Once she had acquiesced, he quite readily managed to place each member of the experimental group into a deep hypnotic sleep.

When they were all on "hold" in their own private limbo, Darmanian began pacing slowly in front of the entranced subjects. For the first time I noticed that he was sweating profusely as if he had been running laps for the past twenty minutes—which was how long the excursion to seventeenth-century Paris had taken us.

"Well, Eric," he asked me, "What are your impressions of the first encounter?"

"I'm not qualified to give any impressions of such an experiment," I answered. "And even if I were, I think I would be as stunned as I am now."

"Can't you give me some kind of intelligent reaction?" he asked sharply.

Pressed, I told him that I thought he should strive for a more structured session. "It seems to me as though you must establish control of the group in a very firm way," I said.

Darmanian considered my responses, and he seemed to reflect upon them for several seconds before he answered my criticism. "I was provided with the means of control tonight," he said.

"I shall assume totally the role of the Marquis Jean de Sainte-Croix."

Chapter Seventeen

"Whatever it was," Ed Vogel told me over the telephone the next morning, "it was *not* hypnotic regression."

"But I saw it with my own eyes, Ed," I told him from the extension in my room just before I went down to eat breakfast. I knew that if I called before eight, I would catch him before he left for work at the lumberyard.

"It was all quite remarkable," I went on. "You should have seen rugged Senator Harrigan flapping his wrists and mincing like a foppish court sycophant. And can you even imagine the oppressively moral Bishop De Shazo behaving as though he were an avowed libertine?"

Ed was attempting to answer me, but I suddenly snapped my fingers. "Hey, Ed, maybe that's it. Perhaps the members of the experimental group are enacting their moral and mental-image opposites in that alleged past life."

"Damn it, Eric Storm!" Ed Vogel roared into the receiver. "Listen to me. In a normal session of past-life regressions, you encounter people who give you what they got in their own private reality—whether true past life or fantasy play. You might hear one member tell about burning to death in a stable fire. Maybe another got eaten by sharks in a shipwreck. You know, like that. Everyone has a catharsis experience, and you might get some reasonable clues about their phobias in their present lives."

"Yes," I conceded. "I was expecting something like that to happen."

"Eric," Vogel persisted, "look at it objectively, man. Isn't it a bit too far-out coincidental that you could take six men and women from widely disparate backgrounds, hypnotize them, and have them all portray bizarre lives during the same era in the same city?"

"You mean it isn't a common occurrence to have such a thing happen during regression experiment?" I asked, remembering Darmanian's curt reassurance of the night before.

"It sure as hell is not." Vogel was definite.

"Shared past-life experiences, then, are not normal in so-called past-life regression work?" I tried it another way to be certain that I had it correct.

Ed grumbled into the receiver. "Look, Eric, I don't want to be dogmatic. Some psychics, such as Edgar Cayce, believed that souls often tended to incarnate in groups, especially if they had to complete Karmic patterns that were left unfinished. Maybe you witnessed an extraordinary example of that kind of thing."

I was puzzled. "Now you're saying that what I saw last night is possible!"

"Eric," Vogel said, his voice assuming a peculiar

earnestness. "I am certain that what you witnessed last night in Woodlands was not a typical example of hypnotic regression. What you saw was a dramatic example of something very different. Something that is potentially very dangerous to you."

"Dangerous?" I repeated with a cutting edge. "Ed, are we back to your prophetic utterances of mounting evil and impending crises?"

"There's no prophecy involved, Eric," Vogel said softly. "Just commonsense concern over what the consequences will be if you stay there at Woodlands."

"Ed, what I saw last night was weird, but it certainly was not evil," I told him. "You know, Ed, I believe that there is nothing that is truly evil except what lies within man. The rest is either natural or accidental."

Ed Vogel was silent for several moments. "Okay, Eric," he said at last. "I've got to go to work now. You keep in touch. Hear?"

I barely had time to promise that I would call soon before I held a buzzing receiver in my hand. I liked Ed Vogel, and I felt certain that he truly believed that he had my best interests as his concern; but I could not help feeling impatience at his perpetual soothsaying of dire events and evil doings.

I found Shelley Eberhart and Don Gruber just beginning their breakfast when I entered the dining room.

"Hey, there, Eric," Gruber greeted me expansively. "Come sit down and join us." His photogenic smile seemed to hang by his broken nose. Don the Jet had the misfortune of having once been a handsome man who decided to become a professional football player.

Too many brutal tackles by hulking linemen from opposing teams had taken their toll of his once near-perfect features. I wagered that even his friendly grin was reinforced by a partial plate.

"Yes," Shelley doubled the invitation. "Come join your fellow lodgers."

"Ah, yes," I said as I pulled out a chair where Agnes had set a place for me. "You two are the only out-of-towners involved in the experiment."

"That's right," she smiled. "The senator, Bishop De Shazo, and Viki all live in either Schenectady or Albany."

Shelley wore a navy blue pantsuit with a flowery blue blouse. She seemed oddly distracted in that manner which professional models develop in order to preserve their sanity while they are being stared at through camera lenses and posed like blank-eyed mannequins. I noticed that she was having only a small glass of tomato juice. A near-starvation diet was the price she paid for being beautiful in the contemporary style of skeletal slimness and sunken cheeks.

"Hey, that session last night was wild, wasn't it?" Don asked, spearing a slice of toast from the tray Agnes set before us.

"Quite," I agreed. "What was your reaction to being spontaneously regressed?"

"A real trip," Don laughed, then became serious about his omelet.

"Shelley," I asked her, "how did you feel about allegedly having been a Satanist in seventeenth-century France?"

She shrugged her slender shoulders and sipped at her tomato juice. It took me several moments before I realized that was the extent of her answer.

"You know, Eric," Don said in a confidential tone, "anything that Darmanian does for me or to me is just fine with me."

"You must really be sold on the man," I said, folding a linen napkin in my lap as Agnes set a savory omelet before me. I winked my thanks at the efficient woman.

"I sure am," Don said around a mouthful of eggs and ham. "That man is a genius."

"I don't imagine either of you would be reluctant to be quoted giving one of your rave testimonials in my book," I asked, smiling at what would seem to be a foregone conclusion.

"Hell, Eric, I'd rent a billboard in Times Square and put it in gigantic neon letters," Don said, chomping down hard on his toast for emphasis.

"Shelley?" I found that I had to keep prompting her.

"Sure," she said in a soft voice. "You can interview me."

"You could build a whole chapter around what he did for me," Don said, reluctant to surrender any attention to Shelley just yet.

"I'll get my tape recorder after breakfast," I told him, "and we can find a quiet spot to commit your story to tape."

"You can interview me in the gazebo," Shelley said. "It looks like such a lovely day outside."

"It is, miss," Agnes confirmed Shelley's visual assessment as she attempted to refill her glass of tomato juice. "And it feels so good after all the cold and rain that we've been having."

"Sure, I'll talk into your tape recorder later," Don

said, "but I just want to tell you a couple of things now before I forget them."

It appeared that as it was on the football field, so it was at the breakfast table: There was no stopping Don Gruber.

"I was just about to be sent off to the boondocks when I came to see Darmanian," Don said, his big fists clenching and unclenching as he relived the anguish of a bad season. "That season of seventy-five was so bad for me that the coach told me his grandma could pass better than me. I almost had to have bodyguards on the field to keep the fans from jumping me when we went into huddles."

"It was that bad, huh, Don?" Shelley laughed at the same flamboyant manner of speech that we had both heard Don displaying on the late-night talk shows.

"I figured I had as much hope of continuing to play for the Jets as a one-legged man has of winning a kicking contest," Don said in mock solemnity. "With the luck I was having, I couldn't make any money selling pot at a rock festival."

"But you had heard of Darmanian and the Woodlands Clinic?" I reminded him, lest the morning trail off into a succession of one-liners.

"Right!" Don said, slamming an open hand down on the table. If the grand old table had not been made of thick oak, every glass on its surface would have been up-ended. "Old Darmanian started right off by looking me in the eye and telling me something one of those smart old philosophers once said. I've even memorized it since. It goes: 'Mark this well, ye proud men of action! Ye are, after all, nothing but unconscious instruments of the men of thought.'

"Now," Gruber explained, wagging a forefinger at

us, "what that meant was I had to start using my head and I had to be a man of thought, as well as action. Otherwise, the smart guys would just keep using me."

Gruber paused in his narrative, sipped cautiously at his coffee. When he found it had cooled to his satisfaction, he downed the cup in three gulps.

"Well," he went on, "there was a whole lot of other things he said, of course. And I'll tell you all about them during my interview. He hypnotized me next, and he taught me techniques of self-hypnosis that have been more valuable to me than memorizing the coach's book of plays."

Gruber hesitated for just a second or two, then he swept his arms wide and roared: "The rest is history. By using the Darmanian method, I went on to become a legend in my own time. Twice voted most valuable player in my league!"

I had to laugh at the man's rampant ego, but Shelley rolled her eyes in disgust. "Jesus, Gruber," she complained. "I hope Darmanian has another quote for you about developing some humility!"

Don appeared hurt. "I'm very humble. Didn't I just give all the credit for my success to Darmanian's techniques of self-hypnosis?"

Shelley's eyes narrowed, and her words were spat out as if they were hard, sharp pebbles. "Don't forget that Hal Clinton broke his leg in practice so that your regaining the number-one quarterback position became assured."

Gruber winced at her recalling the incident to memory.

"And," she persisted, "don't forget the automobile accident that took Bill Lee Smithers, the man breathing down your back for the quarterback slot, out of football for good. He's still blind, you know."

"You bitch!" Gruber hissed. His big hands crumpled his napkin with such vehemence that it was apparent that he wished the cloth was Shelley's throat.

"I only want you to be realistic, Donald," she said, as if she were a mother speaking to a precocious child. "You must remember that there were other factors involved."

Their eyes locked in an impromptu staring contest. I was beginning to feel extremely uncomfortable.

"If I'm going to have to referee," I tried, "I'm going to have to have a whistle."

Don laughed, slapped me on the shoulder with just enough force to be considered friendly rather than punitive. Shelley seemed about to smile but thought better of it.

"These snooty, high-priced models can be real bitchy," Don said with a wink. "Must be pretty hard for you to have humility, too, isn't it, Shelley? I mean, knowing that your body is worth so much an hour."

Her voice was cold. "I knew what I wanted, and I knew what I had to do to get it."

"And Darmanian was also instrumental in your attaining your successes?" I asked her.

Her green eyes were on me at once. "Most definitely. Darmanian helped me in so many ways."

I pushed my chair back from the table. "A genius he is," I said, shaking my head in wonderment. "A professional football player, a leading fashion model, a senator, a respected clergyman. And there are nurses, doctors, lawyers, and thousands of people— people who have been helped by this most remarkable man. Somehow, he has found the proper key to heal them all, to make them whole, to transform them into successful men and women."

"He is a great soul," Shelley said, "and because he himself is by nature half-divine, he takes you with him to the stars so that you may hold a near acquaintanceship with the gods."

"That was lovely," I told her. "Do you write poetry?"

Her eyes lowered, and she smiled like a bashful teen-ager. "I have written a poem about Darmanian and what he means to me," she said. "I will show it to you later if you like."

I was continually being struck by the loyalty and admiration that Darmanian inspired in his patients. "I would like very much to see it, Shelley," I said.

"You know," I mused, folding my napkin and setting it beside my plate. "I cannot help reflecting on what a success story Darmanian himself provides. Here he was, a kid of fourteen in Auburn, New York, both parents dead, alone in the world—"

"Hey, Eric." Don laughingly interrupted me. "If you're going to write a book about a man, you'd better get the facts straight. Darmanian was born in Columbus, Ohio. And his folks are still living back there. I think his old man's a professor in some college there."

"It's a good thing you aren't writing the book, Don," Shelley snickered. "Your information is bonkers."

Relieved by her support, I supplied the data that Darmanian's father was a pharmacist and that both parents had died when the hypnotist was a teen-aged boy.

"I didn't say you were correct, either, Eric," Shelley laughed. "Darmanian grew up in Brooklyn. His father was a Greek Orthodox priest. Or was it a rabbi? I don't know about his mother. A schoolteacher, I think."

It was apparent to me that Darmanian's origins were as shrouded in mystery as they were when I first arrived at Woodlands. Then, to complicate matters further, Viki Chung seemed to materialize from the steam of the fresh pot of coffee that Agnes brought to the table.

"Good morning." She smiled in acknowledgement to our greetings. "Are you exploring the origins of our Darmanian?"

She seated herself next to me. There was a strange but very pleasant odor to her cologne. Her bright green dress suggested that the scent was that of some spring herb. At first I thought the pressure of her thigh against mine was accidental.

"Yes, we are," I answered. "It seems that Darmanian prefers to be a man of mystery. From what I can determine, he has told each of us a different account of his lineage and his childhood."

"Darmanian is actually Chinese," Viki said in mock seriousness. "That is why he is so inscrutable."

Gruber laughed in a kind of snorting cough, but Shelley rolled her eyes ceilingward as if praying to her special deity for strength.

"Maybe Darmanian is really Charlie Chan," the red-headed model smiled in a kittenish verbal jab.

"Hey," Gruber said, grinning, "then I could be his number-one son."

Viki kept her attention on Shelley. "I'll bet Shelley wishes that she could be his number-one hon. Isn't that right, Shelley, honey?"

If Shelley's eyes had been lasers, Viki would have

been scorched black on the spot. There appeared to be little love lost between the two women.

But I didn't know what to make of the steady pressure of Viki's thigh against my own.

At last she gave me a clue.

"Do you ever take a break from your busy schedule?" she asked as she accepted a cup of coffee from Agnes. "Or are you all work and no play?"

"Steady, Eric," Gruber warned me, adding an exaggerated wink. "I think old Viki is about to make you an offer you'd be a fool to refuse."

Viki's eyes held my own in a delicate butterfly's embrace. Gruber's less-than-subtle comment affected her not at all. She was a very confident lady, cool, self-assured.

"I'm always open to suggestions for my rest and recreation periods," I said, tentatively testing the area which Gruber had suggested. Viki was a lovely excuse not to work any day of the year.

"Saratoga Springs has numerous cultural activities available," she said softly. "Perhaps we could take in a concert or a ballet together."

"That would be wonderful," I readily conceded.

Under the table her thigh gave mine a playful nudge. "Yes"—Viki smiled—"I think we could really enjoy ourselves together. It would be an excellent diversion from your note taking and writing."

"Just let me know when you have an evening available," I told her.

Don Gruber chuckled and gave me another of his stage winks. "You'd better take lots of vitamins and eat lots of raw meat if you're going to go out with that pocket-sized Dragon Lady," he advised me.

Viki fixed her cool gaze on the football player.

"Don," she said icily, "promise me you'll start playing with a helmet. Thick as your skull may be, all those vicious tackles are starting to take their toll on your brain."

"Since when have you ever been interested in a man's brains?" Gruber shot back.

"Go play football, Don," Viki said quietly. It's too bad that's the only place where you can give a good performance."

As pleasantly sensual as Vicki's thigh felt against mine, I began to make the appropriate and recognizable preparatory movements of excusing myself both from the table and from their company. Gruber, Viki, and Shelley must have known each other for a long time, because they fought like brother and sisters. I had had enough of such squabbling for the day.

I managed a polite smile as I rose and suggested by way of excuse that I had to get back to work on my note taking and research.

"I'll be waiting for you and your tape recorder," Don grinned. "I've got some dynamite stories to tell you about Darmanian. I promise you that they'll all be interesting. Hell, man, they'll all be about me!"

Shelley seemed embarrassed when she reminded me that she would bring her poem about Darmanian to our session.

"Great, Shelley," I said, nodding approvingly. "How about the gazebo at around three this afternoon?"

Shelley smiled self-consciously, but she made an "OK" with the fingers of her left hand.

Viki caught at my arm just before I turned to walk away from the table. "Don't forget," she said. "We, too, must have a session together. Perhaps more than one."

"Certainly," I agreed, placing my hand over her clutching fingers. "I'm looking forward to it. Just let me know when you're ready."

"I will," Viki promised.

"Perhaps you will be able to provide me with some really exclusive information about Darmanian," I suggested.

The lovely Oriental nodded her head slowly. "More than you will ever be able to use," she said. "More than you would dare to tell."

Chapter Eighteen

The most dramatic aspect of the experimental session held at Woodlands Clinic on the night of Friday, April 21, was the advent of psychokinetic abilities. That is, certain of the group, especially Delores and Don Gruber, began to demonstrate remarkable mind-over-matter phenomena.

At precisely six minutes after eight Darmanian expertly induced a deep-sleep condition in each of the six members of the group and brought them back in time to the year 1679. Earlier that day I had attempted to dissuade him from assuming the role of the Marquis Jean de Sainte-Croix, but Darmanian had dismissed my objections with a wave of his hand. In a manner that firmly suggested that he in no way welcomed my criticisms, he informed me that he considered the task at hand as the most challenging, and potentially rewarding, of his career.

"It is April twenty-first, 1679." Darmanian named the present day and regressed it, too, by three hundred years. "It is evening," he specified.

Then, tapping Delores lightly on the forehead, he spoke to her by the name of her alleged identity in that lifetime. "Catherine, I want you to tell me what is happening. You see it now. You are living it *now*."

Delores's head moved upright, and she took a deep breath. I was hardly prepared for what issued forth from her open mouth. In a deep contralto voice I had had no idea she possessed, she sang: "*Answer us, O Ancient Horned One! Provender and Power are Thine.*"

As with one voice the other members of the circle answered her supplication: "*Hear and answer, Gracious Goddess! Grant us laughter, wit, and wine!*"

Delores—that is, Catherine—joined the group for the next entreaty: "*Descend on us, O Thou of Blessings! Come among us, make us glad!*"

Again the vibrant contralto: "*Since Thou art Chief of our Creation, why, o why, should we be sad?*"

The circle responded to their high priestess's query by singing: "*Beam on us, O joyous Bacchus, banish heavy-hearted hate. Accept our craft, O Greatest Mother, let cheerful brightness be our fate!*"

"So may it be!" Catherine pronounced.

Darmanian interjected himself into the scene immediately after the last note had been sounded. "Good evening, Catherine," he said. "That was a lovely hymn."

"Thank you, m'lord." She smiled and bent her head. "May the master hear it and join us this evening."

I was becoming more ill at ease by the moment. I was also becoming increasingly convinced that Darmanian had made an incorrect decision by surrendering his professional detachment.

And I could not have been more astonished when

Salem, Darmanian's large black cat that Delores so vocally detested, suddenly entered the library, crossed the room to her side, and jumped up on her lap. Incredibly, the trance personality accepted the cat, made it comfortable between the legs of her gray pantsuit, and began to stroke its fur.

Although the members of the experimental group had their eyes closed in trance, I could see that their pupils were moving rapidly under their lids. It was as though they were watching a dream. Rather than each of them observing their own personal theater of the mind, however, it was obvious that they were all watching the same drama. How else could they have all joined in the hymn to Satan?

"Father Jacques!" Catherine suddenly shouted.

Don Gruber sat upright and answered her summons.

"Demonstrate for the marquis your ability to raise a spirit of the dead for consultation and divination."

"Yes, my high priestess," he answered in an obsequious voice. "It is an honor to demonstrate for such a master wizard."

My senses were recording everything, but my brain was beginning to smoke from sensory overload. It was difficult to rationalize what was happening. To hear the rugged, aggressive professional football player actually assuming the role of an obedient devil's disciple was a bit much.

"The chamber is full tonight," Catherine said. "All neophytes in Satan's workshop should observe carefully. I have found this ritual to be most effective when it is performed by a priest who has served at a Christmas midnight Mass. It has been four months since Father Jacques distributed the host at such a service, but the power should still be strong about him."

"Yes, my high priestess," Father Jacques agreed. "I have every confidence that I shall be successful once again. Shall I begin now?"

At his priestess's nod, the man began to chant in a cadence reminiscent of a priest singing matins: *"O Infernal Powers who carry disturbances into the Universe, leave your somber habitation and transport yourselves to the place beyond the Styx. If you hold in your power the one whom I call, I conjure you to allow the unholy spirit to appear before me."*

He made a scooping motion with his hand, as if he were tossing something into the air.

"May he who is dust wake from his sleep," the chant continued. *"May the unholy spirit step out of his dust and answer to my demands—which I make in the name of the Lord of the Earth, my Holy Satan!*

Gruber—Father Jacques—became quiet, his arms extended before him. His face was a mask of rigid concentration.

Viki Chung began to sing as though she had been awaiting a cue: *"O Holy Satan, loose the one thy servant has summoned. Wake him from his troubled sleep. Let him obey our purposeful direction. Grant that we may no more weep."*

Father Jacques maintained his position. Beads of sweat were dotting his upper lip, and large droplets were coursing across his forehead.

"O Infernal Powers," he began again, *"transport the spirit to me from beyond the Styx. Your everlasting majesty has no peer. Wake the unholy spirit from his sleep and bring him to me. I make these demands in the name of my most Holy Satan!"*

I have never been more startled than when the large bust of Pallas Athena suddenly shattered on its stand near the bookshelves. It was as if the loud, explosive retort announced the arrival of the seventeenth-century Parisian coven into the Saratoga Springs of 1978.

"The spirit is here!" Catherine shouted. "Hail, Satan!"

"Hail, Satan!" the circle echoed her tribute.

Father Jacques bowed his head, continued the demonstration with a loud chant: *"Four winds blow! One from each direction. Four winds blow! Spin an object of our election!"*

The small table near Darmanian's chair rose on three legs. I shouted to indicate the activity, but it was obvious that the hypnotist had already noticed it. He was smiling as if he were a small boy in Santa's workshop.

The table slammed down noisily, then rose again and began to hop toward the center of the library like a stiff-legged square dancer. I had heard of such things as levitation of objects, but I never entertained the slightest hope that I might ever witness such phenomena. And I felt a moment of panic as an atavistic fear of the unknown seized me.

"Spin, object, spin!" Father Jacques commanded.

I could not guess what object he was conjuring in his reality, but it was astonishingly evident that the psychic mechanism had spilled over into our world. The table began to rotate wildly.

My attention was diverted by a peculiar flapping and humming sound. I cried out in anger and in fear when I saw that the tape recorder I held on my lap had gone beserk. Within the plastic cassette case, the two small reels were each spinning in a different direction. The tape of the session had been ripped, and loose ends were slapping the recorder head as they rotated at high speed.

Before my disoriented brain could deal fully with that experience, I had the tape recorder jerked from my hands by some invisible agency. My expensive new machine rose several feet into the air, effected a right-angle turn, and smashed noisily into a wall.

"Four winds blow! One from each direction!" the entire group was now chanting.

The heavy drapes on the south wall of the library began to twist and to writhe like frenzied snakes. Several books were torn from their shelves and spun about as if seized by a miniature tornado.

"Stop this, La Voisin!" Darmanian said firmly, his voice edging very close to a shout.

Delores's eyes snapped open. They blinked at Darmanian, as if seeing him for the first time. She turned her head slowly from side to side, studying the room, the people within it. Her eyes fixed themselves sullenly on me, and I felt a chill tingle my body as I saw that the familiar brown eyes had lost their warmth.

When she spoke, her voice was cold, defiant. "There is none better than the Marquis de Sainte-Croix at commanding the spirits."

Darmanian had been challenged.

The library had become an icy maelstrom of swirling objects. A heavy book struck my shoulder, and I winced with the sudden pain. A bookend went crashing through a window. The serpentine drapes were coiling themselves around their supporting rods.

The group continued to chant about the four winds blowing, and the objects kept spinning.

La Voisin's voice rose shrill above the others: "There is none better than the Marquis de Sainte-Croix at commanding the spirits!"

Darmanian raised his hands, and in a booming voice, he declared: "Spirit, return to the Kingdom of the Dead. I have been satisfied by your coming here. I have been pleased by the gift of the Lord of this Earth in permitting you to do our bidding. Now you must return. You must cross again the River Styx. Charon must again guide you to your dusty sleep. I make this demand in the name of my Holy Satan!"

At once the violent psychokinetic activity ceased. Books began dropping to the floor, like birds brought down by hunter's guns. The shattered end table ceased at last its mad dance. The members of the group slumped in their chairs, their heads dropping forward in recognizable hypnotic trance position.

Darmanian was trembling as he surveyed the shambles of the library. His voice was barely more than a harsh whisper when he said: "Next time I shall not permit La Voisin to challenge me. She tricked me! Next time I shall maintain total control!"

I was not at all certain at that moment if it were Darmanian, master clinical hypnotist, who had spoken with such certainty—or if it had been the Marquis Jean de Sainte-Croix, master magician, commander of the spirits.

Chapter Nineteen

Ed Vogel added another teaspoon of creamer to his coffee. It was the only way he claimed to be able to tolerate what he considered the inherent bitterness of the brew.

He had spent the last twenty minutes listening to me give as full an account as possible of the incredible events of the previous night. Just an hour before, I had borrowed the Woodlands Clinic's station wagon so that I might drive into Saratoga Springs and buy a new tape recorder to replace the one that had been destroyed by some unseen force during the group session. Before I left for town, I had telephoned Ed Vogel and asked him to meet me someplace near the lumberyard where he worked.

"My gawd, Eric!" Ed shook his head slowly in wonderment. "I warned you something strange was going on at Woodlands."

We sat at a table for two as far away from the counter as possible in the small diner where Ed had asked me to meet him. The other patrons appeared to be an assortment of blue-collar workers who had probably been on the job since dawn and had by now, ten fifteen, more than earned a coffee break.

Ed hunched low over his coffee, leaned toward me as if to shield his words from the men at the counter. "You saw enough last night to make an orthodox scientist shuck his test tubes and theorems and become a truck driver," he said, jerking a thumb at two stocky men perched on stools near the end of the serving bar. "Any parapsychologist in the country would give his eyeteeth for the opportunity of sitting in on a session like last night's."

"Well, to be honest," I told him, "there were times when I was damn scared. I mean, I didn't think such things existed outside of a Hollywood special-effects scene."

I broke off a piece of my doughnut but left it on my plate. "Ed, the most bizarre aspect of the whole thing was the calm, matter-of-fact manner in which the members of the circle behaved," I said. "They acted as though they were used to seeing such things. Not one of them acted the least bit startled."

Ed considered this, then replied: "I suppose the state of hypnosis in which Darmanian had placed them might have permitted them to better accept levitating objects as part of the reality which they had been sharing."

I popped the hunk of doughnut in my mouth, tucked it to one side. "Hey, Ed," I argued. "Think about it. Books were flying through the air. A table was hopping around the room like a possessed polka dancer. But afterward, when we were all helping to pick up some of the mess, not one person in that group made one comment about what we had just witnessed. How could they have been so indifferent about the incredible things that they had just seen?"

Ed began making concentric circles on the table top with the moist bottom of his cup. "But Darmanian—or should we call him the marquis?—settled everything down, eh?"

"Yes, he did," I said, nodding. "But he has only assumed the role of the marquis for purposes of establishing control. He doesn't believe that he was involved in that lifetime as the Marquis Jean de Sainte-Croix. I know that he believes in reincarnation, but I am certain that a devoted healer and therapist such as Darmanian would not claim a life as a Satanist in seventeenth-century France."

Ed shifted his bulk, dug his wallet out of his back pocket.

"I'll buy," I said, frowning. "But do you have to go so soon?"

Ed laughed, removed a sheet of paper from the bill section of the wallet. "You may wish that I had never come when you see this."

He carefully unfolded the sheet, handed it across the table to me. "I found this in one of my old books. I took it to the library and had it Xeroxed. I am certain that you will recognize it."

On the paper was a reproduction of an ancient woodcut that depicted two winged dragons supporting a crystal on their pointed snouts. The inscription beneath the cut read: "Shield and crest of the Wizard Jean de Sainte-Croix."

"That's Darmanian's medallion," I said, shaking my head in disbelief.

Ed sipped noisily at his coffee, grabbed the remainder of my neglected doughnut. "And it was also the marquis's family crest."

"What an astonishing similarity," I admitted.

Ed arched an eyebrow, unconvinced of coincidence. "I'm not saying that offers absolute proof of anything." He shrugged thick shoulders. "Darmanian could have seen the same old book when he was just a kid. The insignia could have so impressed his head that he copied it—knowingly or unknowingly—and adopted it as his own special symbol."

Ed accepted a refill from the waitress, who was making the rounds of the scattered tables. "But, you know, Eric, from what I can find out from the old reference works, Darmanian and the marquis have more in common than a coat of arms."

He spooned a generous addition of creamer to his cup before he continued. "The marquis was also a skillful manipulator of people. He no doubt applied hypnosis in order to persuade the most influential men and women of his time to accept his leadership. It is said that he was an alchemist, a wizard, as well as a healer. And he did appear to believe sincerely that his approach to matters served the greater good, as well as the individual."

"Then how did such a man become involved with a satanic high priestess?" I asked him.

Ed blew across the rim of his cup, tested the temperature of his coffee. He shook his head, set the cup on the table so that he could spoon some ice from his water glass into the steaming coffee.

"It seems to have been greed, pure and simple, Eric," Vogel answered. "The marquis also appears to have had a powerful lust for power and for control over large masses of people. One historian goes so far as to suggest that the marquis may have been plotting a revolution against King Louis. Another theorizes that the marquis sought to use the satanic underground to foment rebellion."

I was alternating sips of tea with swallows of orange juice, thereby balancing my need for a small amount of caffeine with larger dosages of vitamin C. "Do you mean to say, Ed, that the marquis might have brought about the principles of the French Revolution—liberty, equality, fraternity—one hundred years earlier?"

Ed shook his head. "I doubt it. The marquis was a member of the aristocracy, after all. I think he saw himself as a benevolent despot. He might have established a certain number of reforms, but it is unlikely that he would have relegated a great deal of control to any representative body of elected officials. He no doubt would have applied the principles of magic and his alchemic philosophy to the machinery of government."

"It might have been Camelot reborn," I suggested.

Ed was slowly peeling the wrapper from a White Owl panatela. "I cannot see a Camelot with La Voisin as his advisor. Their affair began when she was in her mid-teens, and she exercised a great deal of control over him. She may have insisted that they demand babies for sacrifice as well as taxes from people they ruled."

I picked up the Xeroxed copy of the de Sainte-Croix crest. It was unmistakably the same as the design on the medallion that Darmanian wore about his neck. I was certain that a rational explanation for the coincidence could be discovered with a bit of probing.

"The marquis was an alchemist of the highest order," Ed told me as he fumbled in his pockets for a match. I got my pipe lighter from my coat, and he bent toward the flame with the cigar in his mouth. I noticed that it seemed as though my friend was always in need of a shave.

"Now the old bit about alchemists changing base metals into gold was only one aspect of their work," Ed said after he had exhaled a thick cloud of smoke. "That was only their material goal. The true alchemist was seeking a transformation, a transformation of himself. He was seeking to achieve a union with the cosmic powers of the universe, a blending of himself with higher consciousness."

"That's a beautiful goal," I commented.

"Yes," Ed agreed, "but, regrettably, there were those who sought that goal so obsessively, so desperately, that they debased their quest by including human sacrifice."

"Some of them became Satanists," I said, studying the ancient woodcut of the sinewy dragons.

Ed tapped a bit of white ash into a tray. "Yes, they considered themselves to be of a superior blend of humanity. Perhaps they felt that if they achieved the goal of transmutation and were able to teach others to attain it, the sacrifice of a few men, women, and babies would be justified."

I could not suppress a slight shudder. "Do you know what became of the marquis?" I asked. "How did he escape going to the stake alongside his lover, La Voisin?"

Ed puffed deeply on the panatela. "The marquis escaped the torture and the stake because of his rank and his money," he replied. "Some authorities say that he went to Switzerland with the intention of raising an army of mercenaries there and in northern Italy. Others suggest that he might have come to America in the hope of creating a new empire dedicated to Satanist principles."

"But," I said, "no one really knows for certain."

"No one really knows for certain." Ed nodded his agreement.

"So what are you suggesting all this means, Ed?" I wanted to know. "This old woodcut that looks like Darmanian's medallion. Your allegation that the life of the marquis bore many similarities to Darmanian's—"

"Not their lives," Ed clarified. "Their personalities. Their attitudes. Their general world views."

He studied the glowing tip of the cigar as if seeking a revelation. "There is no question in my mind that the marquis was totally serious about wanting to help others and to make a better society here on Earth," Ed said softly. "All the reference works agree that he was truly a wizard of the highest degree of accomplishment. Maybe, just maybe, the marquis discovered a way to transmute his soul. Maybe he found a way to control his incarnations."

My hand jerked involuntarily, knocking a salt shaker clattering to the floor. "Oh, come on, now, Ed!"

"What greater accomplishment could a metaphysician achieve than to transmute his soul to such a high energy form that he may rise above time and space and select his own incarnations at any period in the future?" Ed asked.

"You are getting into areas that are, in my opinion, nothing more than speculation," I said, emphatically. Then, I added a bit unkindly: "And, I must say, wooly-minded and weird speculation at that!"

Ed's big hand moved across the small table, and a thick forefinger tapped the crest of the Marquis de Sainte-Croix. "Think of the medallion around Darmanian's neck. His obsession with reincarnation. The incredible manner in which six subjects are all sharing the same regressive experience. The remarkable psychokinetic demonstration you witnessed last night. Think of all those things before you reject what I have suggested."

Ed pushed his chair away from the table. "I've got to get back to work," he said. "Oh, by the way—" He smiled humorlessly. "Here's something else for you to read while you're thinking things over."

He pulled a tightly folded newspaper from his back pocket and handed it to me. "There's been another babynapping," he said grimly. "We seem to have them in spurts around here."

Ed zipped up his jacket, reached down, and squeezed my shoulder. "You have my telephone number if you need me," he reminded. "Please watch yourself. As I told you before, I am convinced that Darmanian is something other than he appears."

I watched Ed Vogel's broad form move toward the door. He was about to put his hand on the knob when he suddenly turned. "You did say you would pay?" he asked sheepishly.

I waved him out the door, then opened the folded newspaper.

The story Ed had referred to was on page three. A young mother had suffered the horror of having her baby snatched from her arms while in their own home.

She had been breast feeding her child when she heard the front door open. Thinking it was her husband returning from his shift at the General Electric plant in Schenectady, she did not look up at once, but only called his name.

Before she had any time to wonder about his peculiar behavior in not answering her, a tall, burly man, his features disguised and distorted by a stocking pulled over his head, rushed in and wrestled her infant son from her arms. He had punched her into unconsciousness before he left.

Police authorities said the incident had taken place about eleven thirty the night before, April 21. Medical examiners verified that the woman had not been molested in any sexual way, nor had any object of value been stolen from the house. The intruder's sole purpose in breaking into the home seemed to have been the theft of the baby. At the time the story had been filed, there were no clues to the whereabouts of the missing child.

It seemed like a good time to drive over to Albany to visit Burt Kandowski. From the directions a trucker at the counter gave me, there seemed little problem getting to the station house before noon. Maybe I could catch Burt before he went to lunch.

Back in the late 1950s I had cut my publishing teeth by writing for detective magazines. I had struck up an acquaintance with Sergeant Burton Kandowski when I did a survey piece on combatting crime in the streets, and it turned out to be the biggest thing in his life. Because of his almost childish pleasure in seeing his name in print and because he proved to be a veritable storehouse of information, I had done a number of articles using the sarge as a quotable reference. It had been some years since we had bent elbows at his favorite neighborhood bar, and until I had run into him the night of Darmanian's demonstration for the police, I had had no idea that he had moved to Albany.

I arrived at the station house just before noon. A slim young cop in shirtsleeves carrying two cups of coffee nodded toward a cubicle between a water cooler and a radiator when I asked for Sergeant Kandowski. Burt swung his feet off a corner of his desk, nearly sent a stack of paperwork to the floor.

"Eric, you old son!" he growled in that rasping voice of his. "You shoulda called first. I was just getting ready to rush out of here."

As I recalled, Burt was always in a rush. His total absorption of the Puritan work ethic required that he be perpetually busy whenever you encountered him, whether it be by telephone or in person.

"Burt, it'll only take a minute. What can you tell me about that babynapping last night?"

"You gonna do an article on those kidnappings?" he wanted to know. "God, Eric, I don't know all the facts, but I can set you up with the right guys, though.

"Hey"—he was off on a nostalgic tangent—"remember back a few years? You musta quoted me in a dozen different articles. Man, the other cops used to get jealous. I still got copies of all them magazines. They had some real nifty chicks on the covers."

For a man in a hurry, Kandowski was chattering like a policeroom parrot. He was the same old Burt.

"Look, Burt, I was only wondering what you can tell me about the babynapping that took place last night."

"This off the record, kid?"

"Off the record."

"It's a real shitty thing, Eric. But I think we've got a major kidnapping ring operating in the area," he said. "We're supposed to play that down so as not to generate panic—or make us look like saps because we haven't nabbed the creeps yet."

"A friend of mine, a local, implied that there have been a number of such incidents involving babies," I pressed him.

"Yeah, that's what I meant," Burt replied. "I figure some well-organized ring is grabbing babies in this area, then probably selling them on the black market in New York City."

"How long has this sort of thing been happening here?" I wanted to know.

"It seemed to start about five years ago. We might go five, six months without a babynapping, then it starts up again. Your friend probably told you that this is the third one in three weeks."

"Do you have any leads at all?" I asked.

Burt took a noisy sip from a coffee cup. "We're up against some real professionals," he admitted.

"And there isn't any kind of pattern evident in the mothers, the families, the homes from which the babies have been stolen?" I wondered.

"None that we can figure out," Burt grumbled low. "Sounds to me like you are thinking about writing an article about the babynappings after all."

"No," I assured him. "Just interested. At least for the time being."

"Well," he said, "if you decide you want to write an article, you could probably get some background quotes from Darmanian."

"Darmanian?" I questioned. "What would he know about such things?"

"I figured you knew that he's been helping us with cases from time to time," Burt reminded me. "He sometimes hypnotizes suspects and witnesses for us."

"Oh, yes, of course," I said.

"And I know that he would have a special interest in solving this case, since a couple of the women have been his clients.

"Darmanian's? For what was he treating them?"

"Well, I know that, according to the gal's medical record, he had worked with this latest victim for emotional difficulties she was having during her pregnancy," Burt said. "Isn't that terrible, Eric? The kid has a tough time carrying her baby, then she has to lose it in this way."

"Yes," I agreed softly. "It's terrible."

"Makes you wonder just what the hell the world is coming to, doesn't it?" Burt demanded.

I shook my head to clear it. *What the hell was I coming to?* Had I been hearing so much lately about men and women who practiced infant sacrifices that I was beginning to make associations where none could possibly exist? By Kandowski's testimony, the babies had been disappearing for five years. The past-life experiments had been going on only for four nights.

I said good-bye to Burt, told him I would buy him a drink some night soon.

As I was walking back to the station wagon, I reached in my coat pocket for the keys and felt a folded piece of paper. It was the copy that Ed had made of the Marquis de Sainte-Croix's crest.

"What greater accomplishment could any metaphysician achieve," I could hear Ed saying, "than to transmute his soul to such a high energy form that he may rise above time and space and select his own incarnations at any period in the future?"

I crumpled de Sainte-Croix's crest and tossed it into a sidewalk trashbin.

Chapter Twenty

"Master, we have gathered tonight to present you with good tidings of great joy," Delores said in the particular verbal cadence that characterized the entity of La Voisin.

"I am most certainly pleased to learn of this," Darmanian said. "I pray that you will not keep me waiting long."

Deep, rumbling laughter came from Bishop De Shazo, as the personality of Abbé Guilborg joined the conversation. "Does the master not like suspense? Life would be flat and colorless without a little suspense."

"Perhaps the marquis has more important things to do with his time, you bloated horse's ass," came the mincing tones of Father Louis from the rugged exterior of Senator Tom Harrigan. "Let us not keep him awaiting the joyous word, La Voisin!"

It was a quarter past eight on Saturday night, April 22. The third group session had just begun.

"Master," La Voisin went on, "our Holy Satan has

come to Angelique, my daughter Marguerite's child, and revealed unto her that she is to present herself as the propitiatory sacrifice that will enable you to attain the highest position of any wizard born to man."

Once again there was a reference to child sacrifice. This time to that of a young girl who was willingly to present herself on Satan's altar. I felt a nausea that suddenly gripped my stomach like the claw of some angered beast. I could see no purpose in Darmanian's decision to pursue such activity with his experimental group.

"How wondrously giving of the child," Darmanian responded to La Voisin's announcement. "Angelique knows, of course, that great will be her reward in lifetimes to come."

"I have been promised that you will be given the power to ensure her coming glory," La Voisin was quick to emphasize. There seemed little of Delores sitting there before us. She wore a tight black gown that accentuated the curve of her hips and her firm bustline. A bright red sash encircled her waist and hung almost to the floor. Salem, the large black cat, lay comfortably curled in her lap.

Darmanian tapped a fingernail against the glass of water that he had picked up from an end table. He seemed to be reflecting on his next course of action.

"I'm going to move you ahead in time," he said to the entranced circle. "It will be exactly three months later. You will all be able to see and to hear everything that is happening, and you will be able to tell me what is happening to you. You will tell me what went wrong with the sacrifice!"

Darmanian's words startled me. Why had he assumed that the sacrifice had never been completed?

With more than two thousand sacrifices to her infamous name, why would the hypnotist suppose she had failed in accomplishing the one deemed most important of all?

The count to three had been reached. The trance personalities had now been moved three months ahead.

La Voisin began to writhe as if in pain. Viki Chung, whom we knew in the regressive state as Sister Marie, was whimpering. Bishop De Shazo, Senator Harrigan, Don Gruber, and Shelley Eberhart—Abbé Guilborg, Father Louis, Father Jacques, and Coco—were sitting slumped with their heads pitched forward.

Darmanian touched La Voisin on the forehead. "You will feel no pain, no distress. My hand heals instantly. You will be able to tell me what is happening to you in a dispassionate way."

"The bastards have me on the rack!" La Voisin spat.

"Are they hurting you?"

"A little. They have not yet begun in earnest. For some reason they are holding back."

Darmanian once again touched her forehead. "Rest quietly, peacefully," he told her as he moved on to Sister Marie.

The lovely Oriental sighed heavily when he tapped her lightly on the forehead. "They were hurting me," she complained. "Thank you, m'lord, for taking away the pain."

"Where are you?"

Sister Marie shuddered. "A terrible dungeon. The rats come at night. And so do the jailers, to force themselves upon us."

"Why are you here?"

Her voice caught in a sob. "We were betrayed! I know it will be the stake for us!"

Darmanian put a forefinger to her anguished brow, reinforced his command to be at peace.

"What of the sacrifice?" he asked Abbé Guilborg.

The voice was soft, emotionless. "I'm just floating. Floating."

"Floating?"

"I guess that . . . I am dead. I don't care anymore."

"Go back!" Darmanian commanded. "Go back to the time of your death. Tell me what happened. Tell me about the sacrifice!"

Abbé Guilborg's voice became a low rumble. "We were betrayed. La Voisin would have my eyes for saying so, but I know that it was her daughter, Marguerite, who betrayed us. She took Angelique away, m'lord. She hid our sacrifice from us!"

"And she also betrayed you to the Chambre Ardente?"

"I am certain of it. Inspector Desgrez and his men burst in on us while we were celebrating the Mass. That little bulldog Desgrez shouted that we could now chant in the dungeons."

"What happened then?"

"We decided to make a fight of it. They were many, but we gave a good accounting of ourselves, m'lord. We had only knives against their swords and muskets. I . . . I am sorry that we failed in the propitiatory sacrifice. But it is Marquerite who is to blame!"

Darmanian lightly brushed his forehead, assured Abbé Guilborg's tranquility, then stepped to Shelley Eberhart, Coco.

"The woodcutter," the trance personality gasped. "He is so ugly. And his privates are as big as a horse's pizzle. The jailers come around and laugh and make wagers if I can take all of him into me. He hurts me very much. I fought him the first time, but the jailers and the torturers only beat me and held me down. I will soon go to the stake."

"What of the great sacrifice?" Darmanian asked her.

"Marquerite took Angelique away and hid her," Coco answered. "It was not our fault that we failed, master. And then Desgrez came to arrest us."

Darmanian tranquilized her, stepped to Don Gruber, Father Jacques, and activated him from what appeared to be a state of bliss. He began sobbing, sucking in great gasps of air, until the hypnotist calmed him.

"My life is as nothing, master, but I would have made the sacrifice happen for you," he said. "I would have done this if the police had not killed me!"

"But Marguerite took Angelique away," Darmanian said. "How would you have made the sacrifice occur?"

"Abbé Guilborg has informants everywhere," Father Jacques said. "We learned that Marguerite had left the child with a family in the country. We were making plans to snatch her away from them."

"You are a good and faithful servant, Father Jacques," Darmanian told him. "Rest now in peace."

The hypnotist returned to La Voisin. "You are moving through time and space," he told her. "You are traveling toward what for you is the future. But you are in a unique perspective. You are able to stand apart from your lifetime as La Voisin. You are also able to view your lifetime as Delores Touraine."

I was baffled by Darmanian's maneuver. Why did he now seek to mix the two realities?

Although I felt again the nausea and sensed a menacing energy or force swirling throughout the library, I was also intrigued by the proposition of that which Darmanian had suggested.

If reincarnation really exists and if to some level of the soul, knowing all time is an eternal now, then might not the La Voisin of the seventeenth century already be a slumbering part of the Delores Touraine of the twentieth century?

If the two personalities shared an essential self, a soul, would not each of them be aware of the other on some level of consciousness, regardless of the ostensible barrier of time and space?

"You are able to see through the dark glass that separates mankind from the cosmos," Darmanian told La Voisin. "You will have knowledge of both lifetimes and special insight into the questions that I shall ask of you. At the count of three, tell me what you see and know! One . . . two . . . three!"

The physical person we knew as Delores Touraine stiffened slightly, her eyelids appearing to clamp down tightly. Her hands moved from her lap and fluttered out to her sides, as if they were young birds suddenly aware of their wings. Then, satisfied with their new strength, the hands returned to their lap nest. When Delores opened her eyes and smiled at Darmanian, the voice cadence was that of La Voisin.

"I . . . I am aware of being in *here*," she said, indicating by an arched hand over the heart to mean Delores's body. "But the *real* me is standing somewhere behind and slightly above the left shoulder."

"Do you know who I am?" Darmanian asked.

"You are now called Darmanian," she answered. "You are considered a master of hypnosis. You are also the Marquis Jean de Sainte-Croix, a master wizard. Both of you," she added with a wink, "are my lovers."

As La Voisin's low, throaty laughter filled the room, I felt increasingly disoriented, and Ed Vogel's voice kept echoing somewhere inside my brain: *"Whatever is happening there at Woodlands, it isn't hypnotic regression."*

Darmanian waited until the laughter had subsided, then he asked his next question: "And the other people in this room? Do you recognize all of them?"

"Most assuredly," La Voisin replied. "Through your wizardry, I am able to pierce the veil and recognize them very well. Abbé Guilborg is nearly as fat in this life as he was before. Sister Marie has a different color. Coco is taller. Father Louis is much sturdier of build. Father Jacques appears very much the same."

La Voisin's eyes met and held my own. I experienced a distinct and decidedly eerie chill that penetrated my entire body. "He is not one of us!" she snapped. "You!" she shrilled at me. "Who are you?"

"I am . . ."

I hesitated, intimidated by those angry, probing eyes. Then a quote from Ralph Waldo Emerson surfaced from somewhere in my memory, and I impulsively paraphrased it as my reply: "I am a man who loves goodness, harbors angels, reveres reverence, and lives with God."

"You are also a fool!" she shouted. Then, like a serpent in human form, her eyes narrowed to tiny slits, her lips compressed in a tight smile, and her pink tongue flicked rapidly from her mouth. When she spoke again, it was in awful mockery. "I see," she said, "that you have purchased a new recording machine."

In a proprietary reflex, I increased the pressure of my grip around my new cassette recorder. I was amazed when I distinctly felt a steady pull, like that from a huge magnet, tugging at it.

"He is here as my guest," Darmanian said irritably. The tension on the machine ceased, and I felt pleased that the hypnotist had come so quickly to my defense.

La Voisin opened her mouth wide and hissed at me. I could not stop my fingers from trembling as they clutched the tape recorder firmly on my right knee.

"Is there anyone missing from this circle who should be in attendance?" Darmanian wanted to know.

La Voisin frowned. "There were so many of us then, but you have assembled the most powerful among us. Of course, Marguerite is not here. And Angelique, her daughter, is again hidden from me."

Darmanian prodded her. "You have the power, you have the ability, to know who these people are in this present-life experience."

"Ah, yes! A-ha," La Voisin said, smiling. "Marguerite is my sister in this lifetime. She is my sister, Sharon. She is a learned one who teaches in this city in a university."

"It is as I suspected," Darmanian said, more to himself. "And Angelique?"

La Voisin once again released that low, throaty laughter. "As before, she is her daughter. Her daughter, Alyse!"

The trance personality shook her head slowly, in wonderment. "Oh, my dearest one. How clear it all is!

How Sharon despaired when her fiancé was killed in Vietnam. How she warred within herself whether or not she would bear his child or have it aborted. She had no choice! Angelique wanted to come through again to serve you, O master!"

"Is Angelique again prepared to serve as propitiatory sacrifice?" Darmanian asked.

It seemed as though my energy was being drained from me in sickening waves of withdrawal. At times I feared for Darmanian's sanity, for it appeared that he was most assuredly utilizing the role of the marquis as more than a control device. He seemed to know too much. He seemed far too insistent on learning about the failure of the sacrifice of the girl. At other times I feared for my own sanity, as I tried desperately to make sense of the techniques that the skillful hypnotist must be employing to explore fully his new concepts of past-lives therapy.

La Voisin reflected upon Darmanian's question for several moments before she answered: "In her inner self, she wishes only to serve Satan and to offer herself as your propitiatory sacrifice. But she does not know of such things at this time. Again, Marguerite has hidden her from us."

My poor brain was scrambling for solutions. Was Delores's lovely body housing a discarnate spirit, mocking us with its fanciful tales?

Had Darmanian's hypnosis permitted us to trespass in some incredible alternate reality?

Or were we acting out our assigned parts in some mutual fantasy being concocted by our unconscious minds, which had somehow combined their energies and ganged up on us?

"Why is Angelique so important, so crucial to you?"

I blurted out. "And why did you wish to sacrifice her?"

La Voisin's gaze was steady, her voice level. "The entity whom we knew first as Angelique, who exists now as Alyse, was fashioned especially for this role of divine service. Her bloodline was cultivated by Satan for this purpose. She has the inner awareness that it is her privilege to serve both her earthly and her supernatural master in this regard. She knows that she will be well rewarded."

"If she expects reward," I pointed out, "then she does not perform this act of sacrifice unselfishly."

La Voisin smiled, as if I were the village idiot. "Satan never expects his servants to work without reward. To receive no reward is to receive punishment by the act of omission. Self-interest is no vice. It is honesty."

As though emphasizing his desire for my silence, Darmanian stepped between La Voisin and me. "And Angelique knows that the opporunity has come again?"

La Voisin nodded. "As I have told you, the child has full soul knowledge of her mission. She has but to be activated. Her greatest desire is to shed her blood so that you might attain your rightful position as the greatest of wizards, the most powerful magician this planet has ever known. Once the sacrifice has been completed, you will achieve powers undreamt of by mortal men. We all stand ready to serve you."

"And you know, La Voisin, that you have one more important function yet to perform," Darmanian said, pointing a demanding forefinger at her.

She bowed her head slightly, then raised it, her eyes afire. "I know, m'lord. And I am ready! Hail, Satan!"

In spite of the fact that Darmanian had left the other members of the group in a tranquil trance state, each of them joined La Voisin's salute: "Hail, Satan! Hail Satan, true Lord of the Earth!"

Chapter Twenty-one

I had had quite enough for one evening. The nausea that had been spasmodically churning my stomach throughout the session was demanding immediate release. I left the library before Darmanian had brought the group back to the present reality, and I had all I could do to keep from running from the room.

I sought refuge in a small downstairs bathroom. I knew that I could never have made it to my room on the second floor. I somehow managed to keep from vomiting, but I sat for quite some time on the toilet, holding a cold, wet washcloth to my face.

I kept flashing images of Delores's angry eyes when she hissed at me, Darmanian's insistence in learning of yet another sacrifice, the group shouting their salute to Satan. I understood that Darmanian was assuming the role of the marquis in order to interact with the regressed personalities so that he might perfect his past-lives therapy. I also knew that he was a very clever, very adept man with an extremely facile mind. Yet he seemed to be becoming too subjective, too involved in the role playing. I saw more marquis at work and less therapist with each session.

At last I felt stronger and I resolved to go to my room. As I left the small bathroom, I could hear Darmanian's voice coming from the entryway.

"We've got to get her involved somehow," he was telling someone, a great sense of urgency in his voice. "I don't care how we do it, but we've got to bring her here."

When I reached the foot of the stairs, I saw Darmanian speaking to Don Gruber, Shelley Eberhart, and a man whom I had never seen before. He was tall, slender, sharp-featured, and dressed entirely in black. Viki Chung and Tom Harrigan stood to one side, and they appeared to be supporting an astonishingly lovely young woman between them. Bishop De Shazo had his back to me, and he was engaged in earnest conversation with a man and woman who were also dressed in black.

The young woman seemed to buckle at her knees, and Viki and the senator clutched at her upper arms to keep her from falling to the floor. The tall, sharp-featured man left Darmanian and the others to help guide the woman to a divan. Her eyes were blank and staring, the only present flaw in her dark beauty. She mumbled something unintelligible as her head rolled from side to side. It appeared as though she might be ill, almost comatose. Perhaps Darmanian had been prevailed upon to help her.

I had started up the stairs when Darmanian called to me. "Eric, we wondered where you had disappeared to."

I leaned on the banister as if it were a crutch. "I was just a bit under the weather in the library," I explained. "I'm feeling much better now, but I'm going to go up to my room."

Darmanian crossed the room to stand next to the staircase. His forefinger traced a column of animals and entwined grains that had been carved on the woodwork of the banister. "Eric," he asked gently, his eyes looking up to probe my own, "you weren't upset by tonight's session, were you?"

"Confused," I told him, "is a better word."

"You are of the opinion that I should remain aloof from the regression experience, that I should retain a more objective control," the hypnotist guessed correctly.

"I have neither the background knowledge nor the right to criticize your methods," I responded.

Darmanian smiled. "Eric, if I am truly going to devise a bold new kind of therapy, then I must dare to become a part of the experience so that I may understand it more completely. I must play my role as the marquis to the hilt if I am going to find a handle on which I might build a therapy to help Delores."

I frowned my inability to comprehend his strategy.

"You must have noticed that her waking behavior, as well as her dreams, have been increasingly disoriented," he said solemnly. "Obviously, she has an important link with her lifetime—be it real or imagined—as La Voisin; and if I am going to help her achieve a meaningful catharsis, then I must enter the experience and guide her through it.

I stood silently, feeling Darmanian's eyes pulling me into his understanding. His hand had left its stroking of the wooden images to play with the medallion, and his deft fingers had set it to spinning. I found myself somehow fascinated by the swirling disappearance and reappearance of the winged dragons. And the coruscating crystal caught the light in a manner that was remarkably beautiful.

"You do understand, don't you, Eric?" Darmanian suggested.

"I can appreciate your desire to explore new perimeters of the mind," I answered after a moment's consideration of his question. I was beginning to feel drained of energy once again.

"We can discuss your procedures more thoroughly in the morning," I said. "I really feel that I must now go to my room."

"Very well, Eric," Darmanian called after my retreating and ascending back. "Good night."

As soon as I entered my room, I walked into the bathroom and turned on the water in the big tub. I wanted baptism, renewal, cleansing. I watched the steam rising from the hot water rushing into the tub. Perhaps, I added, even a purging.

I hung my sport coat and trousers in the closet while I was waiting for the tub to fill. Ever since I was a kid, a good hot bath had been my remedy for depression, anxiety, frustration, nervous tension—whatever ailed me. It was probably an inherited trait from my Viking ancestors who sought the sauna to help them sweat away their problems.

I had just settled myself into the soothing, steaming waters when I heard a sound in my bedroom. The door closed. Footsteps creaked on the old floorboards.

"Who's there?" I called.

Viki Chung opened the door to the bathroom. She wore the bright red dress with the slit to mid-thigh that I had admired during the evening's session. A green dragon with studded rhinestone eyes curled on her left breast.

She entered the room wtihout hesitation, used a forefinger laughingly to draw a Chinese character on the steamed-over shaving mirror. "What you need," she told me, "is an Oriental bathgirl."

I reached for the large towel, prepared to cover my nakedness.

"Eric," she laughed. "I'm a registered nurse!"

"I didn't realize that we were going to play doctor and nurse tonight," I said, attempting to sound gruff. "And I don't remember asking you to make a house call."

"Before the session began tonight," she told me, "I noticed you rubbing the back of your neck now and then. That must be nervous tension, Eric."

I sunk lower into the bathwater. I couldn't help feeling self-conscious sitting there totally nude in the tub while a miniature Dragon Lady scrutinized me. I had placed my washcloth over a crucial area the moment she had poked her inquisitive head into my bathroom.

Viki Chung was really a very attractive lady. She was probably five-three, and if she had not fooled around with Mother Nature, she was very well endowed.

"I have come to give you a massage to relieve your tension," she said, smiling. "When I worked in a public hospital, I was famous for my bedtime massages."

"Are you certain that you didn't create more tension that you relieved?" I asked her.

"I know how to take care of all kinds of tension," Viki assured me. "I can handle whatever might come up," she winked, accenting the double entendre.

She arched an arm behind her back to unlatch a zipper. "It's hot in here," she said by way of explanation for her peeling the red dress over her shoulders.

Viki moved the dress carefully over her hips, then bent her knees one at a time so that she might step out of the encircling fabric. "That's better," she decreed, standing there before me in bra, panties, and strap shoes.

"Much better," I told her. "I wish the tub was larger."

"You wash off, soak a bit to relax the muscles," she prescribed. "I'll go open the rice wine."

"Hell, man," I said to myself as I leaned back in the tub. "Why fight it? This is the best thing that has happened to you since you got here!"

Viki was gone for about three minutes before she reentered, bearing two slim glasses. "Damn cork," she said by way of explanation for the length of time it took for her reappearance.

I sipped the chilled wine, found it dryer than I had expected. "Good," I said. Then feeling the afterglow, I added: "Kind of warms you up, doesn't it?"

Viki sat next to the tub on a small stool. "I can really warm you up." She smiled over the rim of her wine glass.

"I'll bet you can," I conceded. I took another sip of the wine. "I had an upset stomach earlier this evening," I told her. "But, as St. Paul once observed, a little wine is good for the stomach."

Viki studied my face carefully. "Did you really mean what you said during the session tonight? I mean about your being a man of goodness, a man who harbors angels, walks with God and all that."

"I guess so." I shrugged, surprised at her question.

"I've always tried to live as decent a life as I could under whatever circumstances confronted me."

Viki's brown eyes with their delightful almond slant remained unwaveringly on my face. "Delores told me that you only sinned on Saturday nights."

I laughed as I recalled the conversational reference. "We were joking about the cupids and the gargoyles over the doors of various rooms," I explained.

"It's Saturday night," she said softly. "Why don't you get out of the tub now so I can massage your neck and back." Her warm eyes were scant inches from my own.

"I've always had a weakness for blond men." She smiled. "You Nordic types turn me on."

My finger curled around a strand of her lush, black hair. "Opposites attract?"

"*Vive la différence,*" she teased, glancing down at my crotch. The washcloth seemed very small.

"You know," she told me, "you aren't at all bad-looking, Eric. Blue-eyed, blond, good chin line, nice build. You have a really nice sexual magnetism."

"How's your magnetism?" I asked. "Positive or negative?"

Her tongue moved out to lick her lips before she answered. "It is definitely positive tonight," she replied.

She left the small bathroom so that I might dry myself as well as possible in the humid closeness. I wrapped the towel about my middle and joined her as soon as possible.

Viki refilled my wine glass, bade me drink, then commanded me to lie down on my stomach across the bed.

I did as I was told, and I was almost instantly rewarded by her slim, yet powerful, fingers kneading my flesh. "Oh, Viki," I moaned in pleasure. "That is terrific."

After a few minutes, I felt only one handful of fingers working my muscles. Out of the corner of an eye, I saw Viki bending an arm behind her to unsnap her bra, then both sets of fingers were once again massaging my neck, shoulders, and back.

Soon I was aware of the unmistakable tracing of nipples across my upper back. "Ahh," I encouraged her. "They feel even better than your fingers."

Viki giggled girlishly, bent to slide a moist, warm tongue in my ear.

"That tickles!" I laugh-protested, crunching a protective shoulder against the pleasurable invader.

Viki's tongue began tracing warmth and moistness over my shoulders, down my sides, across the small of my back.

I rolled over on my back, put my hands on her smooth, bare shoulders, pulled her down on my chest. Her breasts were round and full, and they flattened against the pressure of our bodies meeting. She stretched her neck so that she could kiss me.

"Drink some more wine," she said. "Then I want to lick you some more."

It was like a kid being told to finish his ice cream so that he could have dessert.

The warmth of the wine blended nicely with the erotic feelings generated by the steady flicking of her tongue against my flesh. I was becoming more euphoric with each moist touch of that tireless instrument of pleasure. I felt as though I were floating on a soft cushion of cloud.

I was dumped back to earth by the fire of pain.

"I'm sorry, baby," Viki apologized. "I gave you a little nibble."

Her legs straddled my lower body, and she propped herself up with straightened arms so that she could bend over my chest and stomach with her mouth. Her long, black hair brushed my skin, adding to the pleasurable sensations as she renewed her tongue play.

"Unnh." I winced involuntarily as she nipped at my chest. There were other small bites after that, but she became more cautious about the depth at which she set her teeth.

Then her hungry tongue was moving below my waist, flicking lower and lower. There was no question that I was in a state of utmost readiness for whatever her next move might be.

I moaned in unrestrained esctasy as her warm mouth encircled me. And her incredibly skillful tongue brought waves of electrical fire as it showed me what it could really do.

But at that moment of heightened sensual awareness, an incredible thing occurred. It seemed as though I were suddenly in a corner of the ceiling looking down at the two of us romping on the bed. My body was moaning and writhing in unrestrained animal pleasure, but my head—my spirit, if you will—was still bobbing up there in a corner of the room. Not as a detached observer, I should explain, but as though it were an emotional motion picture camera, absorbing, reflecting, reacting, as well as recording. It was as if I had three or four perspectives flashing sensory data to my brain at the same time.

I have only a very dim memory of making love to Viki, but I am quite certain that I did.

I seem to remember clutching her firm buttocks,

experiencing the warm wonder of her flesh parting to receive my own. There were love cries, gaspings, whispered profanities.

Then I went wildly spinning into some crazy, runaway roller coaster that catapulted me into liquid flame.

Chapter Twenty-two

I stood naked in the midst of a clearing surrounded by tall, heavily branched trees. The cool night air puckered my skin and drew me nearer a roaring bonfire. Something sticky had been spread over my body. A red, swirling mist made it difficult for me to see things clearly.

There was a pile of stones at one end of the clearing. There seemed to be a platform draped with purple cloth on top of the stones. Some leering, grotesque black thing stood behind the platform. It had horns and a small torch was stuck between them. A gigantic penis curved out from beneath its belly. It was an idol of Satan.

A horn sounded from somewhere in the woods. At the same moment, both of my hands were clasped by someone on either side of me. Viki Chung had my left hand entwined in soft though firm fingers. Shelley Eberhart clutched my right hand. They were both naked.

Our linked hands joined us to a larger circle of living flesh. Naked men and women stood expectant, solemn-faced.

A horn sounded again, and Darmanian and Delores entered the clearing and stood before the image of Satan. Delores wore a purple robe covered with golden eagles. Darmanian's broad shoulders were draped with a robe of black.

Delores knelt, picked up a branch that lay to one side of the pile of stones. Darmanian got one from the opposite edge of the mound. Each member of the naked circle around me released one hand from the linkup and bent to grasp a stick. Shelley thrust a rough branch into my hand, and I felt a splinter pierce my palm.

Delores touched her stick to the flame burning between the dark image's horns. "I have now received Lucifer's light," she proclaimed. "Come ye to the altar to receive his living light!"

A compactly built man prodded me in the buttocks, and I joined the procession to the altar. Shelley Eberhart touched her branch to the flame, then stepped back to scowl at me, as if making sure that I understood what I was to do.

The red mist cloaked me again. When next I could see, I stood before the altar, a flaming torch clutched in my hand. Delores curtsied before the image of Satan. She knelt before his hindquarters and kissed them. Then she rose, moved in front of the idol, and kissed its erect penis.

All around me men and women shouted something that sounded very much like "Hallelujah!" Torches were stuck into the soft earth of the grove, and flagons of wine were produced by two men. Goblets were filled in generous, sloshing movements of the flagons.

"Drink! Drink!" Shelley said, nudging me. It was wine, red wine, but something I could not identify had been added to the brew.

"The Sabbat dance!" Viki laughed in expectation.

I was maneuvered into a back-to-back position with Shelley. Our hands were clasped, and our heads were turned so that we might face each other. From somewhere came the music of flute and drum.

It was a wild dance, circular in motion. I stumbled, fell several times, but there were always strong hands to bring me to my feet. Some of the dancers were wildly chanting words that I could never quite understand.

Shelley spun away from me, and I was facing a dark-haired woman, whose large breasts were bobbing to the eerie music. She turned me around so that I was facing in and she was facing out. We locked hands with other members of the circle, and I could see that all the men were facing in and the women were facing out. The pace became faster and faster until I thought I would surely collapse in a dizzy heap.

A horn sounded a signal to cease the festivities. I stood panting, catching my breath. All around me the other dancers were solemn-faced, sweat-sheened, breathing heavily.

Delores stood before the altar and began to chant what sounded like a jumble of backward Latin. My head suddenly jerked upright when I heard the name "Ansemo Diaz." My thoughts flashed back to my first night at Woodlands, when I lay in the humid closeness and heard Delores crying out that same name. And that next morning when I saw Darmanian in the garden stretch forth his arms and shout: "Ansemo Diaz."

I listened more carefully. "Astaroth" came from her chant. Then Asmodeus. Not Ansemo Diaz. But *Asmo-de-us*.

Delores held aloft something that looked like a black turnip. The circle shouted: "O Master, save us!"

Delores reached for a knife, removed a squirming toad from a cloth sack. With one deft movement she sliced the toad in half and let its blood splatter the pile of stones.

The red mist was again swirling thickly before my aching, burning eyes, but I saw Bishop De Shazo and Senator Harrigan, both clothed in red robes, step forward, each holding one arm of a white-robed girl. It was the same beautiful young girl I had seen earlier that evening. The emergency case.

Darmanian loomed over her, shouted something with Astaroth and Asmodeus in it. He turned her around to face the circle. The girl's eyes were still glassy, her lips moving like an automaton.

Delores squeezed half of the mangled toad over a large, silver goblet. Drops of blood oozed between her grasping fingers and fell into the chalice. Bishop De Shazo poured some wine into the goblet, and Delores swirled the mixture for a moment before she touched the rim to the girl's lips.

Darmanian lifted the white robe from her shoulders. The girl had been stripped naked, and an audible gasp of appreciation went up from the members of the circle. The young woman possessed a body that was not far from physical perfection.

"What a good choice for the preparatory sacrifice," someone whispered from behind my left shoulder.

My knees buckled, but powerful hands scooped under my armpits and held me from falling. *Sacrifice*. How I wanted to awaken from the hellish nightmare!

Viki and Shelley helped the girl lie down on the platform on the pile of stones. Viki placed a pillow beneath her head. Shelley surveyed the girl's slim figure, motioned for Viki to place another pillow beneath her slender buttocks.

Darmanian fitted a leering mask of Satan to his face, then crouched above the young woman. Viki and Shelley parted the girl's legs, and Darmanian lay atop her, his black robe covering them like a velvet nightfall.

The red mist blinded me. The next I knew, the men and women around me were cheering lustily. Darmanian had stepped down from the platform, and Viki was handing him a soft cloth. Shelley offered him a bejeweled chalice, from which he drank deeply.

The girl lay outstretched on the platform, her pillars of flesh still parted.

Sounds around me began to echo and hum in my brain. It seemed as though mouths, lips, tongues were searching out my most private parts. My head was throbbing.

Delores's voice cut through my pain and confusion. "*O Astaroth! O Asmodeus!*" she was shouting. "*O our most Holy Satan, we implore you!*" Her voice had begun to shriek in its intensity. "*We beg you to accept this sacrifice which we now offer to you. O Dark Ones, accept this gift of blood and grant that we may offer you yet a greater sacrifice come Beltane!*"

The red mist had blotted out all around me, but through a wispy parting of the churning scarlet clouds I saw Delores standing beside the dazed young woman, lying on what I now knew to be an altar. She raised the knife as high as her slender right arm could take it, then she plunged the blade into the chest of the beautiful young woman.

My scream echoed down a thousand corridors in my mind.

Chapter Twenty-three

Sunlight stabbed my right eye with a searing branding iron. I closed the lid tightly to escape the pain.

I heard birds happily greeting a bright April morning.

I turned my head away from the light, opened both eyes. My entire skull had been thoroughly scraped clean, dried, and stuffed with mud.

I had no tongue, only a rough, stiff rag that had been provided by the same mad scientist who had reassembled my skull cavity.

I was lying on my bed in the yellow guest room with the cupid above the door.

"Viki!" The sound came out of my mouth like the death bleat of a wounded elk. "Viki!" I tried again with somewhat better results.

No answer. It seemed safe to assume that I was alone. I got one hand and arm under me and pushed up. The mud in my skull had become concrete. It is difficult sitting up when one's head weighs a hundred pounds.

I winced at a new pain in my supporting hand. I sat up, swung my legs over the side of bed, and examined my palm. A wood splinter had provoked a reddened area of flesh.

I sucked in my breath as an image of Shelley handing me a torch rippled across my brain. Then my stomach churned as I saw Delores plunging the knife into the girl's chest.

My bare foot touched the empty bottle of rice wine. "Never again that Oriental ambush!" I vowed. "That stuff gives nightmares that only advanced winos should have to suffer through."

God, with all the sessions' emphasis on sacrifices and satanic rituals, it was no wonder my drunken dream had turned into such a damn, gory nightmare.

It seemed to take me several minutes to walk to the bathroom door, push it open. My shattered eyeballs were having difficulty reassembling themselves into a facsimile of their former, well-functioning selves, but when I was at last able to study myself in the shaving mirror, I was startled to see a dozen or more areas on my upper chest and shoulders where Viki had punctured the flesh with her teeth. Patches of dried blood scabbed swollen skin mounds. On my neck, where the flesh had not been broken, blue sucker splotches indicated where intense mouth pressure had been applied.

I leaned weakly on the edge of the big tub and turned the hot-water faucet as open as it could twist. I needed to soak the booze, the bites, and the bad dream out of my head and hide.

I let the water build to the overflow drain. It was as hot as I could stand it. The entire bathroom was steamed. The shaving mirror was a collection of moisture droplets. I lowered myself into the tub as rapidly as possible without feeling like a lobster tossed in a boiling pot. I scrunched my knees so that the water level came just below my ears. I soaked the washcloth and plastered it over my face.

I had to get some tea, some dry toast, something to settle my stomach. Dream images kept floating up from my unconscious. The naked dancers, the stone altar, the leering idol of Satan, Darmanian mounting the drugged girl, and—worst of all—Delores stabbing the sacrificial victim's exposed chest.

I slid the washcloth from my face, raised my right hand from the hot water. How had I got that splinter in my palm? Again I saw Shelley's impatient scowl as she thrust the branch into my hand. The dream had been so vivid.

"Asmodeus," I whispered. "Astaroth." I wondered how Ed Vogel would interpret my dream.

I stayed in the tub until the steam-hot water was becoming tepid. Then, reluctantly, I removed my wrinkled body from the bath. My hands had become as crinkled as those of the world's oldest man. And as I reached for a bath towel, I had to admit that the rest of my body didn't feel much younger.

I toweled dry, endured the ordeal of shaving, then, towel knotted about my waist, I walked into the bedroom in search of appropriate clothing that would get me admitted to Agnes's breakfast table. I doubted if she would have been impressed by my steamed torso wrapped in a makeshift sarong.

I had just pulled on a pair of gray slacks when I heard Delores calling my name. Her tone was urgent, and her small fist beat a frenzied accompaniment on the door panel. "Eric, for godsakes, let me in!"

The moment I opened the door, she was in my arms. I staggered back, astonished.

"Eric, you've got to help me!"

Her eyes were red-rimmed and puffy. She wore a gauzy summer frock of pale green color. The sleeves were long and flowing, and she seemed almost ethereal.

But as pitiful as she appeared at that moment, I could not banish the image of her standing bedecked in the purple robe embroidered with hundreds of golden eagles. I could not blink out the horror of seeing Delores—even if in a dream—sinking the blade into her naked victim's body.

I put a hand on each shoulder, as if to pacify her by contact alone. I was about to inquire what her distress might be, when Delores's eyes suddenly widened and her mouth became a grim line.

"I see that the saint has become a sinner," she said slowly, weighing each word, her forefinger gingerly tracing the outline of one of Viki's bites.

Embarrassed, I opened a dresser drawer in search of a shirt to match my trousers.

"Don't bother, Eric," Delores smiled, her eyes half-lidding, seductively. "I rather like those decorations on your chest. And neck. And shoulders. Little red badges of courage. Were you brave, Eric?"

I began to unfold a shirt, but Delores snatched it from me and threw it across the room.

"Who got to you?" she demanded. "Viki or Shelley?"

Her eyes were furious, scathing. I was puzzled by her apparent jealousy.

"It was Saturday night, wasn't it?" she said, sneering. "You only sin on Saturday nights. That's what you told me the day you arrived."

She pressed her body against mine and slid surprisingly strong arms about my lower back. "Did you enjoy her?" she asked, petulantly, squeezing us hard together.

Her brown eyes looked almost directly into mine. With her model's height and her heels, she was nearly as tall as I. Her lips were parted, inviting. Then before I had a chance to respond to the erotic suggestion of her nearness, she began again to cry. Her embrace became a desperate kind of clutching for support.

"Eric, you must help me!" she sobbed. "You must help me get away from here. Now!"

"I don't understand," I said, my hands caressing her slender back in a confused gesture that I hoped might be comforting. "What do you mean, you must get away from Woodlands?"

"Are you my friend, Eric?" she pleaded.

"I suppose I am," I answered honestly. I certainly was not her enemy. I could not imagine Delores having enemies. She seemed so fragile and sensitive. That was why the regressive personality of La Voisin was, in my opinion, so foreign to the woman who now stood before me so vulnerable and confused.

"Drive me to my mother's," she asked.

"Where does she live?" I countered. I could envision myself driving a distraught Delores to Montana or somewhere a thousand miles away.

"She lives *here*," Delores answered impatiently. "Don't you remember? She lives here with my sister, Sharon."

"Yes, yes," I said. "I had forgotten."

"Get dressed," she said, crossing the room to pick up the shirt she had only a moment before sent flying. "We'll take the station wagon."

"Can't it wait until after breakfast?" I asked, concerned about my queasy stomach. "What's your hurry?"

She seized both my arms in a grip that drove her fingernails into my flesh. Her eyes were mad with fear: "They are going to burn me, Eric."

Chapter Twenty-four

It was nearly ten that Sunday morning, April 23, when I ran the doorbell of Eleanor Touraine's attractive, one-hundred-year-old Tudor-style home on the outskirts of Saratoga Springs. The bright skies had clouded over, and it looked as though it might soon begin to rain.

While I had been getting dressed, I insisted that Delores telephone her mother and prepare her for our visit. I knew, as the poet Robert Frost had once written, that home is a place where they always have to take you in; but I still believed in giving even one's family fair warning. Especially when you were coming home scattered and trembling.

Eleanor Touraine answered the door in an elegant, blue silk dressing gown. Her fingers pinched the material together at the throat to protect herself from the chill wind that had begun to rustle the branches of the large weeping willow tree in the front yard.

"Please come in, Mr. Storm," she invited. "I greatly appreciate your bringing Delores home."

I stepped aside to permit Delores to embrace her mother, then I entered the warm, comfortable home.

Delores burrowed her face into the nape of her mother's neck and began to weep in great sucking gasps and sobs. Eleanor was even taller than her older daughter, and she, like Delores, might have been a model. I knew, however, that she had been a working journalist for several years.

In the few moments when she hadn't been huddled by the car window, clutching her sides and shivering, Delores had told me bits and snatches about her family on the drive to the Touraine home. Because of her sporadic bursts of lucidity, I knew that the woman approaching me from the room immediately off the entrance hallway had to be her sister, Sharon.

Her voice was pleasantly low. "Please call me Sharon," she smiled.

She was flaxen-haired with brown eyes even larger than her sister's and was walking toward me with her hand extended in greeting. She was dressed in a sensible gray suit with low-heeled black leather knee boots. Considerably shorter than her mother or her sister, she was as voluptuous of body as they were slender. Although there was no excess weight on her frame, she gave the appearance of a buxom Earth Mother.

At her side was one of the most beautiful children I had ever encountered. She was as blond as her mother, but her skin seemed to have the coloration and translucency of pearl. Large eyes appeared to be carried in the Touraine genes, but the child's eyes were almost preternaturally large and expressive. And interestingly, Sharon's daughter's eyes were a brilliant blue.

"This is my daughter, Alyse," Sharon said.

The girl gave me a fleeting smile. Her attention was on Delores.

"What's wrong with Auntie Dee?" she asked, her lovely features distorted by concern.

At the sound of the girl's voice, Delores left her mother's embrace and knelt before Alyse.

"Oh, my darling," Delores said, her cheeks glistening with tears. "Auntie Dee isn't feeling well."

Alyse put her arms about her aunt's neck and kissed her.

Sharon smiled at the two of them. She seemed unaffected by the emotionalism of her sister. "Alyse and Delores have always been very close."

"Yes," Eleanor agreed. "It's enough to make you believe in ESP. This morning Alyse woke up and said, 'Something is wrong with Auntie Dee.' And you know, Mr. Storm, it wasn't but thirty minutes later that Delores called and said that she was upset and had to see us."

"As an assistant professor of biology," Sharon said, "I'm not at all convinced about such things as ESP; but I must admit that those two certainly have a strange rapport that has always made for a very special relationship."

"Really?" I wondered, thinking again of the associations suggested by that damnable circle of Darmanian's.

"Yes," Sharon laughed. "Delores might forget Alyse's birthday, but if the kid skins her knee, I can expect a call from my big sister wondering if anything has happened to her niece."

"Remarkable," I said, "I must say that I am open-minded about such things as psychic links between people, especially people who care about each other."

Sharon shrugged and did marvelous things to the front of her blouse. "It's just pretty hard to test such things in a laboratory, Mr. Storm."

"I imagine so," I agreed. Then I added, "Please, Sharon, Eleanor, let's be on a first-name basis. I'm Eric."

"Very good, Eric," Eleanor said, taking my arm and beginning to lead me into the living room. "Would you like something to eat?"

Delores looked up from her kneeling position on the floor where she still embraced Alyse. "Please, Mom," she said, laughing. "I took Eric away from his breakfast!"

"How gallant!" Eleanor smiled. "You must be rewarded for your self-sacrifice."

Delores straightened to her full height. "Alyse and I will scramble Eric some eggs. Okay, Alyse?"

Before I could politely protest, Delores and the lovely child had left the room, hand in hand, giggling as though they were joining the teddy bears' picnic.

The room into which Eleanor ushered me was a colorful burst of tastefully selected Early American furniture and scatter rugs. The evening before, someone had begun a fire in the large, stone fireplace but had abandoned the project. She bade me sit in an oversized stuffed chair next to a serving cart on which rested a coffee pot and several cups. Eleanor sat to my left on a long sofa with an intricately knitted comforter across its back. Sharon poured three cups of coffee, and when she had served us, she joined her mother.

"Is it the nightmares again, Eric?" Sharon asked, coming directly to the point.

Eleanor sipped at her coffee, then asked: "You do know that Delores has these dreams about being burned alive, don't you?"

I indicated that I was aware of her nightmares.

"These dreams have always bothered her whenever she has been under stress," Eleanor explained. "Delores has always been nervous, even as a child."

"It's probably something that Darmanian has done." Sharon frowned. There was acid in her voice, and it had dripped heavily over the reference to the hypnotist. It was obvious that Sharon did not approve of Darmanian.

"Our Delores," Eleanor said, her eyes lowered, "has never been what you might call a really stable person. She's never been emotionally strong. You see, her father suffered a nervous breakdown at a crucial period in her life, and I think it affected Delores adversely. She's always been so sensitive."

"Mommy, please!" Delores's voice had taken on a little-girl whine. She had somehow managed to walk into the room without any of us having heard her.

Eleanor jumped to her feet, threw a protective arm around Delores's shoulders. "You've always pushed yourself so hard," she said as she guided her to a place between them on the sofa.

Delores's face became pale and drawn. There was an aura of distraction that permeated her every gesture. She began once again to weep, and her mother and her sister each placed a sheltering or protective arm somewhere on her body.

It seemed as though Eleanor felt compelled to

chant a litany of Delores's past difficulties: "In high school you pushed too hard. In college you nearly had a nervous breakdown. You almost killed yourself when you were modeling. You push yourself too hard."

Delores's teeth caught at her lower lip, and her weeping died somewhere in the memory of her most basic fear. "I know now what has always frightened me, tormented me."

She grabbed Eleanor's arms and slid off the sofa. Her eyes were wide with horror. "I don't want to be burned again!"

"It *is* that damn dream again!" Sharon cursed.

"I don't want to be burned again," Delores repeated, her voice raising. "This time I want to live!"

"What does she mean?" Sharon asked rhetorically, her arms dropping noisily to her sides in frustration. "I mean, what does she *really* mean? Does she mean *burned* in the sense of being cheated, swindled, stung, screwed?"

It was at this point that I first detected a peculiar sort of humming or buzzing sound in the room. It began as a little source of irritation in my ears, but it soon became an auditory nag.

I shifted uneasily in my seat, glancing about the room to see if I might detect the origin of the sound. An electric clock, perhaps. A lamp. A neon light. Some appliance.

Delores began to produce an incredible series of sounds—bleatings, whimperings, moanings. Sharon shook her by the shoulders until at last words formed: "Terrible. Torture. The pokers. They put red-hot pokers up inside me!"

Delores grabbed her sister's forearms. "Don't you remember? You were there, too!" she shouted. "And now, because of the terrible thing I did, it will happen to me again!"

"What terrible thing did she do?" Eleanor frowned her concern, looked at me for an explanation.

I could only think of the nightmare I had had. I could only think at that moment of Delores driving the knife into the helpless flesh. But I said nothing.

Sharon put her own hands on Delores's. "Calm down, baby," she said in the tone that seemed reserved for the disciplining of students. It had no effect on Delores.

"Montvoisin!" Delores blurted out, getting to her feet, her breath beginning to come in short gasps. "La Voisin. What does that mean to you?"

Sharon looked up at her sister. "The names mean nothing to me."

Desperate to help, Eleanor suggested, "Your father was of French heritage. Have you discovered an old family name?"

Delores threw back her head and emitted a shrill scream of a laugh that might have been mockery.

Eleanor rose from the sofa to place both hands on her daughter's shoulders. She was startled by the pain in Delores's eyes.

The buzzing sound that I had heard was growing louder.

"Baby, baby," Eleanor cooed, pressing her older child to her breasts. "Baby Dee-dee. Please tell Mommy what is wrong!"

Delores pushed away from her mother, reached down to seize Sharon's wrists, and pulled her to her feet. "You are Marguerite! You are Marguerite!" she screamed at her.

"What the hell are you talking about?" Sharon demanded. Delores's hands had become vises of flesh, squeezing her wrists, and at last Sharon cried out in painful protest.

"I can't stand that noise!" Delores screamed, releasing Sharon's wrists to clamp her hands over her ears. "Stop that noise!"

"Auntie Dee! Auntie Dee!" The distressed Alyse, impatient with waiting for her aunt's return to the kitchen, had come into the room in time to see Delores's frenzy. "Help Auntie Dee!" she begged. "Stop the noise!"

Sharon caught Alyse's arm. "I've got to get her out of here!"

"What is that noise?" Eleanor asked, taking cognizance of the humming sound for what appeared to be the first time. "Is there a timer left on in the kitchen?"

"Maybe it's an alarm clock upstairs," Sharon said. "Let me go see. And I'm taking this young lady upstairs with me."

Alyse squealed angrily, defiantly, but Sharon scooped her into her arms and picked her up bodily.

Delores dropped to her knees, clutched at her mother's legs, and buried her face into Eleanor's waist. Her cries, though muffled, were terrible to hear: "The soldiers! The priests! Keep them away from me! I don't want to burn. I don't want to burn!"

I could see Eleanor wrestling with decision. "Eric!" she demanded of me. "Should we call a doctor?"

"I think we must," I said.

"Soldiers. Priests. Terrible. The burning. The burning!" Delores shrieked. "Oh, my Holy Lover! Why did you forsake me?"

Eleanor tried to pull Delores up from her kneeling position, tried to pry loose her clutching arms. "What has happened to you?" Eleanor shouted in undefinable rage and fear, the tears wet on her cheeks. "What has happened to you?"

Sharon came back into the room from her exploration of the upstairs. Alyse was not with her. "I couldn't find anything that might have been making that humming sound," she said, "but it seems to have stopped."

In all the cacophony of pain, fear, and emotional chaos, I had momentarily forgotten about the humming. Sharon was correct. Whatever it had been, it had left us.

Delores began to intone a chant, a ritual, a meaningless mumble.

"God damn it," Sharon growled. "I know that charlatan Darmanian is behind this!"

"Never again the burning!" Delores was shouting over and over. "Never again the burning!"

"A doctor!" Eleanor told Sharon. "Call Dr. Tosca. Now!"

Eleanor struggled with Delores's maniacal grip on her legs. "Please, Eric," she begged. "Please take Delores."

I pried open Delores's fingers, freed Eleanor, then I took the trembling, chanting, sobbing woman into my arms and led her back to the sofa.

"Eric," Delores said, looking at me as though we had been separated for hours, "I haven't served you your scrambled eggs."

She struggled to get to her feet, but I held her fast. "Let me go, Eric," she whined. "I promised you your eggs."

"Let her go, Eric," Sharon said, reentering the room after calling the doctor. "Sometimes in a time of panic, the best thing you can do is to let a person perform some menial, ordinary task. It can help the person get a grip on reality."

I hesitated but decided to accept Sharon's diagnosis. Delores squirmed free and ran to the kitchen.

"Dr. Tosca said he would be here as soon as possible," Sharon said. "Lucky I got him just after they got home from church."

Eleanor had slumped against the back of the sofa. "Oh, my baby," she weeped openly. "What in God's name has happened to her?"

Sharon irritably cocked her head to one side. "Eric, the humming sound again," she said. "It's coming from the kitchen."

"No! No! Noooo!" we heard Delores screaming. "Stay away from meee!"

Sharon began to race for the kitchen. I jumped to my feet to join her.

Neither of us made it.

The kitchen door burst open, and Delores stood before us, completely wreathed in flames. Her dark brown hair had been transformed into a fiery halo. Her mouth was opening and closing and issuing horrible whimpering sounds. Her eyes were rolling wildly with pain. She raised arms enveloped in fire, then pitched forward, almost at Sharon's feet.

Eleanor was still screaming when Dr. Tosca arrived. Sharon and I had wrapped Delores in a throw rug and had extinguished the cruel flames. Mercifully, she was unconscious.

Her hair burned away, her flesh blackened, seared, charred, Delores died five hours later. She never regained consciousness.

Chapter Twenty-five

The coroner theorized that somehow, as Delores was fixing the eggs, the sleeve of her gauzy, pale yellow dress had brushed against the flame from the gas stove. The man-made fabric had erupted as though it had been spun from kerosene.

Those were the physical reasons for Delores Touraine's death.

Her nightmare had been realized. The reality she feared most had been activated. She died by flames.

Delores Touraine's funeral took place on Thursday, April 27, a bright, sunny day that suggested any number of allusions about life going on, death and resurrection, the process of birth and grave in which all mortals become involved, regardless of personal choice.

I didn't actually notice Darmanian until I had turned to retrace my footsteps toward the station wagon, which I had parked beyond the cemetery gate. I had left early that morning to drive and to think before the ten-thirty funeral service. I had not seen the hypnotist at the formal memorial observation, but he now stood tall and erect at the edge of Delores's grave. Behind him stood Viki Chung, Shelley Eberhart, and Don Gruber.

I hesitated a moment, then decided to join the group at the graveside.

Sharon Touraine got to Darmanian before I did.

As I would come to know Sharon, I soon learned that she was a person who always spoke her mind.

"Darmanian," she began in an even voice, "I know that somehow you are responsible for my sister's death." Sharon's gloved hand indicated the open grave in an accusing gesture.

Darmanian turned toward Sharon, slowly pursed his lips, then directed his attention back to the casket that encased his mistress.

"Hey, kid," Shelley spoke up. "Get hold of yourself. You've got no reason to talk to Darmanian that way. He loved Delores. We all did."

Sharon stared at her as if she were carefully considering her words. She turned to look over her shoulder at the tall figure of her mother standing on the other side of the open grave. Alyse, I learned later, had been left with friends, as the two women had judged her too distraught to attend the funeral.

"It seemed as though you did love Delores when you two were starving together as models in New York City," Sharon agreed with Shelley. "But now it appears that you've thrown your lot in with Darmanian."

"Darmanian pulled my act together when I really needed help," Shelley said. "You've got no reason to badmouth him. You can't blame him for Delores's death."

Sharon would not be placated. "I've heard about Darmanian the miracle worker until I could vomit. I know he did something to totally screw up Delores's head. Maybe you helped him do it. Maybe," she added, her eyes sweeping the rest of the group flanking Darmanian on either side, "maybe all of you helped him do it."

Viki stepped forward. She had worn her nurse's uniform to the funeral, complete with the little white cap. A black cape draped about her shoulders seemed her concession to mourning. "We were all friends of Delores's," she said sharply. "You've no right to speak to us in such a manner."

"If you were friends of my sister's," Sharon accused them, "you would have helped her get free of this quack."

Sharon looked at Don Gruber to see if he would be the next to attempt to run interference for the hypnotist. But the big man just stood there with his hands in the pockets of his trench coat and gave her a crooked, one-sided smile.

Darmanian chose at last to break his silence. "What causes you to say such things, Sharon?"

Sharon's lips compressed themselves to thin, angry lines. "There lies cause and effect," she said in a harsh whisper as she pointed toward the open grave.

"Delores's death was a terrible blow to each of us, Sharon," he told her. "We often look for someone we can blame when such awful tragedies touch our lives."

"Oh, I've found the one to blame," Sharon said, fighting back tears. "Somehow you got inside my sister's head and applied some lever that killed her just as surely as if you had chopped off her head with a sword."

"Come, now, Sharon," Darmanian protested. "I wasn't even present when her terrible accident took place."

"You had already scrambled her brains," Sharon snapped back. "She was almost totally irrational when Eric brought her to our home. If that accident had not occurred, it would only have been a matter of time before she would have suffered a complete breakdown. Or maybe taken her own life."

"How can you suggest that I am responsible in any way for Delores's death?" Darmanian demanded of Sharon. "If you knew the slightest bit about hypnosis—"

Sharon's voice was stern. "I'm not certain that there is such a thing as hypnosis. Maybe it is all power of suggestion. But I'm sure a clever hypnotist can plant all kinds of hooks in a subject's mind and make him do things that would normally be beyond consideration."

Darmanian smiled patronizingly. "And you believe that I could make Delores do things against her will?"

"I believe that you know all kinds of techniques to make anyone do things against his or her will," Sharon asserted.

Darmanian laughed softly. "You give me too much credit."

Viki Chung interceded once again on Darmanian's behalf. "This man's record as an effective hypnotherapist speaks for itself," she stated. "Go home, Sharon. Your grief has distorted your reason."

"And the experimental group sessions have probably distorted yours," Sharon countered.

Darmanian's eyes narrowed with sudden proprietary defensiveness. "What do you know of the experimental sessions?" he wanted to know. His voice seemed tinged with anger.

"I don't know enough," Sharon answered him. "If I did, I'm sure you'd be behind bars!"

"Delores told you about the sessions?" Viki pressed her.

"She said that Darmanian was making her remember things," Sharon said. Then, her eyes smoldering with contempt, she returned her attention to Darmanian.

"No, Darmanian. I don't know what was going on in those sessions, but whatever you were doing, I accuse you of having done it in a manner so irresponsible that you helped bring about the death of my sister."

Darmanian's voice was soft, calm. "Sharon, I think that you must attend one of our sessions and see for yourself what is occurring."

I felt an inner turmoil of confusion and apprehension. Until I heard it with my own ears, I was unaware that I had emitted a rasp of protest deep in my throat. Darmanian turned to glare at me with menace crackling from his glowing eyes.

"I'm certain that Sharon could not consider such an invitation while she is in mourning," I said to Darmanian.

Darmanian's eyes became brilliant globes of blue flame. He opened his mouth to speak to me, but Sharon was the quicker to respond.

"The day after Dad died, Mom got out the next issue of the newspaper and Delores went on one of her most important modeling assignments," she said. "I can't imagine Delores wanting me to wear a black armband and retreat from the world to mourn. I wouldn't miss a chance to attend one of these sessions."

"We are not meeting tonight, in memory of Delores," Darmanian said. "But we come together again on Saturday night at eight o'clock."

Chapter Twenty-six

Miss Lundby had a number of telephone messages for me when I returned from the cemetery. They were all from Ed Vogel.

I heard the voices of Darmanian and the others coming from the library as I ascended the staircase to the second floor. I would call Ed from my room.

It was nine fifteen when I dialed the Vogel's number. Ed picked up the receiver on the second ring.

"Eric! Thank God! I've been hoping you'd get my messages," his husky voice rasped.

"Why wouldn't I?" I wondered. "What's so important?"

"What's important is that you get out of Woodlands," he said, his voice rising insistently. "Go back to New York."

"I've just about reached that conclusion myself, Ed. I've decided to abandon the project. Darmanian is not interested in the biography anymore."

Vogel's laughter was hard, mirthless. "Darmanian is

playing for much higher stakes than the recognition afforded him by a book about his life and work, Eric. Your evil-eyed friend is embarking on the ultimate power trip."

"I'm certain there's a bit of powerplaying in the group experiments, Ed," I conceded. "But I think his primary motive is—"

"Eric, can't you see beyond the end of your nose?" Vogel interrupted. "Haven't things begun to form any sort of pattern in your head? Haven't you begun to see Darmanian for the evil manipulator that he is?"

"Ed,"—I scowled into the receiver—"I resent both the tone and the approach you're using."

"Oh, Gawd!" Ed moaned. "You snatch a man away from the jaws of a tiger and he complains that you ripped a button off his shirt. Eric, just shut up and listen to me! I want to save your ass—and probably your soul!"

I've always been an easy mark for the earnest pitch, so I decided to let Ed have his say.

"I read in the paper about the terrible thing that happened to Delores Touraine," he began. "How she burst into flames."

"Yes," I said, "I was there. It was an accident. Her sleeve—"

Ed seemed determined that I should not complete a sentence. "It was no accident," he snarled. "She was ritually executed."

"That's preposterous!"

"Listen to this," Ed advised me, "then decide what's preposterous."

I could hear him flipping the pages of a book. He took a noisy swallow of what I supposed was his ever-present glass of fruit juice.

"I found this in an old history of the black arts," he said by way of preamble. "*The True History of Necromancy, Alchemy, and True Magick* by Angus G. McWane. It was published by a London press in 1847. It's one of my rarest books, and for some damn reason I didn't think to refer to it until after I read about Delores's fiery death. Some damn bell rang inside my head."

"Okay, Ed," I sighed impatiently. "Ring some bell inside my head."

Vogel cleared his throat, took another sip of his fruit juice. "According to McWane's history, the Marquis Jean de Sainte-Croix first set about to wrest control of La Voisin's coven away from her. Although he had become a wizard of the highest degree, he was no match for La Voisin. Her powers far exceeded his. So he decided to use the ways of a man with a maid to win her allegiance to him. Together they began to practice a unique method of sex magic. By the way, Aleister Crowley later tried to duplicate it."

"So you're saying that the marquis and La Voisin were rivals, as well as lovers?"

"Well, he saw it that way," Ed explained. "She was much more open toward him, much more giving and sharing. Maybe because of her early life in the streets she was a little awed by his position, his wealth, his manners, his education.

"Anyway," he went on, "the account has it that one night the demon Asmodeus—"

"Who?" I asked, feeling my flesh pimple. I had a mental flash of Darmanian lifting his arms to the morning sun, of Delores raising her arms to the idol in my dream, both of them shouting, "Asmodeus."

"Asmodeus is one of the principal henchmen of Satan," Vogel said by way of identification. "So one night the demon Asmodeus appeared to the marquis and told him that he had been judged eligible to become Satan's principal moral emissary on Earth."

"How does one achieve such eligibility?" I asked.

"The marquis's work had been deemed worthy, his devotion found acceptable, and his sacrifices had been received with favor by Satan," Ed replied.

"Sacrifices?" I questioned.

"Yeah," Ed responded. "The marquis was in the habit of regularly sacrificing both infants and young children to Satan. He didn't place as many on the altar as La Voisin, but she conducted commercial Sabbats. The marquis spent more time in fasting, meditation, and cultivating visions."

"Because of his piety, if that's the word," I commented, "the marquis found greater favor in the eyes of Satan than La Voisin."

"Yeah," Ed agreed, then qualified, "but he knew that in ritual magic one must have the female and male balance. And he also knew that La Voisin was the female with the greatest power in all of Paris—if not in all of France."

"So even though La Voisin's magical powers were supposedly greater than the marquis's," I observed, "Satan selected him for the position of ultimate power because his waters ran a bit deeper."

"Right," Vogel said. "And then the marquis really started pressing La Voisin to help him achieve this preeminent status. And according to the account in McWane's book, she did so willingly and with devotion to her lover. She began to take a back seat in the ritual observances, serving as a mute high priestess to his officiating at the ceremonies. She became, in essence, his assistant."

I considered this for a moment. "And La Voisin was willing to surrender her ego to that of her lover's aspirations."

"Well, of course, the marquis promised her that she would always serve as his high priestess and share his throne as the satanic pope, so to speak, of Earth."

"But you're suggesting duplicity on the marquis's part," I prompted him.

"That's right," Vogel told me. "He wanted the candy store all to himself. And things got complicated when Asmodeus revealed that the propitiatory sacrificial lamb had been incarnated in the form of Angelique, La Voisin's granddaughter. Further, it was decreed that eight days before the propitiatory sacrifice was to occur on the Sabbat observance of Beltane, May Eve, La Voisin must perform a preparatory sacrifice of a young woman perfect of limb and preferably a virgin."

My whole body was jolted as my memory banks flashed the dream images of Delores plunging the knife into the perfect body of the beautiful young woman. A dreadful fear seized my stomach and forced me to lean back against the headboard of my bed.

"In addition," Vogel continued, "while the maiden was to be sacrificed, a man of character, goodness, and godliness must be debauched and debased."

I thought of Viki mocking my "harboring of angels" before she began biting my body and making love to me. I recalled Delores's comment that next morning when she asked if the saint had become a sinner. I remembered again within that wretched dream when I presented my torch at Satan's altar.

"Once La Voisin had chanted the preparatory ritual and performed the sacrifice of the young woman perfect of limb, the marquis no longer needed her," Ed said. "Again, according to McWane's book, the marquis at this point betrayed La Voisin to the Chambre Ardente. In other words, he delivered her to the burning."

"And then the marquis became the great satanic pope?" I prodded my storyteller.

Vogel snorted derisively. "If he had, the world would be an even greater madhouse than it is. Armageddon would have been visited upon us in 1679, and the Four Horsemen of the Apocalypse would be running even more rampant then they have been these past couple of centuries."

"You really believe all of this," I said incredulously. "I thought you were merely a student of metaphysics. You are really into all of this. I should have known when you told me you had clairvoyant and precognitive visions."

Ed's voice was soft, yet strongly affirmative. "Yes, Eric, I do believe everything that I'm telling you. Let me finish:

"Although La Voisin was not burned at the stake until February twenty-third, 1680, she was arrested on April twenty-third, 1679."

I wanted Ed to continue his recitation without interruption, but I found myself blurting: "April twenty-third. The day Delores died!"

"The day she died in flames," Ed emphasized. "But to get back to the marquis three hundred years ago, what he had not counted on was Marguerite hiding Angelique from the coven. He had gone into seclusion to prepare himself spiritually. He was not to appear again until the observance of Beltane, the night of the Great Sacrifice—which, by the way, falls on Sunday, April thirtieth, this year.

"When the marquis arrived at the place of worship that night, he found the coven scattered, the principals either slain or jailed by the police," Ed said. "Confused, angry, the marquis fled Paris, probably for Switzerland."

"And there the story ends?" I asked him.

"No, my friend," Vogel replied. "It began again here in Saratoga Springs. I believe Darmanian to be the present incarnation of the Marquis Jean de Sainte-Croix. I believe that he has the soul knowledge to recognize the principal members of his Parisian coven and that he has been activating them over the years by hypnotic regression."

"Oh, Ed, come on, man," I complained. "And you think he's about to become the great satanic pope?"

"He will if he finds Angelique and is able to accomplish the Great Sacrifice," Ed answered without hesitation. "And I think he's found her."

"What makes you think so?" I demanded.

"Because he has once again delivered La Voisin—that is, Delores—to the flames—and much more quickly this time—and I fear that the preparatory sacrifice has already been made," he said, firm in his conviction.

"What," I asked, feeling beads of sweat pop out along my upper lip and forehead, "makes you think that *any* sacrifice has been committed?"

"You don't read the local papers, do you?" he asked. He did not wait for my answer, but he pressed on with his point.

"This morning the *Times-Union* carried a story

about a girl who has been missing since last Saturday night. Her name is Angela Tarrante. Her picture shows a very beautiful brunette. The story says she was a runner-up in the Miss New York beauty contest. It also says that she got the perfect figure award. She was twenty years old. Came from a strict Italian-American Catholic family. She was a secretary in Tom Harrigan's law office—"

Ed's words were beginning to sound as though they were issuing from an echo chamber. The entire room began to waver in sickening, throbbing pulsations. A gory montage of images of Delores plunging the knife again and again into the breast of the beautiful young brunette, "perfect of limb," swirled about my horrified brain.

"Ed," I gasped, "Oh Jesusjesusjesus!"

"What is it, Eric?"

An oppressive bubble was trying to burst free from my stomach. "Ed"—I managed to speak in short, rapid sentences—"I don't know about incarnations and time and space. But the group . . . Darmanian . . . believes that Sharon Touraine is Marguerite. And that her daughter, Alyse, is Angelique."

"Oh, God!" Ed's voice sounded like a great sobbing cry. "And the preparatory sacrifice? Do you know anything about it? Has it happened?"

My fingers gripped the bedspread. I felt as though I might faint at any moment. "I had a dream. Saturday night. I saw a pretty brunette, beautiful figure. I saw . . . in the dream . . . saw Delores sacrifice her on an altar. But I know it was *just* a dream!"

"Eric," Ed said, his voice heavy with concern, "you poor bastard. Listen, you've got to get out of there at once."

"Sharon"—I pushed past my nausea—"Sharon is coming here—"

There was a clicking sound and the line went dead.

My malaise was instantly supplanted by cold fear. Someone had been listening to our conversation.

I sat numbly on the edge of my bed, feeling very much like a punished child who had been sent to his room. At any moment the door would open and someone would be there to administer my spanking.

There was no longer any need to observe the amenities. There was no obligatory knocking. My door swung open on its hinges, and Darmanian stood there, flanked on his right by Don Gruber, on his left by the tall, thin man I had seen on the Saturday night when I had experienced my vivid dream. I still prayed that it had been *only* a dream.

Darmanian was silent for a long moment before he spoke. His eyes were pulling upon my own with such intensity that I felt as though he sought to bring me to my feet by their power alone. The fingers of his left hand stroked his medallion.

"Eric," he began, "I don't want you to speak with Mr. Vogel again."

I tried for the role of the indignant house guest. "What right have you to listen to my—?"

"I have a right to do whatever I wish in this house," he interrupted my attempted tirade. "Everything that happens in this house happens under my aegis, or it quickly ceases to exist."

Darmanian paused, as if wishing the full import of his words to penetrate my total consciousness. "I do not wish you to speak to Mr. Vogel because it is obvious that he is mad. And it is equally obvious that his wild and fanciful tales upset you. The demented fellow has spent so much time studying the occult that it has addled his brains."

Don Gruber stepped into my room, crossed to the dresser, removed the station wagon keys from the place where I had set them with the change from my pocket.

"For your own good," Darmanian smiled in a cold, serpentine manner, "I do not wish you to drive. In fact, I do not wish you to leave the house except for very brief periods in the afternoon. In no case will you leave the grounds."

"Confined to quarters except for exercise periods in the yard." I shook my head slowly. "Am I to consider myself a prisoner, Darmanian?"

Darmanian's attempted smile was more of a grimace. "I am only helping you to discipline yourself. You have spent far too much time on other pursuits. It is time now to devote yourself totally to your work."

"I have no work here, Darmanian," I said, my voice rising higher than I wished. "It is apparent to me that you are not at all interested in having me write your biography."

"That is true," he admitted. "Now you will write the book for which I *really* summoned you to Woodlands. You will write about the miracle of which I have spoken. You will not have long to wait. Not long at all."

His eyes narrowed and I felt their magnetic pull deep inside my brain. "May Eve is but three nights hence. You shall be present to bear witness to all that transpires."

Chapter Twenty-seven

I had at last found a practical purpose for the ugly gargoyle perched outside my window. It was solidly fixed onto the roof and was itself of sturdy workmanship. It would serve perfectly as an anchor for an end of a sheet so that I might hang and drop about another five feet from the opposite end. With all the rain we had been having, I knew the ground would be soft.

I have never been an especially brave person, and I have never sought physical abuse or punishment. But I knew that I had to escape my prison cell within Woodlands mansion and warn Sharon not to attend the following night's session.

I could not accept Ed Vogel's assessment that Darmanian was actually the reincarnation of a master wizard, the Marquis de Sainte-Croix. My own evaluation of Darmanian and his circle was that they had each of them crossed the admittedly blurred, but nonetheless socially defined, boundaries between sane and insane. And I had no doubt the police would wish to question them about the ultimate social violation—murder. Perhaps, mass murder.

It was just after midnight when I decided to make my move. I had opened the door to my room just a crack, checked out the hallway. There was no one in sight, but I could hear the sound of several voices, both male and female, engaged in spirited conversation. As I was closing the door, I heard Darmanian at the piano and a chorus of men and women begin what sounded like a bastardized Gregorian chant. They were in the music room, far away from where my feet would touch grass and soil.

Carefully, quietly, I raised the window behind the gargoyle's pointed buttocks. I set one foot on the roof, pressed down to test the strength of the wooden shingles. Thank God, I wasn't on the third floor!

The shingles seemed supportive of my weight, so I bent through the window and set both feet on the roof. I kept my left hand clamped around the windowsill until I was certain that a loose shingle wouldn't send me flying off into space. They seemed in good repair, however. In the square of light coming from the room, only a few looked spongy with moss or black with water and age.

I was glad it was dark. Just like the first time I went up in an airplane. I had wanted it to be at night so that I couldn't see the ground.

I tied the twisted sheet around the gargoyle's neck. The nightmarish beast had truly been well carved by some forgotten artisan. It looked real enough to complain about the noose that I was tightening about its throat. I gave the sheet an extra-firm tug to be certain that my knot would hold.

The gargoyle's mouth was open, and a long, doglike tongue curled out between its lips. The monster's eyes bulged maniacally. Its nose was more a beak. Its squat body was thick with muscle, and two wings sprouted from its broad back.

I sat on the edge of the roof. A patch of grass was illuminated by the light coming from a first-story window. It suddenly seemed to be a long way to the ground. I wondered if this was really such a good idea. Maybe only movie heroes escaped from eerie mansions by sliding down ropes made of twisted sheets.

But then I remembered the threat in Darmanian's eyes and the promise of what I now believed to be a very real danger to the safety of Sharon and her daughter, Alyse. I had to warn Sharon, and I had to face the true reality of the situation; I had to go to the police.

My biceps swelled against the exertion of supporting my one hundred and eighty-five pounds by my hands and arms. I hung for a moment at the juncture of roof and rope. I could still pull myself back up over the edge without much trouble. My body began to sway in a manner not unlike that of a hanged man.

There was nothing left to do but to do it.

Even as a kid in physical education class, I always came down the rope too damn fast. Friction made the rapid, sliding movement of hand over sheet "burn" my fingers and palms.

Then the soles of my shoes, clamped as tightly as I could make them against the sheet, caught against the large knot I had tied at the end of the twisted cloth. I tensed my muscles as best I could in order to contradict gravity long enough to slow my descent.

Then my hands were around the big knot, and I was hanging . . . and dropping.

I remembered to bend my knees as I landed so that I might absorb shock to my inner organs and sound to any hostile ears.

I straightened, took a deep breath. No sprained ankles. No shattered kneecaps. I had made good my escape from the mansion.

Now I had to get off the grounds.

I remembered my first rainy night at Woodlands when I had seen the light bobbing down from the hills and through the forest. Obviously there was an entrance to the estate on the other side of the woods. Perhaps there was a gate at the far end of the wall that appeared to encircle Woodlands. I'd settle for a hole.

I left the shadow of the great turreted and spired house and ran for the shadow of the guest cottage. I was breathing heavily in my excitement and fear. I could hear the sounds of spirited singing coming from the music room in the mansion. There was no movement in front of any of the first-story windows.

I turned toward the trees and ran into the darkness. God, how I wished that I had been able to bring a flashlight! The sky was generally overcast with very little moon. There appeared to be a forest path, and I decided it would be best to keep on it as well as I could in the dim light.

I ran for about a minute before I slowed my pace to a double-time walking gait. I had not realized how terribly out of condition I had become. In spite of a nighttime temperature of about sixty degrees, I was sweating profusely.

The clouds drifted away from the moon, providing me with a bit more light as I entered a clearing.

Déjà-vu struck me in the pit of the stomach with a velvet sledgehammer. I had been here before!

Dear and gentle Jesus! It was the clearing that I had seen in my dream. *It was real!*

So was the stone altar at the opposite end of the grassy circle. It was very real.

I wanted to charge into the forest in a burst of frantic energy, but something compelled me to approach the altar. This time I had no torch, only my pipe lighter.

I dug the lighter out of my trousers pocket, bent over the upper tier of rocks, and flicked the flint-wheel for illumination. Although there had been one rainy afternoon and one rainy night since Saturday, there were still a number of brownish stains spattered about the stones. I reeled under the impact of envisioning Delores slamming the long knife into the beautiful girl's naked breast.

The sacrifice had also been real.

Darmanian—whoever, whatever he was—had added the ritual slaying of human life to his techniques of hypnotherapy. I had come to Woodlands to work with a healer of human minds. I now had to flee Woodlands to escape the machinations of what would appear to be a dangerous psychopath.

"Eric!"

The harsh whisper came from somewhere in the woods at the edge of the clearing.

Cold prickles of fear stung my scalp, and my heart began to slam at my ribcage as if it were seeking to break free from its fleshly prison.

Something was moving in the woods. A big something.

My peripheral vision caught movement. I swirled to see a manlike thing walking toward me. It was laughing, and the movements of its mirth made its horns slash at the night air.

Primitive horror tore at my brain as I perceived the leering image of Satan stalking me across the open clearing. Then my throbbing senses made out the forms of two men, one on each side of His Satanic Majesty, running toward me.

"Get the sonuvabitch!"

"He knows too much! Get him!"

My edge on them was less than twenty yards, so I sprinted away from the side of the altar and headed for the direction where I felt a gate or an opening in the wall to exist.

"Right into my arms, asshole!"

The man loomed up in front of me. My God! I was surrounded!

He was crouched, his arms weaving out before him, as if he meant to seize me in a violent bear hug.

I had just got up a pretty good momentum when he jumped out from the woods in front of me. I had body velocity and panic on my side. I punched my right fist straight out from my chest and smashed him in the face. I felt a tooth slice my second knuckle.

He fell backward with a shouted curse, then twisted and grabbed at my legs as I ran by him. He caught my heel enough to make me stumble, but I did not fall.

Branches whipped across my face as I shot into the forest with my legs pumping like berserk pistons. My body was a moving machine, and I did not intend to stop for anyone—including Satan himself.

"Wasn't my fault, damn it!" I heard a defensive wail.

"Right through there! Don't let him get away!" Whoever was in charge was angry.

Heavy feet pounded behind me. For a gun, I would give my kingdom. I'd settle for a good stout club!

I struck a tree, hard. I caromed off it into another. They didn't have to be accomplished woodsmen to trail me. They could hear me breathing like a lung-shot deer and follow the sounds of my thrashing through the branches. Thank God it was too early for thick undergrowth to have formed, or I would have tripped long before.

A hand grabbed my coat. Somehow I managed to turn, tear the grasping fingers loose, twist at the wrist, and spin my assailant face first into a tree. His own momentum drove him hard against the rough bark. He slid down without a sound, except for a whoosing explosion of air as the breath was knocked out of him.

My throbbing brain was trying its damnedest to come up with a plan. I was no fighter, so my attempting to stand my ground and punch my way free was out of the question. I didn't even know how many men were after me. I had seen four for certain. One might be out of commission for a while. At least he was in a dazed condition. The man I had punched was probably only madder than hell, not hurt.

Could I somehow luck out if I were able to confront them one at a time? I doubted it. The only sensible plan was to run like a madhouse Mercury in the opposite direction from my pursuers.

Icy water bit my ankles as I splashed through a

small stream. I slipped on something, dropped to one knee. My left hand shot down to balance me, and I slammed my thumb painfully against a rock. It was a good rock, I decided. It had been rounded by the water moving it endlessly against other rocks. I scooped it up, along with another, less round, but heavier, and resumed running.

My lungs were beginning to feel as though they were composed of fiery sandpaper. I had to stop and catch my breath soon.

But not yet! Another dark figure was positioning itself ahead of me. "Hah! Hah!" he shouted triumphantly. His arms were raised above his head as if he were making frightening motions to startle a child.

Once again my body momentum added thrust and pounds to the rock I hurled at his face.

I missed his face, but I heard a solid thud as the rock struck the center of his chest. He doubled over, screaming his surprise and his pain. I brought the round rock down against the back of his skull as I ran past him. He fell without another sound, as if he had been poleaxed.

Under normal circumstances I would not intentionally hurt anyone. But I did not care if I had smashed his skull like an eggshell. All that was important to me was that I now had put two men down. And I still had my round rock to help me deal with another.

But then—O sweet Jesus, thank you—there was the wall! No gate. No hole. But there was a wall.

I tossed my rock aside, leaned against the rough concrete. I stretched myself to full height and stiffened my arms above my head. I could easily reach the top.

My fingers clamped down on the weathered surface,

and I slammed my feet against the wall to help catapult me over the last obstacle to freedom.

I had one leg over the wall when powerful hands tightened about the other. Satan had my foot in a grip that felt like a crushing vise.

"I'll kill the bastard!" someone shouted behind the man in the leering mask. "Hold on to him. I swear I'll kill him!"

"You won't touch him!" It was Don Gruber's voice under the mask. "You won't do anything until Darmanian tells you to do it!"

Gruber jerked at my leg with all of his weight, and I came off the top of the wall as if I were a cat being pulled from a high branch by an impatient fireman. Gruber lost his balance when my weight came down against him, and we fell in a tumble near the wall's edge.

Gruber saw the blow coming, and he tried to move his shoulder to block it, but he could not prevent an angry man's fist from smashing itself into my face.

Chapter Twenty-eight

Sharon's smile of greeting faded instantly into tight-lipped concern. "How did you get that nasty bruise on your cheek?" she wanted to know.

My day had been spent in earnest prayer that Ed Vogel had been able to persuade her of the danger in coming to Woodlands that night, but quite obviously neither the power of prayer nor the warnings I was certain had been made were forceful enough to keep the determined woman from her foray against Darmanian.

"An accident," I told her. "I walked into a door."

"Eric had been working so hard on the book," Darmanian smiled coolly, "that for a moment he became nearsighted. He got up from his desk and turned right into the edge of an open door."

Sharon shook her head sympathetically. "That must have been painful."

"More than you could know," I agreed.

* * *

Earlier that day Darmanian himself had seen to my swollen cheek.

"You have disappointed me, Eric," he had said, his blue eyes sad.

"And you have disappointed me, Darmanian," I had countered. "I came here to work with a man of goodness, and now I find that I must confront a man of evil."

Darmanian sighed, dipped a cotton swab in a bottle of antiseptic. "I am not an evil man," he argued as he dabbed the solution on the open cut on my cheekbone. "I am about to transform the world, Eric. Why can't you understand what a good thing that will be?"

I winced against the sting of the antiseptic, blinked back the tears that formed in my eyes. "But you want to bring about that transformation through human sacrifice and a pledge to serve the essence and embodiment of negativity. How can you imagine that you can accomplish a good end by evil means without sinning against your own soul as well as the souls of others? Such acts of bloodshed cannot help having an evil effect on you."

"All great movements begin with sacrifices," Darmanian said. "The demands of gods, kings, and evolutionary progress have always required the spilling of blood on the altar. I have dared to be great, Eric. The sacrifices of those little ones not yet tainted by the world have enabled me to control the absolute power that is about to be visited upon me. I will then accomplish good with this power, not evil."

"As Swedenborg said," I quoted for him, " 'He who is in evil is also in the punishment of evil.' "

Darmanian's eyes became cold. "Do not presume to judge me, Eric," he warned. "The acts of this life are the destiny of the next. And I cannot shun the destiny that I have crossed the centuries to reclaim. Nothing will stop me now."

I studied his handsome features, probed his brilliant blue eyes. He suddenly seemed as alien to me as if he had just stepped from an extraterrestrial spacecraft with his physical apparatus totally different from mine. But it was not Darmanian's body that was different from mine. It was his head set, his attitudes, his world view, his soul.

"Who," I had to ask, "do you believe yourself to be?"

Darmanian's smile was confident, self-assured. "I am the Marquis Jean de Sainte-Croix," he said. "And I am soon to be Satan's chief mortal emissary on Earth."

I was warned that if I wished to spare Sharon's life and my own, I would have to maintain an air of complete normalcy that night when she arrived to observe a demonstration of the so-called experimental group. I realized now that those who would be in attendance also believed themselves to be the present incarnations of seventeenth-century Parisian Satanists. Whether Darmanian had hypnotized them into believing that they had lived before or whether he had actually "activated" them as he claimed, I had no way of judging. I only knew that I would have to comply with Darmanian in order to buy time for Sharon, her daughter, Alyse, and myself.

True to her word, Sharon arrived a few minutes before eight. She wore a black turtleneck sweater, a gray tweed skirt, and stylish boots. She appeared the very personification of confidence. If Ed Vogel had warned her to stay away from Darmanian, it was apparent that she had not felt threatened. The way her defiant eyes seemed ready for combat, I doubt if she would have left the mansion had I challenged Darmanian's threat and shouted a warning at her at that very moment.

Darmanian introduced Sharon to the members of the experimental group, who, each in turn, smiled at her as though she were a child attending her first grown-up party. Shelley, of course, had known Sharon through Delores, but after the confrontation at the cemetery, they exchanged only cool, mumbled salutations. Sharon had also encountered a silent Don Gruber and a more vocal Viki Chung at the funeral, but she had not had names for them until that evening. She appeared visibly impressed that Bishop De Shazo and Senator Tom Harrigan were members of the group.

Darmanian was everywhere in the library at once, charming Sharon—or earnestly attempting to do so—cajoling the other participants by sharp whispers and burning glances to display warmth and welcome.

"What I have been evolving these past weeks is a bold new therapy," the hypnotist began, once the amenities had been observed and everyone had been seated. Don Gruber had attached himself to me earlier that day, and it appeared as though he did not intend ever to be more than an arm's length away from me.

"This therapy employs hypnotic regression techniques that go somewhat beyond those normally accepted in clinical hypnosis," Darmanian said, smiling conspiratorially at the five seasoned regulars.

Darmanian had arranged us in an open-ended circle with Sharon seated in the gap. I had been placed to her immediate left. The hypnotist stood in the center, leaning on the back of the large black leather chair, which would be his command post during the session.

Darmanian wore a black suit, a white turtleneck sweater, and the ever-present double-dragon medallion. His eyes were spirited and literally glowing with the excitement of the success he judged would soon be his.

"What we do in this therapy," Darmanian continued, "is to suggest that the subject go beyond the birth experience to a prior existence—another lifetime, if you will."

Although the words of explanation were clearly intended for Sharon, Senator Harrigan, Bishop De Shazo, Viki Chung, Don Gruber, and Shelley Eberhart sat is rapt attention, as if they, too, were attending their first session.

Sharon had made a decidedly unsubtle expression of distate the moment that the hypnotist mentioned past lives.

Darmanian chose to ignore her grimaces. "It is not the point of the technique to debate whether or not such a thing as reincarnation actually exists," he said. "It is my contention that in providing the details of an alleged previous existence and its subsequent demise, the subject may unwittingly present the therapist with several valuable clues to current traumas—both physical and psychological."

Sharon stifled a yawn, then blinked, smiled prettily at the hypnotist. "Sorry," she said, shrugging. "It's been a long day."

It seemed impossible to try Darmanian's patience that night. He nodded, made a slight bow. "Of course," he conceded. "Here I am chattering away like the ultimate pedant. You didn't come here for a lecture. You wish to see exactly what the experimental sessions are all about."

Sharon crossed a wonderfully shaped leg over the other, a movement that hiked her skirt disconcertingly to mid-thigh. She took a graceful moment to tug the tweed to a more discreet length, then told Darmanian that she believed that she understood the general idea of his theory.

"I'm beginning to understand what Delores meant when she said you were making her and the others remember things," Sharon said pointedly. "You have been *creating* memories for these people to feed back to you. For no good reason, you have been tampering with these peoples' minds."

Darmanian's professional smile was replaced by a line of displeasure. "I am quite aware that you will be a most demanding audience, Sharon," he said. "But I wish there to be no misconceptions left in your mind."

He turned to face the members of the group. "Although these men and women are conditioned to enter a deep sleep whenever I command it and touch them lightly on the forehead, I realize that such a maneuver would not impress you in the slightest degree. You would think that we had all rehearsed such an act to deceive you."

I was finding it increasingly difficult to maintain my forced role of silence.

I wished that I could leap up and give Don Gruber an incapacitating karate kick, Darmanian a paralyzing chop, Senator Harrigan a debilitating punch. Then I would grab Sharon by the arm, threatening to devastate anyone who might oppose me, and walk her from the mansion to her car.

But I knew that I could barely dent the football player and that somewhere, perhaps just outside the door of the mansion, were at least three men with nasty bruises who would welcome the opportunity to beat me to death. I had no idea who those men were who had helped Gruber chase me through the forest the night before, but I did not doubt their reality.

It was grim realization that counseled me that my only escape—and the only way that I could save Sharon and her daughter, Alyse—would come about through my brain, not my muscle. Somehow I had to stay calm and keep cool.

Darmanian had walked to the side of Shelley Eberhart. "When Shelley first came to my clinic four years ago, she was extremely difficult to hypnotize," he said. "It was difficult for her to concentrate."

Shelley considered this for a moment, then decided the statement required clarification. "I had a great deal on my mind then, Darmanian. I was just really breaking through as a top model, and I had to make the correct career choices. I just really had a lot of scattered energy."

Darmanian smiled his understanding. "Of course you did, darling. But you had to learn that in order to be a good hypnotic subject, you must have the ability to focus attention and to concentrate."

The hypnotist asked Shelley to stand. The model obliged, and Darmanian moved her chair to Sharon's right, so close that the seats were nearly touching. At his gesture, Shelley once again settled comfortably in her chair.

"I want you to be able to observe closely exactly what I am about to do with Shelley," Darmanian said to Sharon. "Shelley has been conditioned to fall instantly into hypnotic trance whenever I employ certain suggestions, but unless I activate those implanted commands, she reverts to being a very difficult person to hypnotize."

With just a trace of mockery in his voice, Darmanian struck a professorial posture. "Since I want this to be a learning experience for you, let me say that in addition to the ability to concentrate, a good hypnotic subject should have an openness to new experience and a willingness to comply with suggestions."

Sharon turned to face me. She seemed about to speak, then smiled and brought her attention back to Shelley and the hypnotist.

"Now, permit me to demonstrate in a step-by-step manner just how one goes about hypnotizing a difficult subject," Darmanian said, the fingers of his right hand reaching up to stroke the dragons on his medallion.

"Just relax, Shelley, and make yourself comfortable," the hypnotist told her. The attractive redhead took a deep breath, leaned back in her chair.

"Find something across the room on which to concentrate," Darmanian directed her. "Relax. Feel the warmth of love flow over your body. Feel it moving gently over your feet. Each muscle in your feet is relaxing. Already your eyelids are becoming heavy. Feel the warmth of love relaxing the muscles in your legs."

Darmanian's voice was authoritative, yet soft, as it assumed the gentle singsong pattern I had heard him utilize with such effectiveness on the police officers at the demonstration in Albany. He singled out each muscle group in progression as he moved from Shelley's toes up the course of her anatomy. Each muscle group was told to relax, to be bathed in warmth, to begin to float away into complete and total peace.

My own eyelids were growing heavy when I finally realized what was taking place. Darmanian was really hypnotizing Sharon Touraine. Shelley was serving as a beautiful decoy, a lovely Judas goat. I brought up thumb and forefinger to rub my temples before I, too, fell into trance.

Sharon's eyes were closed and her breathing rate was that of one who is enjoying the somnambulistic playground between wakefulness and sleep. She appeared about to knock on the door of her subconscious and be admitted to the level of awareness commonly known as the trance, or hypnotic, state.

Then I was jolted into full wakefulness. I glanced up to see that each member of the experimental group, including Shelley, was staring at Sharon. On each of their lips was a strangely anticipatory smile.

"You are moving deeper and deeper, down, down, down," Darmanian was saying. "You are in a deep, deep, sleep. Deeper than you have ever been before. Deeper and deeper than you have ever been before. Do you understand?"

A small sound came from Sharon's lips.

"Louder!" Darmanian commanded. "Do you understand?"

"Yes," came the resonant reply.

"You are moving back through time and space," Darmanian told her. "You are moving back beyond the womb, beyond your conception as a physical shell in this lifetime. You are moving back in man-time to the year 1679. You are moving back to April twenty-sixth, 1679."

My brain was spinning. Darmanian seemed determined to use human minds as if they were but pawns on some psychic chessboard. He was actually attempting to channel the energy from his group's collective fantasy so that he might somehow become a powerful manipulator of humanity.

"Farther and farther back," Darmanian said by way of reinforcement. "At the count of three, you will be in Paris, France. The date will be April twenty-sixth, 1679. One . . . moving back. Two . . . nearly there. Three!"

Sharon sat upright, her eyes wide open. She looked about the room and the smiling men and women who sat staring at her as if she had just arrived late for her own birthday party.

Sharon Touraine shook her head and set her lips in a sneer of disgust.

I wanted to laugh and cheer. It was obvious that Darmanian had failed to hypnotize Sharon. The spunky blonde had resisted his ability to mesmerize.

In spite of his considerable skills, Darmanian seemed blithely unaware of his strikeout.

"What is your name, girl?" he demanded of the scowling Sharon.

Her lips clamped shut in defiance, as if she chose not to indulge the man any longer. Her eyes smoldered with contempt as she took in each of the faces of the men and women arranged in a circle about her chair.

"What is your name, girl?" the hypnotist repeated, his voice assuming a stern rumble.

"Damn you!" Sharon shouted. "You know my name, de Sainte-Croix."

My mouth gaped and my brain blurred in wonder.

"Tell me your name, wench!" Darmanian insisted.

"Marguerite Montvoisin!" Sharon shot back.

Darmanian smiled, satisfied. "Your mother is not here tonight, Marguerite. But as you can see, many of your friends are. And we have some business to discuss with you."

Sharon shook her head slowly, and her words seemed to pierce each of them as if she wielded a finely honed blade: "You'll never find Angelique. I've hidden her where she will be safe from you monsters!"

Chapter Twenty-nine

There had to be some incredible psychic disease that infected the minds of all those who became a part of Darmanian's experimental circle.

Or each of these men and women—including Sharon Touraine—had actually shared a life before—three hundred years before—and had been reborn into the same time sequence to complete a drama whose climax had been interrupted in that previous life experience.

And the majordomo of the entire incredible program of rebirth was Darmanian, also known as Marquis Jean de Sainte-Croix, a wizard who had achieved control of his own incarnations.

I felt extreme disorientation. I was having great difficulty sifting through the layers of reality that were unfolding around me.

Sharon Touraine had entered the clinic a hostile skeptic toward any kind of hypnotherapy—not to mention past-life regression. She had known almost noth-

ing of the content of the previous sessions. Yet with
my own incredulous ears, I had just heard her curse
Darmanian as de Sainte-Croix and identify herself as
Marguerite Montvoisin.

Bishop De Shazo was speaking: "Why are you so
angry toward us, Marguerite? We are your friends."

"I'll have none of your sweet words, Abbé Guilborg," Sharon said. "I find you as disgusting now as
when you tried to have your way with me when I was
but twelve. In fact, I find you even more loathsome
now. Then, you wanted my body. Now, you want my
child's life!"

Viki Chung leaned forward to cajole her. "Angelique herself has always been willing, eager, to serve
her master by offering herself as sacrifice to the Old
Gods. How can you, her own mother, deny her this
honor?"

"Pah, Marie," Sharon spat. "She is but a child. She
cannot know her mind in such matters."

Shelley Eberhart shouted: "She's wiser than you!
She knowns the importance of her mission on Earth!
You think only of your herbs and potions."

Sharon glared at the woman, her eyes revealing her
animosity. "Shut up, Coco! I serve our master in ways
that truly help others. I care nothing to have power
over them."

"But, how," Viki demanded, "can you do anything
that would prevent the marquis from attaining the
heights of mastery that he is destined to achieve?"

Senator Tom Harrigan jutted forth his solid chin.
"Angelique has the soul knowledge that she is to present herself as the sacrifice that shall enable the marquis to attain the position of master wizard of this
planet."

"Oh, Father Louis," Sharon said, shaking her head sadly. "Mother has repeated that suggestion so often that the child has come to believe it."

"Your mother has served us well as our high priestess," Don Gruber said.

"Yes, Father Jacques," Sharon answered him. "And I have mixed herbs and powders for the rituals, and I have healed the bodies of those who sought my help. I have served the master as well as any of you."

"A dozen of my babies have given their blood to the rituals and their bodies to the oven!" roared the Abbé Guilborg through the person of the ostentatiously pious Bishop De Shazo.

Sharon tossed back her head and laughed a high-pitched, mirthless cackle. "Oh, Abbé, you pompous pig! You breed as indiscriminately as a gutter rat. You have no feeling for the 'calves' your 'cows' produce. In fact, the ovens and the sacrificial blades have provided you with a service. They have removed any strain on your purse that the slightest tug of responsibility might have placed on it."

Father Louis cleared his throat, again presenting a remarkable contrast between the compact ruggedness of Senator Harrigan and the mincing mannerisms of the regressive personality. "I think this is shocking, this standing around arguing like this," he said in a shrill voice. "Your mother is devoted to our mission of establishing the Marquis de Sainte-Croix as Satan's most powerful representative on Earth. How can you even think of blocking such a goal?"

Abbé Guilborg shifted noisily in the chair of Bishop De Shazo. "Perhaps we should seize the wench and make her tell us where she has hidden the child!"

Darmanian broke his silence. "There is no need for violence. I am certain that reason can prevail."

"Nothing can prevail against me when it comes to protecting my daughter!" Sharon shouted her rage. "There is no torture that can make me tell where I have secreted Angelique."

Darmanian's voice was soft, yet forceful. "But this is all out of your hands, dear Marguerite. The child has made her own decision. The Lord of the Earth has revealed himself unto her. You are but the instrument who brought her into the world. How can you even consider preventing her from fulfilling the purpose for which she was created?"

Sharon closed her eyes and clamped anguished hands over her ears. How could even the unconscious of Sharon be responding to such dialogue unless she actually possessed the soul knowledge of the previous identity of Marguerite Montvoisin? The last vestiges of my intellectual objections and protests were crumbling away. I was being forced to accept the fact that I must begin to place a literal interpretation on the bizarre events in which I had somehow been placed.

"How dare she seek to thwart the divine plan of Satan?" Father Louis fumed in an effeminate pout that would have shocked Tom Harrigan's fellow senators.

Shelley Eberhart-Coco laughed bitterly. "Yes," she said. "Marguerite of all people. I was bound to the convent when she made herself my friend. All my life I had lived secure from the hardships and terrors of the world. My father had reared me dutifully in response to his answered prayers when my mother nearly died in childbirth. I was to be a nun, a bride of Christ. No mortal man was to touch me."

Abbé Guilborg made a kissing sound against his fingertips. "You made a very juicy bride of Satan, Coco," he leered. "Several wealthy men gave generously to our coffers the night your body was spread-eagled on the altar!"

Coco Shelley rolled her eyes, shrugged her lovely shoulders. "One learns to make the best of life if she is to survive."

Father Louis chuckled in recollection. "You tried to snatch a dagger from the altar to kill yourself."

Father Jacques nodded his head. "And you tried to kill me when I stopped you."

"I had been led to La Voisin's den in wide-eyed innocence," the entity of Coco spoke in halting tones. "Marguerite, the conniving bitch, told me that I could please my father and become a nun in just one night. She said that La Voisin headed a very special order."

Abbé Guilborg roared his laughter. "And you fell for her story!"

"I was but fifteen," Coco protested. "And so stupid and naïve. But Marguerite seemed to be such a good friend. And I did so wish to please Papa."

Darmanian added to her narrative with an aside: "Marguerite has been a most diligent servant of Satan. In bringing you to the altar that night, she accomplished two sacrifices to our Lord."

"Yes." Coco nodded, lowering her head. "Papa took his own life when he learned what had happened to me." Then she snorted contemptuously: "That gentle man who had devoted his life to fulfilling his promise to Jesus was forbidden burial on hallowed ground by the very priests who had so greedily supped at his table and so strenuously tithed his wealth. Papa now lies in the vineyard beyond the ancestral plot."

"No doubt"—Abbé Guilborg laughed in the present bulk of Bishop De Shazo—"he provides an added body to the wine."

"Abbé," Father Louis reprimanded him, "you persist in maintaining a consistently vulgar life."

The big man chortled his reply. "When you die, Father Louis, we shall bury you next to Coco's papa. That way you two can both add tasteful ingredients. You have enough perfume in your flesh to provide a most distinctive bouquet to any grape."

Darmanian silenced the squabble, focused the group's attention once more upon Sharon-Marguerite. "Ever since you were a child, Marguerite, you have served Satan well. You have caught the flow of blood from babies' throats. You have lured virgins to the altar. You have become a master herbalist. How can you think now of delaying his greatest of all plans?"

The entity of Marguerite seemed to be considering her reply carefully. "I have served Satan well so that I might work to change the world," she said. "I reasoned that the sacrifices in which I assisted were necessary. I steeled my heart against the sight of my mother slashing the throats of crying infants. I reasoned that the weeping virgins would have lost their maidenheads sooner or later. Always I told myself that I was working to bring about a better world."

Darmanian's eyes flashed and his voice raised in intensity. "I seek also to make a more perfect world. Once I have attained full power, I shall remake the world into a paradise!"

"But why must it be Angelique who buys your paradise with her blood?" she demanded, her question ending in a sob of frustration and anguish.

Darmanian's tone became almost paternalistic. "Every great goal must be bought with sacrifice," he told her. Deliver Angelique to us so that we can complete the ceremony."

It was as if Woodlands mansion had slipped backward in time, and I was eavesdropping on a confrontation that had taken place three hundred years before. Each member of the group, including Darmanian and Sharon, were speaking as though it were April of 1679 and as if we were in Paris, not Saratoga Springs.

"Even now," Darmanian continued, his voice suddenly urgent, "your dear mother, our high priestess, is in the hands of the Chambre Ardente. She, too, has sacrificed herself by acting as decoy. She permitted them to arrest her so that we might have time to accomplish the ceremony. You must not permit La Voisin's unselfish act to have been done in vain."

My memory cells prodded my brain with the scholarship of Ed Vogel. According to his research, the Marquis de Sainte-Croix had betrayed La Voisin to the Chambre Ardente once she had performed a necessary chant and a preparatory sacrifice. My eyes searched Sharon-Marguerite's face for any sign that she might know the true circumstances of her mother's arrest. Her features, however, remained impassive.

Abbé Guilborg's voice was trembling when he spoke. "Think, Marguerite! Even now your blessed mother may be undergoing hideous torture. Who can imagine what vicious acts those monsters will perpetrate upon her soft flesh!"

The entity Marguerite raised an accusative forefinger toward Darmanian. "You could free my mother now. You have that power!"

"Impossible," he said firmly. "No one has that

power save the king. Release Angelique to me, and I will be the king!"

Father Louis's voice rose in desperation. "For the life of one young girl you would keep the whole world in darkness! You are too selfish to live!"

Father Jacques growled through Don Gruber's clenched teeth: "Kill *her* on the sacrificial altar. Perhaps our Lord will accept a slightly used virgin!"

"Kill Marguerite?" Viki Chung echoed in the persona of Sister Marie. She shook her head sadly. "If we are unable to accomplish the proper sacrifice, we will all be dead within a fortnight. My powers have enabled me to see that death and terrible torture will be the reward for our failure.

"My brothers and sisters, mark my words," she emphasized. "If we kill Marguerite tonight, we have committed an act of supreme generosity. Let her suffer the torture and the flaming stake together with us."

Abbé Guilborg nodded his head violently in agreement with the woman's words. It seemed strangely perverse to see the crucifix on the broad chest of the Bishop De Shazo bobbing up and down in reaction to the movements of the licentious abbé.

"Sister Marie is correct," he argued. "To kill this miserable wench would be an act of mercy. We wish no mercy toward the one who would prevent us from attaining our most worthy goal."

I was startled when I glanced toward Darmanian. He seemed suddenly so very old. His handsome features seemed slack with a vast age. Only his eyes seemed fiercely eternal.

"Marguerite," the hypnotist said in a weary voice. "Can you even begin to realize what you are doing?

What you may be setting in motion? This act of the transfer of power was planned before the births of our parents' parents by the Old Ones. If it is not accomplished now, at its appointed time, here in Paris in 1679, then it must be recast again so that the sacrifice may be received. Your daughter, Angelique, is aware of the enormity of this act. How can her mother be so very wrong?"

"Angelique is a child who has listened to her grandma and to words of sheep who do not think for themselves," Marguerite answered her accuser. "Never will I deliver the child to you."

At that moment I was aware of two men who had entered the library by some unseen door among the bookshelves. Darmanian saw them, raised a questioning eyebrow.

"She wasn't there," the same tall, dark man, who seemed to drift mysteriously in and out of Woodlands, spoke up from the shadows. The light from the table lamp at Darmanian's side cast illumination on the second intruder, a scowling man with a nasty bruise on the side of his face. He was the pursuer I had pulled head first into a tree.

A terrible hissing sound came from Darmanian's lips before he spoke. "What do you mean?" he demanded. "Dare you to tell me that you have failed?"

"My lord," the tall man protested in a voice that had taken on the qualities of a whining plea, "neither the child nor the wench's mother were there."

Darmanian's nostrils flared, and his entire body seemed to be trembling in an all-consuming rage. He stood before Sharon, his hands transformed to huge, grasping claws. I thought for a moment that he would strike her from her chair.

"She . . . she has done it again," Darmanian gasped incredulously. "She is truly the viper in our midst."

I risked a small smile of satisfaction. Ed Vogel must have got through Sharon Touraine's reserves of intellectual objections and convinced her to hide Alyse. It was unfortunate that he had not been able to persuade Sharon to avoid Woodlands as if it were a depository of plague carriers, but it was undoubtedly her own stubbornness, anger, and pride that had driven her to the confrontation with Darmanian.

"Where is the child?" Darmanian demanded. His eyes seemed fixed on Sharon as if they were enraged prisms, focusing to cause her to burst into flame.

It was my hope that Sharon had delivered Alyse into the capable hands of my friend Ed Vogel. It was my prayer that Ed would be able to convince the police that all was not well in the mansion of their occasional benefactor.

One of the women—I believe it was Viki Chung—sounded a strange humming note, which the others in the group replicated almost at once in their own voices. The sound began to swell and to grow as if it were filling the entire room, as though it were rolling out to fill every void in our immediate environment. It rose to a terrible pitch, which, I realized with a horrible shock of recognition, I had heard once before.

The group was reproducing that incredible, unplaceable, buzzing hum that I had heard just before Delores Touraine had burst into flames!

Sharon began to writhe on the chair, as if some electrical force were wrenching and twisting her muscles in painful spasms. She clenched her teeth, made pitiful whimpering sounds. She seemed determined not to cry out.

"Darmanian," I shouted, finding my voice at last, defying the muscular threat of Don Gruber at my side. "Stop this! Stop this ter—"

And then I could no longer breathe. No one rose to place a finger on me. Gruber sat with his eyes closed, sounding the vibratory hum along with the others in the circle.

Yet it was as if my own lungs and chest muscles had suddenly rebelled against the familiar old inhale-exhale routine that constituted my breathing. Sweat literally squirted from my pores as I panicked. *I could not breathe!*

I strained against the invisible force pressing me to my chair. My thigh muscles bulged against my trousers. I placed my hands on the edge of the seat and tried to straighten my arms upward.

Colored lights were beginning to explode in my brain.

Incredibly, it was Christmas back in Minnesota when I was seven years old.

I was unwrapping a jigsaw puzzle, and my mother's father, Grandpa Johann, was laughing. "Dat'll keep da little monkey's fingers busy," he said in his Danish singsong accent.

"I said *no* presents before the candlelight service," Mother was scolding. "Now hurry or we'll be late for church."

I had a clear image of putting on a white robe sewn together from a discarded sheet.

I was nervous. In five minutes I would be singing "Away in a Manger" and "Silent Night" in front of all those people of St. Olaf's Lutheran Church.

Thank God, I was not alone. All around me were angels, wisemen, and shepherds.

But I got dizzy.

In front of the entire congregation, I got dizzy. It was as if I could not breathe.

I turned to the altar behind us, and I said, "Dear Jesus, help me! If something terrible is going to happen to me, please help me! Help me, Jesus!"

And then I had fainted. In front of everyone. Blip. Blackness.

Until I became aware of my father holding me in his arms outside the church door.

It was below freezing Christmas Eve, and the cold air felt good in my lungs. I sucked it in like a drowning man. I filled my lungs with the cold Minnesota air until it felt as though they would burst.

I sat up with a start. Blackness was all around me. My senses desperately shot input to my brain so that my heart would stop thudding against my chest, and I could know where I was.

A crack of light from a door. Softness under me. I was in my room. On my bed.

I heard soft sounds of weeping from beside me. I touched the swell of a woman's hip. Sharon lay on her side next to me.

Had she told them where she had taken Alyse?

I lay back on the bed, and with fear and anguish warping my voice, I said aloud words I had not uttered for so many years: "Dear Jesus, help us. If something terrible is going to happen to us, please, please, help us, Jesus!"

Chapter Thirty

Sharon and I said very little to each other until morning. We gave each other reassurance of our identities, then lay huddled together like two children frightened of the dark.

Somehow I managed to fall asleep, for I sat up with a start at the sound of the bathroom toilet being flushed. By the time Sharon had finished with the lavatory, I was sitting on the edge of the bed, trying my best to look confident.

"Eric," Sharon smiled weakly as she reentered the bedroom. "You're awake. I thought I had better let you sleep. I tried not to wake you."

Then she was rushing into my arms. "Oh, God, Eric," she sobbed. "What happened to me last night?"

She pulled back for a moment. "How did we get in this room?"

"It's mine," I told her. "Sharon"—I gripped both of her shoulders—"did you bring Alyse to Ed Vogel?"

Her eyes widened, moved about the room as if

seeking a hidden enemy. She nodded, and her answer came in a low whisper. "I thought he was crazy when he knocked on our door. But he kept talking, and he was so convincing. And he seemed to know so many things."

I grinned, breathed deeply. "And your mother?"

"With Vogel," she whispered. "She went with Alyse."

"If Ed was able to convince you," I said as though it were a prayer, "maybe he can convince the police that we're in trouble."

Sharon's eyes stopped their darting about, fixed themselves on the telephone on the bedside table.

"It's been disconnected," I told her. "I lost telephone privileges the same day I lost the keys to the station wagon. That was when I tried to escape to warn you. But," I added, gingerly touching the bruise on my cheek, "I didn't quite make it."

"Darmanian," she gasped. "He's crazy. And so are the people in his group. I couldn't believe it when I saw Senator Harrigan and Bishop De Shazo. And the things Darmanian made me see . . ."

"What things?" I wanted to know. "What did he make you see?"

Sharon's mouth opened and closed as if reliving the horror and pain of the previous night. "It was as if"—her eyes narrowed as though to focus the images more clearly—"as if I were in a big underground room. And I was ringed in by Darmanian and the others. They were angry, accusing me of thwarting some plan."

Sharon could not check a shriek of fear and loathing. Her nails dug into my shoulders as she pulled herself close to me. "Alyse!" she sobbed into my chest. "They want to kill Alyse. They want to sacrifice her!"

Her eyes came up to plead with my own. "Eric," she asked, tears streaming down her cheeks. "I didn't tell, did I? I didn't tell them where they can find Alyse, did I?"

I hugged her close to me. "I don't know, Sharon," I had to admit. "Somehow, in a way I simply do not understand, they put me totally out of commission."

"The buzz." She shook her head increduously. "Did you hear the buzz? It was the same sound that we heard just before Delores had her terrible accident."

Sharon dealt intellectually for a moment or two with the incredible, unthinkable connection. "Eric, oh, no," she said, her chin quivering with the horror of it.

We were both having a difficult time with reality.

"The past two days I've had to accept so much that would normally be unacceptable to me," I said, my fingers tightening on her back. "Darmanian believes himself to be the reincarnation of the Marquis Jean—"

"De Sainte-Croix," Sharon completed my identification. "And Bishop De Shazo is Abbé Guilborg. That . . . that mean Oriental girl, Viki, is Sister Marie. And Father Louis, he's Senator Harrigan. And . . ."

Sharon pushed herself away from me, rose shakily to her feet. "How do I know these things?" she seemed to be asking the ceiling. "Coco is Shelley Eberhart. And, oh God, Delores. Delores was Catherine Montvoisin. La Voisin."

She whirled to face me again, her eyes wide, her nostrils flared. "My mother!" she screamed. "Delores was my mother, Catherine Montvoisin!"

Sharon began to sway unsteadily, as if she were about to faint. I got up from the edge of the bed, took her once again in my arms.

"How can I know those things, Eric?" Her voice

was soft, discordant, fluttering between levels of reason and being. "Darmanian made me know those things," she accused, her voice gaining strength once more. "Darmanian—"

"*Helped* you to remember, my dear," came the hypnotist's deep voice from the doorway that neither of us had seen open. A grinning Don Gruber slouched at his side. In back of them, her eyes confused, her mouth a thin, tight line, stood Agnes bearing a tray of coffee and toast.

"I thought you might like some breakfast," Darmanian said, his voice pleasant, almost cheery. Then he added: "Sharon, you'll have plenty of time to eat, but I'm afraid Eric will just have to take a couple of swallows of coffee before he runs off."

"And where am I going?" I questioned, feeling my stomach clutch at Darmanian's suggestion that I was about to be taken somewhere.

"You have a visitor downstairs." Darmanian smiled. "A Sergeant Kandowski has come inquiring about your well-being."

My heart began to pound at my ribcage with renewed hope. I shot a meaningful glance at Sharon, as if to say, "Hang on, baby! We're about to go home free!"

"I told the sergeant that I would probably have to awaken you, since you are in the habit of sleeping late," Darmanian said, stepping aside so that Agnes could set the tray down on the low dresser in front of the bed. "Take a sip of Agnes's good-morning coffee, Eric, and I shall help you receive your guest."

My hand was shaking as I held the cup to my mouth. I only pretended to drink, just in case Darmanian had drugged the coffee. I wanted all my wits about me when I talked to Kandowski. That big, beefy cop was going to be our ticket out of Darmanian's mad circus of horrors.

"Don will stay with Sharon so that she won't become lonely while you're chatting with the sergeant," Darmanian said, smiling.

Gruber moved into the room, his half-lidded eyes crawling over her body as if he were a starving man glimpsing a full-course dinner. Sharon was not oblivious to the big man's thinly disguised lechery. She walked over to me and put her arm around mine.

"I want to go with Eric," she said. I could feel her arm trembling her apprehension.

"I'm afraid that won't be possible," Darmanian said. Then, as if to allay her fears, he added, "Don't worry about Don. He will need all of his energy for tonight."

"Tonight?" I echoed, feeling Sharon's fingers clutching for my hand.

"Oh, yes," Darmanian smiled, "I forgot to tell you. You two are invited to a costume ball. It is more or less a 'come as you were' party. Shelley will be dropping your costumes off sometime this afternoon."

"I imagine the 'come as you were' applies to the Paris of 1679." I said.

"Oh, good, Eric." Darmanian winked. "You have been paying attention."

I shrugged. "Too bad I won't be able to come," I told him. "I wasn't around then."

"Oh, but we didn't want you to miss the party," Darmanian countered. "Since you are a writer and a scholar, we are preparing a becoming academic gown for you to wear. Sharon, of course, remembers what she enjoyed wearing on dress-up occasions."

Sharon's teeth caught at her lower lip. Her eyes

were suddenly drawn to the dragon medallion about Darmanian's neck.

"A . . . a blouse of pale pink," she began, haltingly at first. "A black waist cinch that I can tighten to make my waist really small and—" she broke into a girlish giggle—"to make my bust really big!"

I could only gape in astonishment. Darmanian seemed inordinately pleased, and his fingers stroked the twin dragons as if they were pets being rewarded for fetching a ball.

"I'll wear my rose-colored skirt with the pink satin trim," Sharon continued. "And . . ." She paused, touching her hair.

"Yes," Darmanian said, nodding in agreement, "roses in your hair. You shall appear exactly as you did then."

The hypnotist reached out and touched my arm. "Come, Eric, Sergeant Kandowski will be getting restless."

I left Sharon sitting on the edge of the bed. Her features were expressionless, and her eyes were open and staring.

"You will be very careful not to spoil things for me, won't you, Eric?" Darmanian asked as we walked together down the elegant open stairway.

I said nothing. I surely would not be held by any promise I might make to the devil at this point in the incredible morality play in which I had become so embroiled.

Sergeant Burt Kandowski was standing in the library. His thick hands were clasped behind his back, and he was rocking nervously forward and backward on the heels and toes of his scuffed black shoes.

He grinned at the sight of me, made some mumbled

comment about sloth and sleeping late, then he scowled as he zeroed in on the bruise on my cheekbone.

"You didn't get that nasty bruise from the bedpost, did you?" he asked solicitiously.

I could feel Darmanian's eyes burning the back of my head. "I walked into an open door," I said providing Kandowski with the lie that the hypnotist had already approved.

Kandowski squinted one eye and arched the shaggy brow of the other. "Some guy in Saratoga Springs telephoned the station with a complaint," he said, getting directly to the point of his visit. "Since it involved you, the fellas passed it on to me. This guy said you were in some kind of trouble."

Sergeant Kandowski cleared his throat, turned to face Darmanian, who had seated himself behind his large, ebony desk. "I couldn't imagine any trouble here, sir," he said by way of apology to the hypnotist. "But Eric has been a friend of mine since a long time back."

Darmanian smiled pleasantly. "I understand, sergeant. It is your sworn duty to follow through on any call for police assistance. Even if it should come from a crank or a crackpot."

Kandowski winced—ever so slightly—but the gesture betrayed his embarrassment at having disturbed so august a personage as the great Darmanian.

"It was no crackpot who called you," I spoke out, my voice quavering with desperation. "I need your help. I'm being held here against my will. Upstairs there is another person, Sharon Touraine, who is also being kept prisoner here."

Kandowski blinked his astonishment. Darmanian,

on the other hand, appeared indifferent to my charge. His eyes flicked from Kandowski, back to me, as if he were watching a tennis match.

"What the hell, Eric," Kandowski found his tongue. "You told me you came here to do a book on Darmanian."

"I did, Burt," I told him. "But my research has uncovered a madman. And a murderer!"

"Jesus, Eric," Kandowski shouted, his voice nearly becoming a squawk of surprise. "What the hell are you talking about?"

My heart was thudding my chest so hard that I feared it might drown out my words. I felt suddenly dizzy, and I wanted to sit down. But I knew I must stand there before Darmanian and defy him. I must assert myself against the evil he represented.

"I'm talking about that young secretary, Angela Tarrante, for openers." I was startled at the strident quality my voice had assumed. "I'm talking about maybe dozens of babies. You know, Burt, the ones that have been disappearing around here for years now."

"Jesus, Eric," Burt repeated.

Darmanian leaned back in his black leather desk chair and began to rock slowly. His indifference to my accusations was disconcerting. He appeared almost serene.

Sweat matted my hair and moistened my forehead and upper lip. "Yes, Darmanian," I said, pointing a trembling finger at him. "I finally figured out what I saw that man bring you on the first night I came here. I know now why the furnace suddenly kicks out so much heat on certain nights. I want to cry in outrage when I think of what I must have seen you burying that morning. *Bones!* Babies' bones!"

Burt's arms flapped helplessly at his sides. He was having difficulty assessing what was happening. "Eric," he pleaded. "Hey, buddy, slow it down a bit. Let's start getting things straight."

But I would not be slowed. Once I had become bold enough to accuse the smugly confident hypnotist, the words were becoming a torrent.

"It is certainly convenient that Viki Chung is the director of a home for unwed mothers, isn't it?" I challenged Darmanian. "You learned that trick from La Voisin, didn't you?"

Kandowski moved to my side, put a powerful arm around my shoulder. His strength was marvelously reassuring. "Let's take it easy, kid," he said.

"Arrest him!" I shouted at Sergeant Kandowski. "Arrest Darmanian."

Kandowski turned to look at Darmanian, who had stopped his complacent rocking. He now sat tall and confident.

"Sergeant Kandowski." Darmanian spoke his name slowly. "Sergeant Burton Kandowski. How terrible it is for you to have to work so hard and then to have to listen to such nonsense. You policemen are so overworked. It is no wonder that you always look so tired. So very tired. So sleepy."

Darmanian's long, slender fingers had moved up to caress his medallion, to make it spin slowly on its chain.

"The moment I saw you, sergeant," Darmanian was saying in a soft, friendly voice, "I could see how sleepy you were. You looked so tired, so very tired."

I grabbed Burt by his bulky shoulders, shook him

"Don't look at that medallion!" I begged him. "Don't listen to him!"

Burt seemed not to hear me. He was staring at the dragons. He was listening only to the sound of Darmanian's voice telling him to relax, telling him to sleep, telling him to forget about all his troubles and problems. And, Darmanian urged him, he must certainly forget about what I had said and about why he had come to Woodlands.

The medallion in Darmanian's practiced fingers seemed to become animated, seemed to glow with a life force of its own.

I could have continued to shake Kandowski for hours without his responding to my entreaties. He was deep in hypnotic sleep.

Tears of anger and frustration stung my eyes, as Burt Kandowski, obeying Darmanian's suggestion, began to walk out of the library. I begged Burt to take me with him, to wait until I got Sharon, but he did not respond to anything I said.

"Drive carefully, sergeant," Darmanian called after him. "You will drive home and have a nice, long sleep. When you awaken, you will remember nothing of this conversation. You will not remember having come here at all."

I started to follow Kandowski out of the library, but the tall thin man and my angry nemesis with the bruised face, whom I had battered against the tree, blocked my path.

"That was a foolish thing to have done," Darmanian scolded me, slowly shaking his head like a disappointed schoolteacher who has caught a defiant student drawing nasty pictures on the blackboard. "I warned you not to try to spoil things for me. You can't blame me for being upset with you, Eric."

I could say nothing. I knew that my anguish and my rage would only make me stammer impotent curses and threats.

Darmanian cradled the medallion in the palm of his left hand. "You should have guessed that I was not donating all my time to the police officers purely for civic-minded purposes. During the course of my annual presentations and my occasional visits to the station houses, I have been steadily conditioning the key officers. If that had been Chief Weyerhaus, I would only have had to tap my medallion once and tell him, 'Deep sleep.'"

"You really are a devil," I accused him.

Darmanian lowered his eyelids and smiled contentedly. "One second after the stroke of midnight, and the spirit of Satan will enter me fully. From that moment until the sun dies, I shall be his mortal emissary on Earth."

"Only one thing prevents that from occurring," I reminded him.

He scowled his puzzlement. "One thing?" he repeated. "One thing." Then he snapped his fingers, grinned. "Oh, you're referring to Angelique, that is, Alyse, aren't you?"

Before I could taunt him further, Darmanian told me: "At this very moment the child is being prepared for her glorious role in tonight's observance. Nothing, dear Eric, can prevent me from achieving my destiny!"

Chapter Thirty-one

The monstrous situation seemed completely hopeless. Kandowski had been sent from Woodlands like a mindless automaton. The terrible fact that Darmanian now possessed Alyse must mean that Paula and Ed Vogel, as well as Sharon's mother, Eleanor Touraine, had probably been murdered.

Although I did not want to nurture the ghastly thought for even an instant, I saw nothing that could stop Darmanian and his circle from carrying out their sacrifice of Alyse at midnight. Nor could I conceive of anything that would prevent them from disposing of Sharon and me after their grim and perverse ceremony.

I did not tell Sharon about Alyse because I was uncertain of the bizarre mental states between which she perpetually fluctuated. When we were alone in the room, she was Sharon Touraine, desperate mother, angry prisoner. Whenever Darmanian or one of the circle entered our makeshift prison cell, she seemed to become Marguerite Montvoisin. Although, as Marguerite, she was still the protective and defiant mother, so many of her other attitudes appeared unstable. If we were to escape, it would be left to me to devise a method by which that extraordinary good fortune might occur.

At ten minutes past six Shelley Eberhart entered our room with two black-robed women with cowls shadowing their features. It was time, Shelley said, as she led Sharon into the hall, that she be prepared for the evening's festivities.

I did not wait alone for very long. No more than three or four minutes after Sharon had been escorted away to receive her costume, Don Gruber walked into my room bearing a scarlet robe, which I assumed to be my scholar's gown.

Gruber himself was dressed in the manner of a Roman Catholic priest of seventeenth-century France. His black robe was loose and flowing, fitted only slightly at the waist. I noticed that the crucifix he wore hung head down and had been dipped in red paint.

"Put on this robe," he said, thrusting the folded gown into my arms. "And hurry up. We're supposed to join the party as soon as possible."

"Gruber," I sighed, "the indignities are enough. I refuse to put on this robe and to join your cruel charade."

He pushed the gown hard against my chest. "You'd better cooperate, Eric," he snarled. "And call me Father Jacques."

I took the robe from his large, thick hands, and threw it to the floor.

Gruber grabbed my lapels, whirled me across the room, and slammed me against the wall. He didn't do it as hard as I've seen him hit a football foe on Sunday afternoons, but it hurt.

I threaded my fingers together beneath the outstretched arms still gripping my lapels, brought my linked hands up fast, and broke his hold. He stepped back, furious, his hands coming up like a boxer's.

"Enough!" Darmanian shouted from the doorway. Gruber stepped back, cursing me in brusque monosyllables. "Put on the robe, Eric."

I turned to glare at the hypnotist. I wanted to scream my outrage at the man, but I permitted the anger to die with a dry, choking stammer in my throat.

"You will do nothing to upset the ceremony for which we have waited for three hundred years," he said. Darmanian was dressed in a black satin suit trimmed with white lace. Highly polished boots with flashing silver buckles granted another two inches to his height. A thin-bladed rapier with a highly ornate handle hung from his left hip, a dagger from the right. The dragon medallion with its brilliant crystal at last seemed appropriate with this manner of dress.

"I refuse to participate in this insanity," I told him. "I see no reason to put on that gown and enter your world of madness."

"I gave you the opportunity to participate in the glorious destiny that will accrue to us once I have received the power," Darmanian said. "If you cooperate tonight, I may give you a second chance."

"And what chance will you give Alyse tonight?" I asked him. "Can you really believe that any kind of meaningful power could come from the act of sacrificing a young girl?"

"Perhaps not just *any* girl," Darmanian answered

impatiently. "But this is a very special girl, one whose bloodline has been carefully nurtured for centuries. Her very reason for being is to shed her blood over the altar and baptize the most powerful wizard this planet shall ever know.

"With the abilities granted to me," Darmanian continued, "by the shedding of that girl's blood, I shall become the most spellbinding of men. Others who have acquired talents nearly as powerful have become tyrants. I shall become a most benevolent despot, a potent expression of Satan's mighty force."

"Primitive garbage," I spat at him.

He narrowed his eyes, slowly nodded his head in agreement.

I felt a burning, twisting sensation in my chest. Cold droplets of sweat beaded my forehead. The pain became excruciating, and I sucked in a hoarse gasp of agony.

"Primitive," he repeated. "But most effective."

Instantly the pain was erased from my chest, and I realized that I had been provided with another personal demonstration of psychokinesis—Darmanian's mind influencing the matter of my flesh.

"Put on the gown," Darmanian commanded me.

"I will not be a party to murder," I replied.

Gruber moved in fast, slammed me back against the wall. This time he did it with conviction. Bright spangles of pain splashed before my eyes. Then, before I could react to the body blow, he backhanded me twice, hard, fast.

The dagger came from somewhere beneath his robe, and its point was now pressed against my throat. "Put on the robe, Eric," Gruber threatened. "Or I'll kill you now."

Darmanian turned to leave the room. "It has reached the either-or moment," he told me. "The choice is yours. I must leave."

I dabbed at the trickle of blood oozing from a corner of my mouth.

The dagger's point still pressed my throat. Gruber's eyes were cold, emotionless.

"Father Jacques," I called him by the name of his regressed personality. "I'll put on my robe now."

Chapter Thirty-two

Sharon had correctly described the costume that she would be wearing that night. How sensually alluring she would have appeared under circumstances other than what I suspected to be our last supper.

She wore a pale pink blouse that was low-cut to display her full breasts to marvelous advantage. A black cummerbund had been laced about her waist, and the cinched effect nearly made her bust spill out over the top of her blouse. Her rose-colored skirt was trimmed with a pink satin ribbon. Her long blond hair had been done in ringlets that hung to her bare shoulders. Fresh pink roses had been placed atop her head.

We sat at a long banquet table that had been set up in an enormous ballroom on the third floor of Woodlands mansion. Shelley Eberhart sat on my left side, Sharon on my right. Shelley wore her hair pulled back, a false wiglet of curls adding length to her auburn tresses. Her black velvet dress, with white lace trim around her neck and wrists, indicated the lady of breeding she had been in seventeenth-century Paris.

Viki Chung sat directly across from me. Her usual smoldering sensuality was clothed in a crisp white blouse with a heavy white shawl. A long, tan skirt with a white apron bedecked with many pockets, burgeoning with herbs and potions, completed her costume of Sister Marie, nun turned satanic herbalist.

Farther down the table were Bishop De Shazo, Senator Harrigan, and Don Gruber, each attired in the clerical robes of Roman Catholic priests of that time. Each wore their red-dipped crucifix with the head of Jesus changing downward. In addition to the principal members of the circle, there were at least a dozen men and women in black, cowled robes. Darmanian was nowhere to be seen.

"Don't look so glum, Eric," Shelley told me. "Eat the food. Enjoy. This is going to be a great night."

"Eric is afraid of being a bad boy," Viki mocked me. "But we already know that he can be a little wicked now and then."

Shelley leaned close to me, gave me a slow, lewd wink. "Everybody eventually falls into evil," she said. "We're always doing things that aren't good for us. We eat too much or smoke too much or screw around too much."

Viki laughed. "Eric knows. Don't you, Eric?"

Sharon sat quietly. She had not touched her food. From time to time her chin would quiver, her eyes would brim with tears, and she would shift restlessly in her chair as if she were about to speak. Twice, I had reached for her hand and squeezed it reassuringly, giving her my gamest smile. She had only lowered her eyes and looked away from me.

The sound of a trumpet split the air, startling

Sharon and me, but apparently answering the expectations of the others.

"The master will soon be here," Shelley said, her fingers grasping the arm of my scarlet robe.

The ballroom had been decorated in what I assumed to be the ostentatious opulence of King Louis XIV's France. Lush velvet curtains and drapes of purple and red were hung from floor to ceiling on each wall. In addition to the obligatory statues of gargoyles and demons, there were other works depicting men and women in every imaginable erotic posture. In certain cases the naked humans were wantonly and ecstatically joined in sexual intercourse with succubi, incubi, and other lusty denizens of Satan's Kingdom.

"Here comes the master!" someone shouted. "Aha! Look, he comes riding on the back of an ass!"

A raucous chorus of shouts, cheers, and laughter was supplemented by enthusiastic applause and the noisy stomping of feet. Darmanian entered the ballroom from between the parted halves of a curtain of purple trimmed in gold. He sat astride the broad back of Ed Vogel.

I felt like crying at the sight of this kindly man's terrible debasement.

Costume donkey ears had been clipped to Ed's head, and he had been shoved in a gray comedy outfit, complete with dragging tail. He had an ugly welt on his forehead, and the flesh around his left eye was puffy and discolored; but, thank God, he was alive.

Ed Vogel's presence meant only one thing to Sharon. A terrible sob shook her body, and she turned to me, her eyes wild with fear and desperation. "They've got Alyse!" she cried, unable to check further the brimming tears.

I put my arm around her, pulled her to me as best I could with the impediment of the chairs separating us. I could think of absolutely nothing to say to her that could possibly minimize the horror of the situation.

Several of the hooded initiates had grouped themselves around Darmanian and were placing red-colored palm fronds in front of Vogel's "hoofs." When they had reach the area directly in front of the massive dining table, Darmanian lifted himself from his mount's back and stood to his full height, his arms outstretched toward the arched ceiling of the great ballroom.

"Hosanna!" the cowled men and women shouted.

"The glorious night has come at last," Darmanian said, his eyes lively with the rapture of one who is about to see his vision become others' reality, as well as his own.

"Hallelujah!" answered his disciples, as though with with one voice.

Then everyone was getting to his or her feet. Sharon was pulled away from me by two men and taken to the far side of the room. Each member of the circle seemed to know a task or assignment that must now be fulfilled.

I knelt beside Vogel, helped him to his feet. "Ed," I whispered. "Are you hurt? Are you okay?"

I unfastened the donkey ears; and as I did so, Vogel winked at me with his unblackened eye. "I'm sorry about the kid," he rasped. "But I've brought reinforcements with me."

Don Gruber—that is, Father Jacques—pushed us apart. He had a rope with him, which he wrapped about Vogel's ample girth. He laughed as he fashioned a knot and drew the rope tight. "The ass must be tied to the old hitching post," he said, handing the rope to a giggling redhead, who tugged Vogel after her.

Hope dies hard within the human psyche. What had Vogel meant by "reinforcements"?

I shouted after Ed: "What about Paula and El—?"

Don Gruber slapped the back of my head hard with an open palm. "You should know better than to shout at a solemn ceremony," he said, scowling. "What kind of a scholar are you?"

He stood there for a moment, his eyes narrowed, obviously deep in thought. Then, realization achieved, he smiled. "Sister Simone," he called to the giggling redhead who was leading Vogel about by the rope. "Come back here. It seems we have another ass in our midst. I think we should tie them both together."

Gruber tied a tight knot.

"Brother Maurice," he barked at one of the nearby Satanists. "Are you one of the doorkeepers tonight?"

"Yes, Father Jacques," the man replied.

"Have you your cudgel?"

The man wrapped his hand through a leather loop that hung over his belt. With a rapid, quick-draw movement, he withdrew a stout wooden club.

"Set these two on yon bench," Gruber told him. "And if either of them makes a disturbance, crack his head. Understood?"

The man smacked the thick end of the club against the palm of an open hand. "Yes, Father Jacques. Understood."

As we were being pushed toward the bench, trussed together with two feet of loose rope between us, Ed whispered: *"Alive. At police."*

I was happy the two women had somehow escaped

murder at the hands of the coven, but I was dismayed to think of their reception at the local police department. "Police," I hissed back. "No good. Darmanian has them—"

The blow from the cudgel made red stars spin before my eyes. I stumbled toward the bench, pulling Ed after me.

"That was a tap," Brother Maurice warned me. "Talk again without being asked, and I'll crack your skull!"

I shook my head to clear my vision. The fingers I sent to my hair to inspect the damage to my head came back with a smear of blood on their tips.

A curtain beside Sharon suddenly parted to reveal a large ebony altar that was draped with a black cloth. A trumpet sounded, and Viki Chung lead Alyse Touraine to the side of her mother.

Alyse was dressed in a gown of purest white satin. A gold chain was looped about her middle. A single red rose crowned her blond hair. Even from my observation point across the ballroom, I could see clearly her enormous blue eyes. She truly was the most beautiful child I had ever seen. Anguish and despair tore at my heart. How could I stop the foul obscenity that sought to spill her blood on a satanic altar.

Both mother and daughter were obviously in hypnotic trance, for neither of them responded in a normal manner. They simply stood side by side, facing the coven, which had now arranged itself in a circle about the room.

I heard the sound of a pitchpipe. A woman's voice sounded a note, and a chorus of voices began the ceremony:

O Satan,
Holy Satan, Mighty Satan:
Remove the weakness from our limbs,
And give us your strength.

O Satan,
Holy Satan, Wise Satan:
Remove the fetters from our eyes,
And give us your wisdom.

O Satan,
Holy Satan, all-powerful Satan:
Remove the weakness from our hearts,
And give us your resolution.

O Satan,
Holy Satan, Lord of the Earth:
Remove the restraints of ill-determined purpose,
And give us dominion!
May this be so!

Darmanian stood before the altar and raised his arms in prayer. He now wore a robe of purple over his black velvet suit. He threw back his head, and in a deep baritone, he chanted:

O Satan, take the weakness of my back,
And give me strength instead.
Give me power in all things.
Grant that I may be as resolute in purpose,
As are you, Great Lord of the Earth.
Let me stand tall between the heavens and the Earth.
Let every fiber in my body be blessed.
Let me have your scepter, your rod, your staff.
Let me have dominion over all the Earth.
May this be so!

"May this be so!" the coven echoed his supplication.

Bishop De Shazo, once again the Abbé Guilborg, stepped to the side of Darmanian and turned toward Sharon. "Marguerite Montvoisin," he called. "bring forth thy daughter to the altar of Satan so that she might be prepared."

Viki and Shelley approached Sharon to guide her in her presentation of Alyse.

But Sharon suddenly roused herself, as if waking from a deep sleep.

"Burn in Hell, Abbé Guilborg," she shouted at him. "You'll not have my daughter on that altar."

Abbé Guilborg's mouth dropped in astonishment. Then, a strange growling sound coming from his lips, he strode purposefully toward Sharon and the girl.

"You brainless slut," he cursed, brandishing his ceremonial dagger. "You'll not interrupt this ritual on this night of nights with your blasphemous words and deeds. Give me that girl!"

Sharon encircled Alyse with her arms, her eyes glaring at Abbé Guilborg in fierce defiance.

The fat man slashed at her bare arms with the blade, and thin lines of blood streamed from the wounds.

Alyse stood quietly in the harbor of her mother's arms, oblivious to all around her.

Sharon looked across the ballroom at me and shouted: "Desgrez! Help me. Help me as you did before!"

I sat in stunned amazement. Why would she identify me as the police inspector who had broken up the coven after La Voisin had been taken to the dungeons? Why would she name me as Desgrez, the hated officer who had prevented the completion of the Great Sacrifice three hundred years before?

A hooded coven member whirled, his dagger poised for ripping and killing. "Where is the dog, Desgrez?" he demanded.

Two men were advancing on me with drawn blades. "I want his gizzard," one of them said.

A cowled, gray-haired woman who to my astonishment turned out to be none other than Mrs. Lundby snarled: "I want to drink his blood."

"His blood will make you retch and vomit," said the redhead who not long ago had giggled as she led Ed Vogel about the room. "I want his skull to hollow out and use for a chamber pot."

"Enough, you fools!" Darmanian's voice boomed from the altar. "He is not Desgrez. Desgrez has not been reborn in this time, I was certain to see to that! The wench seeks only to delay us!

"*But*," Darmanian demanded of the woman twisting to free herself from Abbé Guilborg's determined grip, "what did you mean, Marguerite, when you asked your imaginary Desgrez to help you *as he did before*?"

Sharon laughed at his question. "Yes, O great and wonderful Marquis Jean de Sainte-Croix. I betrayed you to the Chambre Ardente! I betrayed the coven to Desgrez rather than permit you to slay your own granddaughter in order to achieve your selfish goal."

"What mean you when you say my granddaughter?" Darmanian frowned his disbelief.

"True!" the entity Marguerite shouted back at him. "You first had my mother when she was but a fifteen-year-old guttersnipe. You took the ragged little street seeress for a diversion from your perfumed ladies.

How surprised you were when you discovered the range of her talents! How amazed you were when she ended up mastering you! How stunned you were when you learned that it was she who could teach you!"

"You lie," Darmanian said coldly.

"I tell the truth on all counts," she said calmly. "I am your daughter. Angelique is your granddaughter. And you were La Voisin's pupil, not her superior!"

Abbé Guilborg brought his thick arm up to clamp about the woman's throat. "Bitch! You betrayed us to Desgrez and the Chambre Ardente. You were the one who delivered us into the hands of the enemy!"

Her blood-streaked fingers formed claws to pull at the bearlike arms that were squeezing the breath from her chest and throat. "Why . . . why should I not . . . betray the marquis?" she gasped. "He . . . he betrayed my mother."

The abbé loosened his grip. "What say you?" he demanded of his captive.

"Don't listen to her!" Darmanian snapped. "Bring the child forward. Precious minutes are being lost."

I glanced at my wristwatch. *Eleven-forty-two.* Perhaps if we could stall past the crucial moment! I decided to risk another blow from Brother Maurice's cudgel.

"It is true!" I shouted. "History testifies that the marquis betrayed his own high priestess to the stake!"

The skull-shattering blow never came. I risked a glance over my shoulder. Brother Maurice had become absorbed in the remarkable drama unfolding before him. And I took advantage of his distraction to begin working on the knot that joined Ed and me together.

"He was always jealous of my mother," the entity Marguerite shouted, seizing a momentary advantage. "He always resented her. He knew that the throne of power rightfully belonged to her."

"Ridiculous!" Darmanian snarled. "Bring me the girl!"

Viki and Shelley reached for Alyse, but the abbé held up a restraining palm. He, too, had become intrigued by the exchange between his high priest and the defiant mother of the sacrificial lamb.

"Listen to me!" Sharon-Marguerite shrieked. "Even though La Voisin acquiesced, even though she yielded the position of might to him, he still resented her. He hated her because he knew within himself that she was the greater, the truer, magician. That is why he betrayed her to Desgrez. And that is why—"

The entity paused, furrowed her brow, as she seemed to be struggling with her perspective of two worlds, two times, two identities. "That is why," she continued, "he killed her in *this* life. Once again, he delivered her to the burning! He has that power. And he used it against his own high priestess!"

The abbé released his hold and let the woman fall to the floor. "Marquis de Sainte-Croix"—he wanted to know what the others dared not ask—"did you betray our high priestess in that other time, *too*?"

Darmanian fixed his questioner with a cold look and a practiced sneer. "Would you believe the lies of a desperate woman, an admitted traitor? Would you believe the lies of the same woman who betrayed our noble purpose nearly three hundred years ago?"

The cleric brought up a beefy hand to wipe the sweat from his eyebrows and forehead. "It is suddenly . . . all so confusing. This time . . . and that other time," he said softly, almost wistfully.

"It is time!" Darmanian said urgently. "Bring me the girl!"

Eleven-forty-nine. I looked at Ed, who sat beside me as calmly as though he were watching all this on the late show. He sensed my attention directed upon him, and he turned slowly to give me another of his conspiratorial winks, which suggested confidence, but offered no tangible display or force or counterattack.

"Fetch the child," Senator Harrigan—that is, Father Louis—shouted at the abbé. "She has yet to be annointed, and the blade must pierce her heart at the stroke of the midnight hour."

"It can never be!" the entity Marguerite screamed from the floor.

The abbé hesitated, then nodded his agreement. "It must be," he said. "We have waited too long. Satan would punish us by setting us another three hundred years in Limbo."

The priest of Satan scooped up Alyse in his arms. "Here she comes, my lord. The sacrificial lamb who shall make us all free and make us lords of the Earth."

"No!" Sharon-Marguerite shouted her maternal protest.

"It cannot be!" She reached out for the abbé's leg, caught it in a desperate grip.

Father Louis ran to her and directed a vicious kick at her face. She caught it on her shoulder, but the blow sent her rolling away from the abbé.

"Set the child on the altar so we might prepare her!" Viki-Sister Marie directed the abbé, as she and Coco began uncapping bottles of ointments and herbs.

Eleven-fifty-three

"Begin the chant," Darmanian commanded the coven. "It must be sung once more as they prepare the sacrifice for our Most Holy Satan!"

Again the pitchpipe sounded, and the chorus swelled its litany to their master:

> O Satan,
> Holy Satan, Mighty Satan:
> Remove the weakness from our limbs,
> And give us your strength.
>
> O Satan,
> Holy Satan, Wise Satan:
> Remove the fetters from our eyes,
> And give us . . .

Merciful God in Heaven! It was happening. As the two women annointed Alyse with various potions and oils, Darmanian was slowly removing the ceremonial dagger from its sheath at his side. He turned to face the altar, gracefully, as controlled as a finely, disciplined ballet dancer. The whole affair now seemed to have been skillfully choreographed, as the chanting coven swayed to their hymn, as priestesses bent to their work, as the high priest raised the gleaming blade at arm's length.

Father Jacques held the struggling Marguerite in his powerful hands. Someone had affixed a gag to the anguished mother's mouth.

> And give us dominion!
> May this be so!

It was twelve o'clock. Midnight of Walpurgisnacht. Beltane. May Eve. The time of the Great Sacrifice.

From somewhere a bell began tolling the hour, one of mankind's oldest rituals.

Bong.

Darmanian's voice was a supplicant's wail: "O Most Holy Satan! Accept this purest of sacrifices!"

Bong.

The shining blade quivered for a moment before it was to begin its flashed descent into Alyse's virginal heart.

Bong. The third stroke! I could not help counting!

That was the crucial, shaved-edge moment that Ed Vogel leaped to his feet, yanked me upright beside him, and began reciting in a loud voice:

"Adjuro ergo te, draco neguissime, in nomine Agni immaculati, qui ambulavit super aspidem et basiliscum, qui conculcavit leoneum et draconem, ut discedas ab hoc Angelique!

"O Master Magician, conqueror of time and space, manipulator of thy soul energy, stay thy hand! The Most High, the Holy of Holies, knows that thou hast perverted the Dragon power, that thou hast corrupted the energy of the feathered serpent of wisdom. Stay thy hand and be shamed!"

Ed Vogel's words seemed to hold the dagger suspended. Darmanian's eyes bulged, and he appeared confused.

The fifth stroke of midnight sounded.

Darmanian shook his head as if he were a fighter clearing his senses after he had recieved a powerful blow.

"You *are* a scholar, Mr. Vogel," the hypnotist said, smiling. "You did not deserve those ears of an ass. You did your homework well. But the priest at Notre

Dame only *thought* that incantation stopped me. Reference books cannot always be relied upon."

The members of the coven had turned as one with Vogel's first utterance; and now, as he made the sign of the cross and began again the incantation, a hideous, frightening, hissing sound was issuing from their open mouths, as if they were angry serpents. I understood at last Ed's reference to "reinforcements." He had memorized an incantation that one of his arcane texts declared had subverted the Marquis de Sainte-Croix three hundred years before. Unfortunately, the chant was only partially effective.

Bong. The ninth stroke of midnight.

"To paradise on Earth!" Darmanian shouted as he once again brought the bejeweled dagger to full arm's length above the supine Alyse.

The knot that linked Ed and me together was at last undone. With a swiftness and daring borne of desperation, I pushed the two cowled figures directly ahead of me roughly to one side and sprinted for the altar. The distraction forced Darmanian to hesitate for one second.

It was all the time I needed.

My open palm slammed into his chest at the eleventh stroke of midnight. Darmanian staggered backward, wild-eyed when he saw his medallion dangling from my curled fingers. The twin serpents with their ruby eyes and dazzling crystal were now leashed by the chain that hung from *my* fist.

Midnight had passed. Alyse was safe.

Darmanian's knuckles were like whitened marbles as he clutched the dagger in his own trembling fist. He was livid with rage, yet he was strangely impotent to strike out at the two men who had robbed him of his crucial moment, the night of nights for which he had waited for three hundred years.

Vogel's eyes narrowed, and his voice raised in accusation. "Darmanian, you are a man who has vomited out of his soul all remnants of true goodness. You have cherished a pride in evil, falsely calling it good. You have served your selfishness, greed, and iniquity so constantly that there is not even the shadow of glory left for you!"

"Fool!" Darmanian cursed Vogel in a voice made shrill and strident by anger and frustration. "You have cheated the entire world of paradise!"

Vogel snorted contemptuously. "Your paradise would have been a bottomless pit of wickedness. It is easier to keep from falling if you never enter the pit! Once we would stumble over your version of paradise, we would find out too late that the sides would be too smooth to stop our falling for infinity."

Darmanian stepped back from the altar, his piercing blue eyes flicking back and forth from the beautiful child lying before him to the confused coven muttering their despair and anguish at having failed in their mission of performing the Great Sacrifice. He held the ceremonial dagger at arm's length.

The hypnotist stood straight and tall before his disciples, a commanding figure robed in purple. "Am I your high priest, a most exalted Master of True Magic?" he demanded of them.

With one voice they answered in a shout: "Yea!"

"Has anyone served our Holy Satan with greater fidelity and devotion than I?"

"No!"

"Has anyone else achieved mastery over time and space and control over his incarnations?"

"None!"

Satisfied, Darmanian smiled at their spontaneous responses. "When you combine as a unit," he told them, "I have shown you how to move objects, how to control men's minds. If you blend your psyches into one, you have the force, the energy, the power to restore life to the dead!"

I had rejoined Ed and had set to work at the rope tightened about his wrists. "What's he talking about?" I asked him.

Vogel shrugged. "I have the feeling that he's building up to an awfully big point. Get this rope off me! We may have to get out of here in a big hurry!"

"Satan demands a sacrifice," Darmanian reminded them. "Every great movement requires a sacrifice. There is no one better prepared than I!"

"My lord!" Shelley Eberhart shouted. "No!"

"I shall be my own sacrifice!" Darmanian told them. "You have the ability to restore me to life. You have the power to bring me back to my full strength. *Do not fail me.*"

Without another word or sign of deliberation, Darmanian plunged the dagger into the center of his chest. Perhaps that was when he fully realized that I still held his special totem, his medallion, in my fist.

He clenched his teeth, but the sound that forced itself from deep within him was hideous. He staggered against the altar, dropped to one knee. He propped himself up on an elbow while the other hand instinctively tried to claw the blade from his chest. There was a mournful gasp, and Darmanian sprawled at the foot of the altar.

The coven stepped back in awe, then froze as if a paralysis had seized each one of them. The only sound in the room was that of the awakening Alyse crying out for her mother.

Sharon got to her feet, rushed to the altar, and gathered her daughter into her bloodied arms.

I undid the last of the knots that bound Vogel, then pushed my way through the dazed men and women to kneel at the side of the hypnotist.

The face that looked up at me was softer than I had ever seen it. The eyes were frightened, injured. His left hand came up to clutch at my sleeve.

"Eric, I—" His voice cracked. "I promised you . . . a good book. Eric—"

I closed the dying, staring eyes, lowered Darmanian gently to the black-carpeted floor.

As I did so, Darmanian's eyes snapped back open, and a peculiar spasmodic twitching of his facial muscles contorted his features into a mask of malignant menace. For a fleeting moment the brilliant blue eyes of the hypnotist appeared to blaze with renewed anger.

"*I will be back!*" was the hoarse whisper that seemed to come in a cold breath against my ear.

Don Gruber pushed me roughly aside, knelt beside Darmanian, and pulled the ceremonial dagger free of the ruptured flesh. Blood moved easily from the open wound.

"Sister Marie," he ordered in a crisp, professional voice. "Get some bandages. Two of you men, help me pick him up and put him on the altar. We must begin the restoration ritual at once!"

"Gruber, Darmanian is dead," I told him.

His eyes narrowed angrily, as if I were the vilest infidel defiling the sacred and the holy. He grabbed Darmanian's upper body and with the help of two hooded coven members placed the hypnotist on the altar.

"Our high priest is not dead," Bishop De Shazo informed me in stentorian tones. "He is but waiting in Limbo for us to restore him to life."

"Wait, wait," I pleaded. "That was in that other time, that other place. Darmanian is—"

Ed caught at my arm. "Forget it, Eric," he told me. "Get Sharon and Alyse. Let's get out of here before these butchers start looking for someone to blame for their failure."

Chapter Thirty-three

When the police arrived the next morning at seven forty-five, they found the body of Darmanian encircled by eighteen black-cowled men and women. The corpse of the hypnotist still lay on the black marble altar, and a number of the zealous group solemnly told the officers that they had the power to bring him back to life.

The investigating police officers did nothing to disguise their distaste at what they discovered in the third-floor ballroom at Woodlands. It was, to them, as if they had pried open a festering cesspool that was about to burst and disseminate its foul contagion throughout the beauty and uncluttered city of Saratoga Springs.

Although we had prepared Sergent Kandowski with a hurried dossier of whom he might expect to find among the faithful disciples gathered around the funeral bier, the officers still expressed their shock at finding certain members of the praying and chanting circle to have reputations that extended far beyond the perimeters of upstate New York. It proved to be quite mind-boggling for a number of the officers when they found a United States senator, a Roman Catholic bishop, a professional football player, and the fashion model of the hour kneeling among incense burners, black candles, and obscene idols, beseeching Satan to deny the death of the famous hypnotist. The other men and women involved in the grotesque resurrection day project were area residents of no great or special accomplishments, but the investigating officers knew that their names, once released, would startle the community. The local citizenry would be confused that so many of their neighbors could possess a secret life and a world view so morbid, so bizarre, so different from their own.

Paula Vogel and Eleanor Touraine had been awaiting an audience with Police Chief Weyerhaus when Darmanian's thugs had attacked Ed and grabbed Alyse. The two women, unaware of the posthypnotic suggestions that Darmanian had planted within the chief's psyche, felt they were lost behind Alice's looking glass. Every time they had mentioned the hypnotist's name, Chief Weyerhaus merely smiled and told them what a fine man Darmanian was.

They had returned home to Vogel's around seven that evening to find the house in a shambles. Fearing the worst, they returned at once to the station house in Albany and demanded their charges be taken seriously. Darmanian's campaign had been an extensive one, however. Each ranking officer had given them the same saccharine smile and enthusiastic endorsement of the man whom they believed might even then be murdering their daughter, granddaughter, and husband.

Sharon, Alyse, Ed, and I arrived at the station house at about two A.M. Paula and Eleanor were still there, physically exhausted, emotionally distraught, mentally disoriented, and increasingly desperate in their attempts to get help. I knew that Burt Kandowski had succumbed to Darmanian's hypnotic conditioning, but I also knew that he had no posthypnotic suggestions implanted in his unconscious. I called Burt, got him out of bed, explained the incredible situation, and had him raising hell at the station house by three. By six, he had enough officers for the raid on Woodlands.

That evening, the *Albany Times-Union* filled their front page with photographs, banner headlines, and double-column stories detailing the incredible double life of Darmanian and his coven. By the next afternoon, May 2, the New York *Daily News* headlined their front page with the spooky promise of "How Famous Hypnotist Forsook Healing for Hoo Doo Models, Athletes, Politicos, Church Leaders join in Rites to Raise Dead." *The New York Times* assessed the affair as "a tragedy of the misuses of power and the exploitation of the human psyche . . . the sad deterioration of a distinguished career."

No one mentioned the Marquis Jean de Sainte-Croix, reincarnation, or the satanic master plan. No one knew of those things other than the coven and us, its survivors.

At first we decided not to say one word of such things to anyone.

Sharon and I talked a lot about Darmanian, Delores, and her own peculiar role in the bizarre drama. As a kind of side benefit of the whole trial by ordeal, we found that we were developing a deep and growing affection for each other. If a lasting relationship between Sharon and I should come to fruition, I would consider that ample reward for having endured the nightmare of Darmanian's circus of horror.

The body of Darmanian lay in the morgue, unclaimed. No living relative could be found.

Ed challenged me to begin at once to set down an accurate account of the hypnotist's master plan, the sacrifices of the infants, and all the rest before some other writer, ignorant of the true facts and their monstrous implications, set forth an incomplete account. But I argued that I was yet too close to the diabolical drama to write with perspective.

On May 3, three days after Darmanian had taken his own life in sacrifice to Satan, an event occurred which gave the media prime sensationalistic news copy. On that morning, although the police loudly protested such an act to be impossible, the body of Darmanian disappeared.

There were those who said that police officials had been bribed by members of Darmanian's coven, who had quietly infiltrated the ranks of local, state, perhaps national government. But most of the accusations directed against the police dealt with their inability to prevent a group of fanatics or perverts from stealing the corpse of the notorious hypnotist.

When we learned that Darmanian's body had vanished, Sharon recalled that the medallion, which I had cautiously placed in a safe-deposit box in a Saratoga Springs bank, had now achieved even more importance as the last tangible link with the incredible shadow world of the hypnotist.

I think it was a peculiar sort of awareness that

made us visit the bank to inspect the serpentine artifact. A bank official helped us withdraw the box and left us in a private cubicle in the safe-deposit vault. Somehow I believe we both knew that we would find the box to be empty.

It was.

The medallion had disappeared as completely as its owner's body, and I was left with Darmanian's final words echoing in my mind: *"I will be back!"*

It was then that I knew that I must face my responsibility toward humanity and set down the whole truth of what had happened behind the chained gates of Woodlands mansion. I must warn others about the tyrannical parasites who may inhabit the dark side of the soul. I must seek to make all men and women aware of the infinite variety of powers and principalities that may exist around us and operate through us. I knew that I must remind all who would take heed that even though evil must be conquered anew in each confrontation, it can never vanquish those who arm themselves with love and who strive to live in light rather than in darkness.

A novel of terror aboard the President's plane, as one desperate man holds the passengers and crew at gun point, high over the skies of America!

"The right ingredients. A top notch yarn." *Pittsburgh Press*

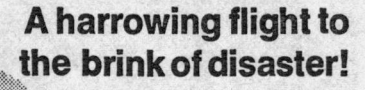

A harrowing flight to the brink of disaster!

AIR FORCE ONE

by Edwin Corley author of *Sargasso*

A Dell Book $2.50

(10063-1)

At your local bookstore or use this handy coupon for ordering:

Dell	**DELL BOOKS** Air Force One $2.50 (10063-1) **P.O. BOX 1000, PINEBROOK, N.J. 07058**

Please send me the above title. I am enclosing $ _____
(please add 75¢ per copy to cover postage and handling). Send check or money order—no cash or C.O.D.'s. Please allow up to 8 weeks for shipment.

Mr/Mrs/Miss _____

Address _____

City _____ State/Zip _____

THE TRITON ULTIMATUM
by Laurence Delaney

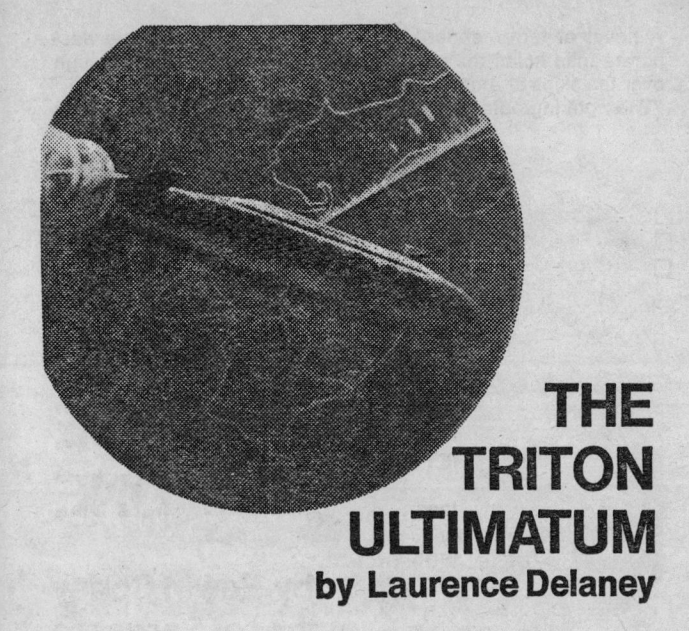

The terrifyingly unforgettable story about the mysterious disappearance of the newest, biggest, deadliest weapons platform in history! Ten desperate men have brutally commandeered a Triton sub and 24 Poseidon missiles, more than enough to raze the world! They demand 4 billion in gold. But not even a golden ransom can save every major city on the globe once they make THE TRITON ULTIMATUM!   A Dell Book $2.25   (18744-3)

At your local bookstore or use this handy coupon for ordering:

Dell	**DELL BOOKS** The Triton Ultimatum $2.25 (18744-3) **P.O. BOX 1000, PINEBROOK, N.J. 07058**

Please send me the above title. I am enclosing $ _____
(please add 75¢ per copy to cover postage and handling). Send check or money order—no cash or C.O.D.'s. Please allow up to 8 weeks for shipment.

Mr/Mrs/Miss _____

Address _____

City _____ State/Zip _____

Dell Bestsellers

- ☐ **CRY FOR THE STRANGERS** by John Saul $2.50 (11869-7)
- ☐ **WHISTLE** by James Jones $2.75 (19262-5)
- ☐ **A STRANGER IS WATCHING** by Mary Higgins Clark $2.50 (18125-9)
- ☐ **MORTAL FRIENDS** by James Carroll $2.75 (15789-7)
- ☐ **CLAUDE: THE ROUNDTREE WOMEN BOOK II** by Margaret Lewerth $2.50 (11255-9)
- ☐ **GREEN ICE** by Gerald A. Browne $2.50 (13224-X)
- ☐ **BEYOND THE POSEIDON ADVENTURE** by Paul Gallico $2.50 (10497-1)
- ☐ **COME FAITH, COME FIRE** by Vanessa Royall $2.50 (12173-6)
- ☐ **THE TAMING** by Aleen Malcolm $2.50 (18510-6)
- ☐ **AFTER THE WIND** by Eileen Lottman $2.50 (18138-0)
- ☐ **THE ROUNDTREE WOMEN: BOOK I** by Margaret Lewerth $2.50 (17594-1)
- ☐ **DREAMSNAKE** by Vonda N. McIntyre $2.25 (11729-1)
- ☐ **THE MEMORY OF EVA RYKER** by Donald A. Stanwood $2.50 (15550-9)
- ☐ **BLIZZARD** by George Stone $2.25 (11080-7)
- ☐ **THE BLACK MARBLE** by Joseph Wambaugh $2.50 (10647-8)
- ☐ **MY MOTHER/MY SELF** by Nancy Friday $2.50 (15663-7)
- ☐ **SEASON OF PASSION** by Danielle Steel $2.50 (17703-0)
- ☐ **THE DARK HORSEMAN** by Marianne Harvey $2.50 (11758-5)
- ☐ **BONFIRE** by Charles Dennis $2.25 (10659-1)

At your local bookstore or use this handy coupon for ordering:

Dell **DELL BOOKS**
P.O. BOX 1000, PINEBROOK, N.J. 07058

Please send me the books I have checked above. I am enclosing $_____
(please add 35¢ per copy to cover postage and handling). Send check or money order—no cash or C.O.D.'s. Please allow up to 8 weeks for shipment.

Mr/Mrs/Miss_____

Address_____

City_____ State/Zip_____

Paul Gallico
BEYOND THE POSEIDON ADVENTURE

NOW—ONE STEP BEYOND THE DISASTER THAT CLAIMED THE POSEIDON!

When the luxury liner Poseidon is capsized by a tidal wave, only six out of sixteen hundred survive the shipwreck. Rescued by a French naval helicopter, the six are soon returned at gunpoint to the sinking ship and into a trap of some very deadly predators.

A Dell Book $2.50

At your local bookstore or use this handy coupon for ordering:

Dell	**DELL BOOKS** **P.O. BOX 1000, PINEBROOK, N.J. 07058**	BEYOND THE POSEIDON ADVENTURE $2.50 (10497-1)

Please send me the above title. I am enclosing $_____
(please add 35¢ per copy to cover postage and handling). Send check or money order—no cash or C.O.D.'s. Please allow up to 8 weeks for shipment.

Mr/Mrs/Miss_____

Address_____

City_____ State/Zip_____

Gerald A. Browne
GREEN ICE

"RIVETING! ..

Browne does for EMERALDS what he did for diamonds in *11 Harrow House*!"—*Robert Ludlum*

When Joseph Wiley fell in love with an eccentric heiress, who had fascinating appetites, a gift for the mysterious, and a taste of danger, he stumbled into a wonderland of greed, corruption, and boundless wealth. **"A Cliff-hanger! Sparkling! Entertaining suspense! The double twist ending is as satisfactory as the heist!"**—*Cosmopolitan Magazine*

A Dell Book $2.50

At your local bookstore or use this handy coupon for ordering:

Dell	DELL BOOKS P.O. BOX 1000, PINEBROOK, N.J. 07058	GREEN ICE (13224-X) $2.50

Please send me the above title. I am enclosing $_____
(please add 35¢ per copy to cover postage and handling). Send check or money order—no cash or C.O.D.'s. Please allow up to 8 weeks for shipment.

Mr/Mrs/Miss_____

Address_____

City_____ State/Zip_____

Cry for the Strangers

John Saul
author of Punish The Sinners

A chilling tale of psychological terror!

In Clark's Harbor, a beautiful beach town on the Pacific, something horrible, violent and mysteriously evil is happening. One by one the strangers are dying. Never the townspeople. Only the strangers. Has a dark bargain been struck between the people of Clark's Harbor and some supernatural force? Or is the sea itself calling out for human sacrifice?

A Dell Book $2.50   (11869-7)

At your local bookstore or use this handy coupon for ordering:

| Dell | **DELL BOOKS**
P.O. BOX 1000, PINEBROOK, N.J. 07058 | CRY FOR THE STRANGERS $2.50   (11869-7) |

Please send me the above title. I am enclosing $_____
(please add 35¢ per copy to cover postage and handling). Send check or money order—no cash or C.O.D.'s. Please allow up to 8 weeks for shipment.

Mr/Mrs/Miss_____

Address_____

City_____State/Zip_____